"The minute I saw you, I knew I wanted to get to know you better.

"Intimately, in fact," Paul continued. "But you were pretty good at avoiding me. Did you do that deliberately?"

"Avoid you? Well . . ." Layla hesitated for a moment. "Maybe."

"But why?"

She stared at him helplessly. How could you tell a man you were scared? That the thought of craving someone's love and approval was tantamount to a living death. And if you let yourself get close, there was always that chance that before you knew it, you'd be repeating the patterns you'd worked so hard to overcome. Before you knew it, you'd be wondering if what you did met with his approval. Before you knew it, you'd be jumping through hoops over and over again to prove your own worth.

"Answer me, Layla," Paul demanded softly.

Dear Reader,

Welcome to Silhouette **Special Edition** . . . welcome to romance. Each month, Silhouette **Special Edition** publishes six novels with you in mind—stories of love and life, tales that you can identify with—romance with that little "something special" added in.

April has some wonderful stories in store for you. Lindsay McKenna's powerful saga that is set in Vietnam during the '60s—MOMENTS OF GLORY—concludes with *Off Limits,* Alexandra Vance and Jim McKenzie's story. And Elizabeth Bevarly returns with *Up Close,* a wonderful, witty tale that features characters you first met in her book, *Close Range* (Silhouette **Special Edition** #590).

Rounding out this month are more stories by some of your favorite authors: Celeste Hamilton, Sarah Temple, Jennifer Mikels and Phyllis Halldorson. Don't let April showers get you down. Curl up with good books—and Silhouette **Special Edition** has six!—and celebrate love Silhouette **Special Edition**-style.

In each Silhouette **Special Edition** novel, we're dedicated to bringing you the romances that you dream about— stories that will delight as well as bring a tear to the eye. And that's what Silhouette **Special Edition** is all about— special books by special authors for special readers!

I hope you enjoy this book and all of the stories to come!

Sincerely,

Tara Gavin
Senior Editor
Silhouette Books

SARAH TEMPLE
The Liberation of Layla

 Silhouette Special Edition

Published by Silhouette Books New York

America's Publisher of Contemporary Romance

For my sisters, Linda Domholt and Nanette Caldararo, both of whom have given me more than they'll ever know.

SILHOUETTE BOOKS
300 East 42nd St., New York, N.Y. 10017

THE LIBERATION OF LAYLA

Copyright © 1992 by Cheryl Arguile

ISBN: 0-373-09736-0

First Silhouette Books printing April 1992

All the characters in this book have no existence outside the imagination of the author and have no relation whatsoever to anyone bearing the same name or names. They are not even distantly inspired by any individual known or unknown to the author, and all incidents are pure invention.

®: Trademark used under license and registered in the United States Patent and Trademark Office and in other countries.

Printed in the U.S.A.

Books by Sarah Temple

Silhouette Special Edition

Kindred Spirits #593
Lifeline #674
The Liberation of Layla #736

SARAH TEMPLE

has been a jack-of-all-trades throughout her adult life. She worked her way through college as a waitress, motel maid and pool-hall clerk. Then she traveled to Europe and met her husband in England. For the past eight years, she has been employed by a Chinese steamship company where she moved her way up to personnel manager.

Sarah says that the biggest influence on her writing has been other writers. She loves to read their stories, then dream up her own.

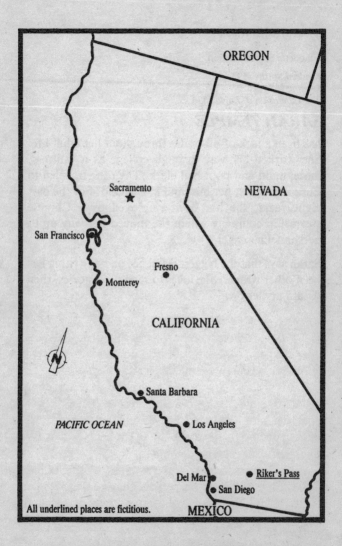

OREGON

NEVADA

Sacramento

San Francisco

Fresno

Monterey

CALIFORNIA

N

Santa Barbara

PACIFIC OCEAN

Los Angeles

Del Mar

Riker's Pass

San Diego

All underlined places are fictitious.

MEXICO

Chapter One

"**Y**ou want me to what?" Layla Jane Odell stared in horror at the tall man lounging against the back door of the examination room. She wasn't sure she'd heard him correctly, or, more to the point, she hoped she hadn't.

Dr. Paul Tressler grinned lazily and crossed his arms over his chest. "I want you to take Stanley, he needs a good home. You want me to hire Tank, don't you?".

Layla stifled a groan. How had this gotten so complicated? She'd come across the street to Paul's office to convince him he needed a part-time employee, but the man had neatly turned the tables on her. *He* was trying to convince *her* she needed a dog.

"But that's different," she protested, staring at him in astonishment. "Tank's a person, that's a dog."

Paul glanced down at the large lump of black-and-brown fur lying by his booted foot and shrugged. "Theoretically, you're right. Stanley is a dog. But all he ever does is sleep. Believe me, he'll be no problem.''

Layla shifted uncomfortably. A flat-out refusal would kill Tank's chance and she didn't want to risk that. On the other hand, she wasn't sure she wanted a pet. Stalling for time, she cocked her head and stared at Paul curiously. "Is there something wrong with him? I mean, why do you want to give your dog away? Aren't vets supposed to love animals?''

"I do love animals and he isn't my dog."

"Then why can't you keep him?''

Paul straightened. "Miss Odell, Layla," he corrected. "My loving animals isn't the issue here. But just to keep the record straight, so far this year I've had two dogs, one cat, a sick parakeet and a three-legged lizard dumped on my doorstep." He sighed. "And they're all still in residence. My house isn't exactly small, but with that menagerie, I'm running out of room."

"Stanley was abandoned on your doorstep?" She felt a flash of unwanted sympathy for the dog.

He shook his head. "No. Stanley belonged to old Joe McCain. When he died, his landlady brought the dog over here. Joe didn't have any family and none of his neighbors volunteered to take the dog. So I'm stuck with him." Paul glanced at the animal.

Stanley snorted in his sleep.

Reluctantly accepting his explanation, Layla nodded. Her mind worked furiously as she tried to calculate the odds of Paul Tressler hiring Tank if she didn't take the darned dog.

She began to pace the length of the examination room. Her high-heeled pumps clicked against the hardwood floor as she watched the sleeping animal.

He hadn't moved a muscle since she'd walked in. Maybe it could work, she thought. A vision of Tank's scared white face flashed into her mind and nudged her conscience.

Paul squatted down and absently began to stroke Stanley's soft fur as he studied the lovely woman in front of him. Petite and slender, Layla Odell projected a fragile beauty that drew his gaze like a magnet. Her high cheekbones, deep-set hazel eyes and full, soft mouth were as delicately carved as the face on the cameo brooch at the neck of her lace-trimmed blouse.

She moved her head a fraction, and caught a ray of sunlight in her light honey-colored shoulder-length hair, which she wore pinned up in an elegant topknot. Paul dug his fingers deeper into the dog's silky coat as his gaze drifted to the stray curls dangling against her delicate neck. Stanley grunted.

She'd fascinated him ever since the day he'd looked out the front window of his office and seen her fumbling with the lock of the Old Emporium, which she'd just inherited from her great-aunt. But she couldn't see him for dust. No matter how charming, friendly and agreeable he'd tried to be, Layla Odell had proven as elusive to get close to as the pot of gold at the end of the rainbow. In the three months she'd lived in Riker's Pass, she'd been polite, friendly, courteous . . . and as remote as a cloistered nun.

At first it had simply been a case of a damaged male ego. He was no Casanova, but he didn't think he looked like a troll, either. But now it was more. He wanted, no, he needed to know why she kept herself so apart from everyone in town except the local juvenile delinquent.

Layla turned suddenly and smiled. For a moment, he was too stunned by the impact to do anything except stare at her. Finally he managed to find his voice.

"Come on, say yes," he cajoled. "This poor thing's got nowhere else to go. Besides you live alone. You sure don't go out much. Stanley will be company for you."

Layla's smile vanished. Good Lord, he was practically calling her an old maid! Indignation gripped her and she stiffened. Without thinking she snapped, "I don't need any company, Dr. Tressler, and I certainly don't need a dog."

Paul rose to his feet and came toward her, stopping on the other side of the table. "And I certainly don't need a delinquent teenager working for me."

The intimidating expression on his face caused Layla to step backward until she bumped into the supply cupboard.

He was a big man. Six foot four and so heavily muscled he could easily be mistaken for a professional body builder. Beneath the thin material of his white cotton shirt, she could see the outline of muscles lining his chest, arms and shoulders.

Paul watched her coolly, his gray eyes now the color of storm clouds. She flushed but forced herself to meet his steady stare.

Despite the faint frown on his face, he was a handsome man. High cheekbones, a stubborn-looking slanted chin, and a prominent nose with a tiny bump at the bridge that indicated it had once been broken. His hair was a deep rich brown and he wore it parted on the side and brushed casually away from his face.

Layla's fingers tightened around the small clutch bag in her hand. Much as she'd like to turn on her heel and walk out of his office, she couldn't. Tank's whole future was at stake here. She had to back down. If the boy was going to have a chance, she must be the one to apologize for snapping at the vet.

She turned and stared out the window as she fought off a wave of bitterness. She was good at backing down. Lord knew, she'd had plenty of practice.

But then she realized she was angrier at herself for reacting to his words than she was at him. His opinion of her social life shouldn't matter. No one's opinion of her life should matter except hers. Hadn't she spent the past ten years trying to achieve that very goal? Then why was she getting so upset because he knew she had less social life than a hibernating bear?

"Hey," he said softly, his voice apologetic. "I'm sorry. I didn't mean that the way it sounded. Tact isn't one of my strong points. I was just trying to reassure you that taking Stanley wouldn't affect your social life. Heck, you could stay out every night and the dog wouldn't care as long as you fed him." He paused briefly, then added, "I didn't mean to offend you."

Paul didn't really think he'd been all that offensive, but her quick retreat and the flash of panic in her eyes when he'd moved toward her had confused him. For a split second, she'd actually looked scared of him. The thought left a decidedly bad taste in his mouth. The last thing he wanted from any woman, but especially this one, was fear.

Surprised that he had apologized when she'd been just as at fault as him, Layla turned to see him staring at her. There was no trace of anger or mockery in his expression.

"You didn't offend me," she said with a weak smile, "and I'm sorry for snapping at you. You're right, of course. I don't go out much. I guess the fact that everyone knows how I spend my evenings made me a little defensive." She shook her head. "There isn't much privacy in a small town, is there?"

"You've got that right," he agreed quickly, grateful that she was smiling again. "In this town, if you sneeze twice in one morning, the local gossips will have you down with the flu by noon." He hesitated for a moment. "Anyway, do we have a deal?"

She took a deep breath. "You get Tank and I get Stanley? Is that it?"

"That's it." Paul laid his hands flat on the top of the table. He fully intended to hire Tank Mullins. It was the only way he could keep an eye on the kid. But he was enjoying the conversation too much not to spin it out. Besides, if she took Stanley, maybe it would give him an excuse to see her again. "That seems like a fair exchange to me."

"Not to me." Layla replied honestly. Silently she commanded her heart to slow down. Confrontations of any sort upset her, but she forced herself to ignore the butterflies fluttering in her stomach.

You can handle this, she told herself, you can handle him. Just keep your head and stay calm. After all, the worst he could do was say no. And that wasn't the end of the world or a measure of her worth as a human being. The thought made her feel better.

Yet there was a lot at stake here.

Tank's freedom depended on getting this man to say yes.

"After all," she continued in a deliberately calm voice, "you'll be getting some pretty cheap labor. Tank's willing to work for minimum wage. All I'll be getting is a dog." She glanced uncertainly toward the corner. "I don't know anything about dogs. I'm not even sure I like them."

"That's ridiculous," Paul exclaimed, looking genuinely shocked. "Everyone likes dogs."

Layla shrugged. "That's not true. And don't try to change the subject. The fact of the matter is you'll be getting something really worthwhile. Despite what everyone thinks, Tank's a hard worker." She paused and gathered her nerve. "I think the least you could do is give him more than ten hours work a week." She flicked another look at the dog and the sight bolstered her courage.

The animal didn't look violent. As a matter of fact, he didn't look like much of anything except a large slug with hair.

"I'll tell you what," she said briskly, "I'll take…what did you say the dog's name was?"

"Stanley."

"Right, Stanley off your hands if you give Tank fifteen hours a week." She held her breath.

"Fifteen hours," Paul yelped, clearly outraged by the suggestion. He put his hands on his hips and tried to scowl. It was difficult, he was having too much fun.

"I think that's fair." She smiled sweetly.

"In case you've forgotten," he pointed out, still trying to draw the negotiations out as long as possible. "I don't need anyone at all. I'm doing you a favor even offering him *ten* hours of work a week."

Layla refused to be intimidated. Paul Tressler might loom over her like one of the mountains fringing Riker's Pass but he was still just a small-town veterinarian. She had to think of a way to convince him that he needed an employee. And more importantly, that he needed that employee for *fifteen* hours a week.

Paul was her last hope. No one else in town was willing to give Tank work, that was for sure.

"I appreciate that," she said pleasantly. "And from all appearances, there wouldn't be much for Tank to do in here. But I'm told there's lots to do out back."

From the gossip she'd heard, Paul Tressler was in love with old and unusual collectibles. Behind the high wooden fence surrounding the back of his office, word had it that there was everything from a circus calliope to a completely refurbished Model T.

"I understand you've got a lot of valuable things out there." Turning, she pointed toward the back of his office, and missed the wide grin on Paul's face. "I'm a collector, too, so I have firsthand knowledge of how much attention old things need. Tank could keep the place clean for you and do a lot of the maintenance work. That would give you more free time."

"Now that I could use," Paul agreed. He gazed at her thoughtfully. "Well, there *is* a lot to do around here and I really could use another pair of hands. Okay, we've got a deal. I'll give Tank Mullins fifteen hours of work a week and you'll give Stanley a good home."

Layla smiled brilliantly in relief. "Oh, that's wonderful," she gushed. "Thank you. You won't be sorry, I promise you. Tank is a good worker and I'll give that dog a good home—" She broke off and eyed Stanley warily.

"Is there something wrong?"

"No, not really." She looked worriedly at Paul. "It's just that I've never had a pet before. Do you have a book or something?"

"I've got some pamphlets I can give you. But if this is your first time as a dog owner, I think it would be better if you came directly to me with any problems. I'll give you all the help you need." He smiled suddenly. "As a matter of fact, I'll drop by your place a couple of times in the next few weeks to see how the two of you are getting along."

Alarm bells sounded in Layla's head. "But that would be a lot of trouble for you."

"Not at all," he replied smoothly, "and it'll give us a chance to get to know each other better."

Layla went utterly still. She had no choice but to agree. She didn't want Paul backing out of their deal now. "All right, if you're sure it's no bother," she answered, trying to infuse some enthusiasm into her voice. "That would be nice."

He looked amused. "I'm sure."

Flustered, she dropped her gaze and looked at Stanley. The reality of being a dog owner slapped her squarely in the face. "Oh, gosh," she muttered, flicking a quick glance at her watch. "How am I going to get him home and what am I going to do with him today? I have to open the store in ten minutes."

"Leave him here for now," Paul said calmly. "I'll bring him over this evening. It'll give me a chance to talk to Tank and fix his hours. What time do you close?"

"Five." She picked up her purse and edged toward the door.

Paul trailed behind her, successfully hiding his triumphant smile. His luck was holding; she didn't know a darned thing about animals. That should be good for dozens of excuses to drop by her place.

"Don't look so worried," he said soothingly as they stepped around the sleeping animal. He opened the door. "I'll be over right after work to give you your first lesson in owning a dog."

Stanley didn't move.

* * *

"What did he say?" Tank Mullins stopped washing the front window of the Emporium and dropped the sponge into a bucket of soapy water as soon as he heard Layla's footsteps approaching. He'd been watching her out of the corner of his eye ever since she'd come out of the vet's office across the street.

"He's going to do it," she replied brightly, stepping around Tank's mess and pushing open the door of the Emporium. "Come on inside. I've got to get ready to open up."

The moment she stepped into her store, she forgot all about her awkward conversation with Paul Tressler. This was her kingdom, her domain, her ticket to freedom. She thanked her lucky stars every time she walked into the place.

Tank trailed behind her as she marched up the center aisle. The Old Emporium was a genuine old-fashioned country store, carrying everything from dry goods to farm tools. The bins, barrels and shelves were filled with a healthy mix of the frivolous and the practical. The air was heavy with the scent of licorice, horehound candy and sassafras tea. Toiletries and razor blades nestled next to a bin of imported silk flowers, a rack of paperbacks stood beside a display of stationery, and a row of hand-crafted mugs stood proudly behind a bin of potting soil. Layla thanked the gods for Great-Aunt Velma and her uncanny ability to stock exactly what her customers wanted.

Layla hadn't changed a thing since she'd inherited the place. The tourists thought the store quaint; the locals were used to it. She liked it the way it was.

Coming to a halt by the cash register, Layla glanced at Tank's face. Immediately she felt a wellspring of sympathy for the boy. Even his nickname—picked up heaven only knew how—seemed wildly inappropriate. Skinny, pale and cursed with the thinnest white-blond hair she'd ever seen on a teenager, Norbert Osgood Mullins hardly looked like the town scourge.

But that was precisely what he was—a rebellious, troubled kid from a lousy home who hadn't had the luck she'd had herself at a similar time in her life.

"Uh, what's the deal?" Tank tried hard to be nonchalant, but his voice was edged with worry.

"I think Paul will probably want you to start as soon as possible," she said crisply, wanting to take that haunted fear out of his eyes. "But I'm not sure what hours he needs you. He said he'd drop by at closing time and we'll work out the details then."

Tank gave her a worried frown. "I gotta go to Escondido to see my probation officer. The doc won't get mad if I'm not here, will he?"

"I thought you did that on Monday."

He shook his head. "I did, but when I got there, Mr. Beals had the flu so they told me to come back this afternoon. You can call if you don't believe me."

"I believe you." Layla knew how important trust was to a seventeen-year-old. God knows, it had been a commodity lacking in her own life. "And don't worry about Dr. Tressler, he doesn't strike me as the kind of man to get upset about your not being here. I'll take care of everything."

"Thanks, I owe you, Layla." He looked away in embarrassment. Clearing his throat, he asked, "Does he know?"

Oh Lord, Layla thought helplessly, the whole town knew. Surely Tank was aware of that. She marveled at the ability of youth to delude itself. "He knows you were arrested for stealing a car and he also knows the terms of your probation.''

The terms of Tank's probation were very clear. Stay out of trouble and find a forty-hour-a-week job or face a year with the California Youth Authority.

''Then he knows that if he hadn't given me the extra work, I'd have been up for CYA.''

''That's not true,'' she protested, trying to make him feel better. ''You've got a job with me. I know it's not as many hours as the judge wanted, but it's a start.''

''Yeah, but Beals already said that unless I worked full-time, he was going to pull me in.'' Tank smiled bitterly. ''They don't want me to have too much spare time on my hands. I guess that's my punishment for actually being dumb enough to graduate from high school a year early.''

''No,'' she corrected softly, ''that's your punishment for stealing a car.'' Layla frowned. ''And stop putting yourself down because you're smart. If that probation officer had any brains at all, he'd be having you go to college, not working. But you're not going to do time. You've got the hours you need now, so there's nothing to worry about.''

''There's always something to worry about.'' Tank looked down at his feet. ''Maybe I should have just let them lock me up. Maybe I'll end up being nothing but trouble for you no matter how hard I try to keep my nose clean.''

Layla's heart went out to him. ''Tank,'' she murmured quietly, ''you're not going to be trouble for me. You made a mistake...and you're paying for that mistake. You're not a bad person. For goodness' sake, you didn't do anything violent or vicious and you certainly didn't hurt anyone.''

He gave a short, humorless laugh. "Yeah, but you're the only one around here that sees it that way. You were the only one willing to give me a job."

Sighing, she turned and walked behind the polished oak counter. She hated the cynicism in the boy's face, but she could easily understand it.

Tank Mullins had lived here all his life but when the chips were down, when he'd really needed a friend, he'd had to come to a stranger. She supposed she couldn't blame the town. Tank might be bright, but he'd been in one scrape after another since he was twelve. Getting arrested for Grand Theft Auto seemed to be the straw that broke the camel's back as far as the people around here were concerned. Layla had been uncertain of the whole situation herself. She wouldn't like having her car stolen, either.

But when Tank had shown up at the store and literally begged her for a job, she couldn't refuse. There was something in his face and eyes that was all too familiar to her. Something that tugged at her heart and reminded her all too painfully of her past. Something she'd seen in her own face for years every time she'd glanced in a mirror.

Fear.

A terrible, naked, mindless fear. And she couldn't turn her back on him.

Layla knew all about fear. She'd spent a lifetime living with it and then she'd spent the past ten years teaching herself to overcome it. It was a long, hard road and she was determined to help Tank Mullins take that first step. Just like Miss Pine had helped her.

"That's not true," she replied calmly. "Paul Tressler was willing to give you a job, too. So you see, I'm not the only one in town willing to take a chance on you."

"Yeah, I guess you're right." Tank said. He grinned, and she was amazed at how his thin face was transformed. "I won't let you down," he promised, "and I won't let Dr. Tressler down, either, I swear it."

"Don't let yourself down," she said gently, fighting a twinge of guilt as she remembered how she'd had to negotiate to get the vet to hire Tank. It was odd, really, she thought. She'd chosen to approach Paul because the man was known for being a soft touch for every hard-luck case around. Yet she'd had the distinct impression he didn't feel the least bit sorry for Tank Mullins. Layla wondered why. "By the way, I'm getting a dog."

"A dog." Tank's grin got even wider. "Hey, neat. I love animals."

"Good. You can help me take care of him." She opened her purse and took out the keys to the cash register. "But don't get too excited, I don't think this dog has much personality."

"What kind is it?" he asked excitedly. "Shepherd, lab, retriever . . . ?"

"Kind?" Layla frowned. "I don't know. I forgot to ask. He's big and sort of lumpy-looking and he's got dark brown-and-black fur . . . oh, yes, and he's fat."

She broke off as she heard the tinkle of the bell over the front door announcing their first customer. Tank nodded and headed back to his windows while Layla quickly counted out the cash and opened the register. They were busy that day and the hours flew by.

But by five o'clock Layla was as skittish as a teenager waiting for her first date. The feeling unsettled her because she knew what caused it. Paul Tressler. He'd be here any minute. She grimly concentrated on counting the day's take.

Glancing at her watch, she put the receipts into the bank bag. When Paul hadn't shown up by ten past five, she decided he'd probably been called out to an emergency.

She was both disappointed and relieved. The relief she could understand. The good doctor made her nervous. But the disappointment? Now that was strange. Determinedly she pushed the unfamiliar feeling to the back of her mind and forced her attention back to filling out her deposit slip.

After she'd finished, she sighed and gazed at the front door. Through the plate glass, she could see the steady glow from the barber's pole at Fisher's and the twinkling lights of Lili's House of Beauty.

Absently she put the bank bag beside her purse and started up the aisle toward the door. She might as well lock up and go home, Paul obviously wasn't coming.

She'd almost reached the door when she spotted him crossing the street, pulling Stanley on a leash behind him.

Paul was dressed in his pale green doctor's coveralls, a stethoscope dangled from his neck and he was grinning from ear to ear. She held the door open for them.

"Hi. Sorry I'm late."

"That's all right," she murmured politely. "I had to close out the register anyway. Why don't you take Stanley up front and I'll lock up? We can leave by the back door when we're finished."

Tugging on the leash, Paul headed up the aisle. "Busy day?"

"Yes," she answered as she shut the front door and slid the bolt into place.

She stared at his broad shoulders as she followed him up the aisle. He walked with a natural grace, a litheness and ease of movement that hinted at superb coordination and controlled strength.

There was an almost overwhelming air of masculinity emanating from him. Paul seemed totally unaware of it, but the effect was there nonetheless. He possessed an almost primitive maleness that reached out and touched her deeply on some level she couldn't control, a sexuality he wore as comfortably as that stethoscope around his neck.

That was why she'd ignored his friendly attempts to get to know her better. Her response to him frightened her half to death.

Layla's footsteps slowed as she came toward him. She fixed a polite smile on her face. "Tank isn't here right now. He had to go to Escondido to see his probation officer. But you can fix his hours up with me. Is that all right?"

Paul's face hardened a fraction. "I guess it'll have to be."

"Good," she said crisply. She turned her attention to the dog. "What do I need to do with him?"

"The same you do with any living creature," Paul said calmly. "Give him food, shelter and love."

"I suppose he eats a lot of dog food. Is there any special kind you'd recommend?"

At the mention of dog food, Stanley looked at her for the first time. His deep brown eyes were hopeful. Then he dropped his gaze and stared at the glass case of candy in front of him. His tongue came out and he licked his lips.

"Yes, he does need a special kind, something without too many calories. This dog is way too fat. He needs to go on a strict diet. And you'll need to walk him a couple of times a day, too." He watched Layla's face. "But other than that, just keep him clean, give him lots of affection and flea him whenever he needs it.''

"Fleas?''

On cue, Stanley sat down and began to scratch behind the ears. "I have to flea him?''

"Yeah, I've got a bag of supplies out in the truck for you. There's some dog shampoo in it. Use that for starters and it should take care of the immediate problem.''

"I have to give him a bath?''

Paul stared at her curiously. "Of course you have to bath him. He's an animal, he needs to be taken care of.''

"Oh, God, this is getting complicated. . . .''

"Hey,'' he said. He stepped toward her, his lips breaking into a reassuring smile. "It sounds a lot more complicated than it is. I'll help you. Tell you what. Why don't I take Stanley home with me now and feed him? I've got a really good pamphlet at home, too, then I can bring him by your place around about seven and give you a complete rundown on what you have to do. How does that sound?''

Relief swamped her. She wouldn't have to be alone with that animal just yet.

But if she agreed, she would have to be alone with Paul. Her relief evaporated.

Layla looked from Paul and his unsettling smile to the still-drooling form of Stanley and tried to decide which was the lesser of the two evils.

A low rumble came from deep in Stanley's chest.

Decision made, she smiled nervously at Paul and said, "That'd be wonderful. I think I'll need to write everything down.''

Chapter Two

Layla pulled the pan of cinnamon rolls out of the oven and set them on top of the stove to cool. Leaning back against the counter, she picked up the glass of white wine and took a sip. She was nervous. Paul and that dog would be arriving any minute. She closed her eyes for a brief moment and concentrated on analyzing why the arrival of a man and a dog should have her so rattled.

The best way to conquer a fear was to face it, she told herself firmly. All of her self-help books had been clear on that point. She frowned. Fear?

What did she have to be afraid of? It couldn't be Paul. The man was capable of arousing some pretty unusual emotions in her, but fear wasn't one of them. In fact, even when the negotiations this morning had gotten a little testy she hadn't been really afraid. Then what was it? Why was she so antsy that she'd had to rush home and soothe her nerves by baking for two hours?

Because he was an unknown quantity. The uncomfortable thought flashed through her mind with the speed of lightning. She straightened away from the counter, turned and put her half-finished wine in the sink. But Paul wasn't really a stranger, she told herself. She'd known him for over three months. He'd been one of the first people in town to introduce himself. Then why this uncertainty? Why this uneasiness because a nice man, really nothing more than a neighbor, was casually dropping by?

Glumly she concluded it was because she just plain didn't know how to react to him. For the first time in her life, she wished she were more experienced with men. Most women her age wouldn't have any qualms about spending an hour with an attractive man. But she wasn't most women and that was a fact.

Relationships had never come easily for her. Oh, heck, she thought, be honest. You've never even had a serious boyfriend, much less a real social life. Layla sighed. The truth was, dating had always seemed too much like a highly competitive game to her, one where there were very few winners and a lot of losers.

Paul slowed as he came to the short gravel driveway in front of Layla's house. She'd turned on the outside lights. The straight, boxy lines of the small bungalow were softened by several long redwood planters filled with shrubs and flowers. There were two new apple trees planted in the front yard and a flower bed had been dug alongside the concrete walkway.

Paul pulled up behind Layla's car and switched off the engine. As he flicked off the headlights, he turned to the dog and said, "Come on, mutt, it's time you saw your new home."

Grasping the leash firmly, he pulled Stanley out of the truck and across the lawn. At the door, he hesitated a second, then rang the bell.

Layla answered immediately. "Hello." She ushered both of them inside. "Go right on in," she said giving the dog a wary glance and then pointing toward the living room.

"Hi." Paul tugged the dog into the room a few paces before stopping and turning to Layla. He studied her with unabashed pleasure. She'd changed into an emerald-green turtleneck sweater and a pair of figure-hugging tight jeans. The outfit wasn't in the least flashy, but on her, it was sexy as hell. "Stanley was eager to see his new home. I think he's getting tired of bunking down in my back room."

Layla's throat felt dry. She found it hard not to stare. Paul had changed into a pair of faded denims that clung to his muscular legs and a long-sleeved V-necked black sweater that exposed the curly dark hair of his upper chest.

For a few seconds they studied each other, then Layla persuaded her voice to work. "How long have you had him staying with you?" she asked.

"Three days." Paul looked curiously around the room, his eyes widening in surprise. "My God," he exclaimed. "What have you done to this place? It looks fantastic."

"You've been here before?" She hadn't realized Paul had known her great-aunt so well.

"Yes." He grinned as he surveyed her living room. "Velma used to hold committee meetings here. We were both members of the Business and Merchants Association." He shook his head. "But this room didn't look anything like this when I was here before."

She flushed as the compliment sent an unfamiliar shaft of delight spearing through her. "I know, Aunt Velma was into white paint and serviceable plaid furniture. I wanted something a little softer."

Paul turned in a slow circle and surveyed the changes. She'd made it soft, all right, he thought, and very much a reflection of herself.

The walls were painted a pale peach and the old plaid furniture had been recovered with a dainty flowered fabric. Delicate white lace curtains hung at the windows. Velma's houndstooth carpet had been taken up to reveal gleaming hardwood floors.

"I'm envious as hell," he admitted, turning to smile at her. "You've only been here three months and you've done wonders in here. I've had my place for five years and it's still half-finished."

Layla laughed, inordinately pleased that he liked her house. "Thanks, I'm glad you like it. Would you care for some coffee and a cinnamon roll? They're homemade."

"So that's what that great smell is." He sniffed appreciatively. "My mouth has been watering since you opened the door." He didn't add it wasn't just the sweet rolls that had him drooling.

For once, Paul didn't have to give Stanley's leash a sharp tug to get the animal to move. The dog took out after Layla like a shot. Paul wasn't sure if it was the word "kitchen" or the smell that had the dog running, he only knew the mutt was practically dragging him now.

Paul threw up his hand against the doorjamb to slow them down. The dog stopped, strained on the leash for a second and then just stood there.

"Easy, boy," Paul muttered softly, "you don't want the lady to think you're ill-mannered." He glanced quickly at Layla and saw that she was busy at the coffee-pot. He took a moment to gaze around the kitchen. That, too, had changed. The walls were covered in cheerful yellow-and-white flowered wallpaper, the cabinets had been stripped down, sanded and stained a rich brown and the old aqua linoleum he remembered had been replaced by a hardwood floor like the one in the living room.

Instead of Velma's bulky old kitchen furniture, a simple pine table and matching chairs stood in the center of the room. His eyes narrowed speculatively as he spotted a bright red object by the back door.

"What's that?" he asked, thrusting the leash at Layla.

Startled, Layla took it. "Hey," she yelped as Stanley, now freed from Paul's restraining hand, galloped full force toward the stove. "Hold on." She tugged sharply on the leash and to her surprise, the dog stopped. She felt a spurt of satisfaction at her first attempt to bring the animal under control, but the feeling quickly faded as Stanley plopped down in front of the oven and stared at her cinnamon rolls.

His tongue came out.

"What did you say this was?" Paul asked.

Layla looked over. Paul was squatting in front of her prize possession, running his hands over the top of it.

"I didn't," she replied pointedly, holding the leash like a loaded gun. "But it's a horizontal butter churn."

He leaned forward to examine it more closely. The iron-banded wooden barrel sat in an oak sawhorse. It was painted a bright red and a crank stuck out one end. "A horizontal butter churn," he repeated. "I've never heard of that. How old is it?"

"I'm not sure. I bought it from an elderly lady at an estate sale. It had been shoved up in an attic for years. No one knew how long it had been there. It's my greatest find, though."

Layla decided to risk dropping Stanley's leash, since the dog didn't look as though he was going to budge. She went to the cupboard and pulled out mugs and plates. "How do you take your coffee?"

"Black," he replied. He straightened and stared at her slender back. "Do you do that sort of thing often?"

"What sort of thing?" She poured the coffee and moved to the stove, stopping at a drawer long enough to pull out a knife.

Paul was aware of an intense pleasure at the idea that he and Layla might share a hobby. "You know what I mean," he said. "Are you one of those people who spend their weekends haunting antique shops or stopping at every yard sale you see?"

She laughed. "I wouldn't exactly describe it as haunting them, but, yes, I will admit to having a lamentable weakness for collecting. But I have some tough rules for myself. I never stop at more than three yard sales on the same day."

She maneuvered around the dog, deftly sliced two rolls out of the pan and popped them onto the plates. As she picked them up and walked to the table, she looked at the dog. Stanley was staring at the plates in her hand. He was drooling.

"Are you sure he isn't hungry?" Layla asked as she took the chair across from Paul. "He's been staring at these rolls ever since you walked into the kitchen."

"Believe me," Paul replied fervently. "The last thing that dog needs is more food. You're going to have to toughen up, cut him back and make him get some exercise, no matter how much he begs."

She sighed. "All right, you're the vet."

Paul launched into a short, concise lesson on the care and feeding of grossly fat dogs. Layla grabbed the notepad she'd laid on the counter earlier and began taking notes. By the time Paul was finished, her head was spinning and she was wondering what she'd taken on.

"Now that we've taken care of Stanley," Paul continued briskly as he saw her lay her pencil down. "Why don't you tell me more about this lamentable weakness of yours. How long have you had this affliction?"

It took her a moment to realize what he was talking about. "Oh, my collecting. About ten years?" She cocked her head and stared at him curiously. "How about you? From what I've heard, you've got enough stuff behind your office to stock a swap meet." She was amazed at how easy it was to talk to him.

He contrived to look offended but didn't quite pull it off. "I see Ida Ingles is still moaning about my pack-rat tendencies."

Layla laughed. "According to Ida, you've got so many antiques behind your office you could charge admission and give tours."

"I probably could," he agreed. "But most of the stuff back there is from my wild, unrestrained youth. That's how I ended up with the circus calliope and the hay wagon. Used to be that if I saw anything that halfway interested me, I'd buy it. But I'm more discriminating now."

"What's your main area of interest? Antique cars?"

"No." He shook his head. "The old Model T was on the property when I bought the building. I just restored it. But I'm not really interested in old cars, that's a hobby all on its own. I found I enjoy working with my hands, so for the past couple of years I've concentrated on restoring old furniture."

"I've always wanted to try that," she said. "Is it hard?"

"It's not difficult. I started out by refinishing a small stool I found in the back of Ted Allison's barn and worked my way up from there."

"Maybe I'll give it a try," she murmured, excited by the prospect. "There must be some good books on the subject at the library."

"I've got some books you can borrow." Paul grinned. "It'll be nice having someone close by who shares my hobby."

His grin faded as his eyes focused on her smiling face. A tiny crumb of icing was caught on her lower lip. He stared at the speck of white, gripped by a fierce urge to lean across the table and lick it off her luscious mouth. Unconsciously, his tongue slid out and traced the edge of his lips.

Mesmerized, Layla watched his eyes darken and his color rise as the pink tip of his tongue skirted along the rim of his mouth. The movement was slow and sensual. Her heart thudded against her ribs and a hot sizzle of excitement raced through her veins.

She was suddenly scared to death.

It wasn't the desire in his eyes that had her wanting to leap from the table and run. No, she'd seen passion on a man's face before and could cope with that.

What frightened her was the way her pulse pounded and her stomach tightened in response to that hot, seductive motion.

She smiled uneasily and willed her nerves into deliberate silence. "We really should talk about Tank. He was thrilled that you're going to hire him."

All traces of sensuality vanished from Paul's face. His eyes narrowed and his jaw tightened. "I wish I could say the same. But I've got to be honest with you. I'm not looking forward to having him work for me. But we made a deal and I'm willing to stick to my end of it.''

Layla was absolutely dumbfounded. "What have you got against Tank?" she asked in bewilderment. "All he did was go joyriding. Car theft isn't a good thing but it's hardly the crime of the century. For goodness' sake, it's not like he hurt someone." She snorted in derision. "What's wrong with this town. Why is everyone so down on this kid?"

Paul cocked his head to one side. "You haven't been here very long," he informed her bluntly, "so you can't be expected to know. But take my word for it, he's not as innocent as he looks. This isn't a case of the whole town turning against some poor kid from the wrong side of the tracks."

Outrage sizzled through her like electricity down a wire. "Oh, really. Well, that's exactly what it sounds like to me. Just because he's poor and he's been in a little trouble doesn't mean he's scum. For God's sake, Tank's only a kid."

Paul put up a hand in a placating gesture. "Stop putting words in my mouth. I'm not calling him scum and I know he hasn't had it easy. Life with an alcoholic father and no mother doesn't give a kid the best start in life. But that doesn't excuse some of the things he's done." He leaned forward, his expression serious. "Did you know he almost killed my goddaughter, MaryBeth Harrison, last Christmas?"

Layla's jaw dropped. "What are you talking about?"

"It was a month or so before you arrived. Tank had been pestering MaryBeth for a date for ages. Finally, maybe because she felt sorry for him, she agreed to go out with him. Tank took her down to Escondido to the movies and on the way back, he started drinking. By the time they hit the outskirts of town he was so drunk he rammed her dad's new car into a tree and almost killed them both. But that's not the worst of it..." He paused. "Mary-Beth was knocked unconscious but Tank wasn't hurt. You know what he did?"

"What?" she asked, her voice almost a whisper.

"He got out of the car and walked away. Bud Harrison and I found MaryBeth at six the next morning. Tank hadn't even bothered to call anyone."

Layla felt a sinking sensation in her stomach as she listened to Paul's story. She'd wondered why no one in town was willing to give Tank a job, but she couldn't believe this of him. Was her own judgment so far off? He'd only worked for her for a few weeks, and she'd be the first to admit he wasn't a paragon of virtue. But Tank wasn't callous. There had to be more to the story. "Did anyone ask Tank what happened?"

"Yes. As a matter of fact, *I* did. We found Tank hiding out behind my office. Bud was ready to deck him, but between the sheriff and I, we managed to cool things down."

Paul smiled coldly. "Your fair-haired boy got his chance to talk and he didn't say one damned word. He just stood there and glared at everyone. MaryBeth still felt sorry for him, though, and she talked her dad out of pressing charges. The sheriff had to let him go."

Layla couldn't believe what she was hearing, but she knew Paul wouldn't make up such a fantastic story. She stared into her empty coffee cup while she tried to sort things out in her own mind. On the one hand, she couldn't condone what Tank had done but on the other, she couldn't abandon him.

Lifting her chin, she looked at Paul and asked, "Are you still willing to give him those fifteen hours?"

"We have a deal, Layla," Paul said as he stood up, "and I'm not looking for an excuse to back out of it. I just wanted you to know the facts and take a few precautions. A lot of people around here, and I'm one of them, think Tank's capable of violence. According to MaryBeth, the boy's got a temper as hot as his old man's used to be."

She shook her head and rose to her feet. "I don't believe that. I've never seen Tank lose control."

"Believe it. MaryBeth and Tank grew up together. She should know." He paused briefly as he watched Layla's eyes narrow. "Just be careful, that's all. What hours does he work for you?"

"Eight to one," she replied, wanting to continue the discussion. Then, changing her mind, she moved quickly toward the door and led the way into the living room.

"Okay," Paul said from behind her, "I'll give him two to five. But I'm going to be keeping my eye on him. You might tell him, there are no drugs available in a vet's office."

She stopped dead and spun around to glare at him. "Tank doesn't take drugs."

"Alcohol's a drug," Paul shot back. He caught himself and sighed. "Look, I admire you for giving him another chance. And I'm willing to do my bit, but that doesn't mean I'm going to turn a blind eye to how he behaves."

"Does that mean you're going to be standing over his shoulder all the time, watching every little thing he does?"

Layla crossed her arms over her chest to keep her hands from shaking. She hated arguments. All in all, Paul was being reasonable. But it wasn't fair to Tank to send him into a no-win situation where the odds were already stacked against him.

"You tell me," Paul replied softly. "Do I need to play the heavy-handed boss man with the kid?"

"No. Tank's worked for me for weeks now and he does a good job." She forced herself to remain calm. "But it's not fair to hire him unless you're really willing to give him a chance."

"I agree," Paul said. "Don't worry, he'll be treated fairly." When she continued to stare at him, a doubtful look in her big hazel eyes, he smiled gently and said, "You have my word on it. Okay?"

She stared at him uncertainly for a moment. Then her mouth curved into another one of her breathtaking smiles. Paul wondered if she knew what that smile did to him.

"All right." She turned and pulled open the front door.

He stopped in the doorway. "Will you be at the Business and Merchants meeting tomorrow night?"

"Is it tomorrow night?" She looked surprised. Then she smiled weakly, feeling drained. This skirmish had taken too much out of her already. Paul Tressler confused her and angered her and made her admire him all at the same time. "Yes. I'll be there. Aunt Velma wanted me to continue the tradition of the Emporium taking an active part in the Association."

"Good. You can let me know how you and Stanley are getting on." He moved onto the top step and turned to stare at her as though he wanted to say something else.

Layla silently took a slow, deep breath. A familiar sinking feeling coiled in the pit of her stomach. Her mask of confidence was slipping. "I'm sure I'll have a full report for you," she replied, forcing her voice to a lightness she wasn't feeling. When he continued to watch her, she asked, "Was there something else?"

"Yeah, tell Tank I'd like him to start tomorrow." He nodded briefly and strode out into the darkness toward his truck.

Layla closed the door with relief. Intriguing as Paul Tressler was, she was glad he was gone. It had taken every ounce of nerve she possessed to argue with the man about Tank.

She glanced at the bookcase in the corner and smiled wryly. Despite dozens of volumes on assertiveness, positive thinking and being your own best friend, confrontations of any kind still left her feeling weak and nauseous.

Her gaze drifted up and stopped at an ornately framed photograph of an elderly woman. The stern but kindly face in the picture stared back at her. Miss Violet Pine: spinster, teacher, mentor and friend. With her ramrod-straight spine, her iron-gray hair pulled back in a severe bun and her twinkling blue eyes hidden behind those thick horn-rimmed glasses, she looked like a stereotypical mean old maid. Layla grinned.

Nothing could be further from the truth.

Miss Pine was the best thing that had ever happened to her. Even now, she could almost hear her old teacher's clear, crisp voice saying, *I won't have you caving in over this, Layla. You've got to stand up for what you think is right. And that includes standing up for yourself. You're worth it.*

And she was worth it, but sometimes it was still hard not to be afraid. Sometimes she had to keep reminding herself that the past was over and done with. Sighing, Layla sank onto the couch.

She knew where the sick feeling and the fear and the shame came from. It came directly from Daniel Shepley Odell.

Her father.

She tensed as his harsh and disapproving face flashed through her mind. Like a flame sparking against dry kindling, anger flared deep inside her and made every muscle in her body go rigid.

She fought against the anger, knowing it was self-destructive and defeating. She was free of him now and that was all that mattered.

But for so many years she hadn't been free. For so many years she and her poor, ineffectual mother had lived under that man's hard and dominating will.

Her mother had been his slave. Layla had been his whipping post. She smiled bitterly. He hadn't been physically abusive and she supposed that was something to be grateful for. But maybe emotional abuse was just as bad. It was the kind of ugliness that was so easy to hide. There was no damning evidence, no scars, no bruises. There was just a small child with a mind that believed every horrible word that Daddy said.

And her father had said plenty. She was never smart enough or pretty enough or clever enough. Nothing she ever did was right. Nothing she had to say was worth hearing. Nothing she ever gave him was enough. No matter how high her grades, they were never good enough. No matter how polite she tried to be, she was never enough of a lady to suit him. No matter how she tried, she could never please him. Never get him to say anything to her that wasn't negative. She couldn't remember her father ever giving her or her mother a compliment, let alone a kiss or a hug.

By the time she was fourteen, she was an emotional wreck. Riddled with self-doubt, she'd been terrified to open her mouth in case she said the wrong thing. Then her mother died.

Sadness filled her as she thought of her mother's bleak existence. Elaine Odell had escaped by dying. Layla had escaped by meeting Miss Pine.

Flattening her hands against her thighs, she focused her eyes straight ahead and took ten long, deep breaths. With every breath she silently commanded her muscles to relax and her mind to clear. By the time she'd finished counting, she was feeling better. In control.

She dealt with her father with a monthly phone call and an occasional letter. Since his remarriage ten years ago, she was free. She intended to stay that way.

Layla gazed at the picture and felt the last of the anger fade. You were right, Miss Pine, she thought, smiling wistfully at the picture. Despite my father's best efforts to convince me otherwise, I'm worth something.

And so is Tank Mullins.

Things went pretty well, Paul thought as he put his truck in gear and pulled out onto the county road.

He whistled softly as he drove. He was pleased at the way he'd gotten past Layla's coolness in the last twelve hours, even though he'd hated having to argue with her over Tank Mullins. His whistling stopped abruptly and he scowled into the darkness. After the way Layla had defended the Mullins boy, she'd have a royal fit if she ever found out he'd only hired the kid to keep an eye on him.

Two weeks ago, when he'd realized she'd gone and done a fool thing like hiring the young hoodlum, he'd started to worry about her safety.

A short, humorless laugh escaped him. The irony of the situation was almost absurd. Up until that incident with MaryBeth, he'd been one of Tank's few defenders in town.

But his blood had boiled when he'd seen how callously the boy had treated his goddaughter. Then, when he'd stuck his head out of his office and seen Tank washing the Emporium's windows, his anger had crystallized into fear.

Tank might be troubled, but the kid was also potentially dangerous.

Thank God, he thought fervently, easing his foot off the accelerator, Layla had come to him asking for those extra hours. Now he could make sure she was safe. If necessary, he could put the fear of God into Tank Mullins.

He turned onto the tree-lined road leading up the hill to his house and started whistling again. Things were on track. Fate, for once seemed to be working in his favor. Not only did he and Layla have Tank in common, but Stanley as well. If nothing else, he could pop over from time to time to make sure things were going all right on that front. And she was a collector, too. That was like frosting on the cake.

Paul pulled up in front of his modern Spanish-style home set on the crest of a hill. Before he'd switched the engine off his ears were filled with loud, joyous—at least to him—barking.

Digging into his pocket for his keys, he took the steps two at a time. He could hear his dogs thumping against the double front doors. "Okay, fellas, just a minute." He pushed the door open and hit the light switch. Immediately, three dogs leaped around, barking and jumping and generally doing whatever it took to get their master's attention.

"Hello, boy." He kneeled down and petted an Irish setter with one hand while stroking a cocker spaniel with the other. He made eye contact with Rhea, a shy mixed breed with more brains than the other two combined.

Several minutes passed before he could stand up and survey his home. He grew thoughtful as he took in his half-finished house. The bare white stuccoed walls looked good, as did the red tile floors. They should, he'd done them himself, but the only furniture in the room was one black leather sofa, a TV stand with a twenty-five-inch color television, a stereo sitting in lonely splendor by itself in the far corner and a couple of heavy southwestern-style end tables.

He didn't particularly like living in a half-furnished house; it was just that when he'd bought the place five years before, he'd known he wanted to make a home, to fill the rooms with pieces he'd redone himself. But, what with the demands of his job, he never seemed to find the time. And, anyway, doing it alone wasn't much fun.

Paul sighed, tossed his keys onto one of the end tables and promised himself he'd eventually find the time to do some more antique hunting. Maybe he and Layla could find some great old pieces and refinish them together.

Enormously cheered by the thought, he headed for the kitchen. The dogs trotted right behind him.

"Yes, fellas," he said to the canine trio. "I think I finally made some headway today. God knows it's taken me long enough."

In the gleaming modern kitchen, he pulled open the refrigerator and grabbed a beer. Paul perched on a stool at the breakfast bar and took a sip of his drink. His offhand comment had gotten him to thinking.

Why had he worked so hard to get closer to Layla Odell? It was a question that came up often.

True, she was gorgeous. But he'd seen lots of beautiful women before. Hell, he'd even been married to one once. So what was so compelling about Layla that he practically jumped through hoops just to get her attention?

He didn't know.

But he damned well intended to find out.

Chapter Three

The Business and Merchants Association meeting was held in the community room of the Riker's Pass Town Hall. The large wooden building also housed the fire department, the city council chambers and the now-defunct city jail.

Layla jumped out of her car and hurried toward the front door. She was running late. The meeting was due to start at seven sharp and she'd been delayed because of that wretched dog. Dashing inside, she quickly scanned the crowd for Paul. She had to talk to him.

Twenty-four hours with Stanley was driving her crazy.

A dozen or more people milled around a semicircle of folding chairs at the front of the hall. Layla surveyed them quickly. She didn't see Paul. Whatever trepidations she'd had about approaching the man after the way her hormones had reacted to him yesterday vanished. This was an emergency. That dog was just plain weird.

When her first glance failed, she started again, looking carefully at the various clusters of people huddled at the front of the room. Arnold Dunphy, the tall, balding owner of the hardware store was talking to Lillian Metcalf, the owner of Lili's House of Beauty. Her disappointment mounted as she studied each group. No sign of Paul in any of them.

She spotted Elliot Thaxton, a prosperous chicken farmer and the chairman of the association, heading toward the microphone. Her apprehension mounted. The meeting was starting and Paul wasn't here. Damn. He'd probably been called out on an emergency. She'd have to phone him now.

Sighing, Layla headed for a chair at the edge of the circle. It wasn't that Stanley was hard to take care of. Quite the contrary, he was very polite about going outside and doing his business. But she knew something was seriously wrong. Paul had forgotten to give her that pamphlet on dog care yesterday and she was just about at her wit's end.

Layla hadn't taken two steps when someone tapped her on the arm and a familiar voice said, "Looking for somebody?"

She whirled to see Paul smiling at her. "Oh, thank goodness you're here," she said. "I've got to talk to you."

His warm smile vanished and was instantly replaced with a worried frown. "What's wrong? Is Tank giving you trouble?"

"No, no, no," she said impatiently, shaking her head. "It's not Tank. It's Stanley."

"Stanley. Oh. Well then, it'll have to wait. Come on, I've saved us a couple of seats up over there." He pointed to the center of the circle, grabbed her hand and tugged her toward two folding chairs smack in front of the microphone.

If Layla hadn't been so rattled by the feel of his hand enveloping hers, she'd have noticed that everyone in the room was watching them. But her attention was so focused on Paul that she missed the knowing grins passing from person to person.

Paul's grip was strong and sure, his flesh, callused and warm. Layla could feel the heat of his hand rippling through her entire body. This was the first time he'd touched her and the effect was startling. She stared at their clasped hands in confusion. She wanted to pull her hand away while at the same time she had the ridiculous urge to hold him tighter. How could so casual a touch have such an impact on her?

"There'll be a big crowd tonight," he continued as he released her hand and sat down. "We're supposed to start planning the Centennial Celebration."

"But I've got to talk to you about Stanley," she said, her voice breathless. "And about Tank."

"There isn't time now. Elliot's already at the microphone. But the meeting shouldn't last long. We can go for coffee afterward."

Layla nodded and sank onto the metal folding chair next to Paul. She peeked at him out of the corner of her eye. He grinned at her.

Flustered, she hastily looked away and glanced at the other members of the Association. They were all merchants or business people from the area in and surrounding Riker's Pass. Several of them were smirking at her. Layla blushed.

"We have several items on the agenda tonight," the chairman said, after he called the meeting to order. "So let's get a move on."

Layla only half listened as the meeting got underway. They were talking exclusively about the upcoming Centennial and as she didn't intend to get very involved with that, she allowed her thoughts to wander.

Was Paul asking her for a date? No, she decided quickly, he'd only suggested coffee because she'd made it clear she had to talk to him. The thought sent a twinge of regret through her. She flicked Paul another surreptitious glance.

Though it was early spring, he wasn't wearing a jacket, only a short-sleeved blue sports shirt that contrasted sharply with the deep tan of his exposed arms. He was leaning forward on his elbows, his hands clasped casually between his knees.

Of their own accord, her eyes locked onto his thighs. Through the tight jeans he wore, she could see the long, sculpted muscles of his upper legs straining against the denim. The contrast between the golden skin of his bare arms and the faded blue fabric was mesmerizing. She stared at him, wondering if he was the same warm brown all over.

An image, a very erotic image, flashed into her mind.

Paul, his gray eyes smoldering with passion, his hands reaching for her half-naked body...standing beside a canopied bed in a candlelit room. A room filled with shadows and moonlight and sensual mysteries. His long-sleeved white shirt was unbuttoned to the waist and she could see the rapid rise and fall of his chest. His fingers touched the bare flesh of her shoulders and she shivered in anticipation....

"Mr. Chairman—" Arnold Dunphy's booming voice shattered her reverie "—I'd like to second that motion."

Startled, Layla quickly tore her eyes away from Paul's legs and stared at the floor. Deeply shocked by her sexy fantasy, she kept her gaze lowered and prayed that her face wasn't beet red. Willing her pulse rate back to normal, she held her breath and darted a quick look at Paul. He was staring straight ahead, his attention focused on the speaker.

She expelled the breath she'd been holding and sagged against the chair. Her reaction to this man was getting ridiculous. Why, for two cents she'd slip out the door as soon as the meeting was over. But she did have to talk to Paul and not just about Stanley. There was a thing or two she wanted to ask him about Tank.

She'd run into Tank after closing the store and his report hadn't been encouraging. All the boy had said was that the work was dirty, but he could handle it. Layla wondered exactly what that meant. She wanted to make sure Paul wasn't riding roughshod over the kid.

"I'll volunteer for that one." Paul spoke for the first time since the meeting had begun.

"Good." The chairman smiled encouragingly.

"But I'd like Layla Odell to serve as the cochair of the committee."

Layla's head snapped up and she stared at Paul. "Cochair of what?" she whispered.

"Haven't you been listening?" he admonished. "I've volunteered us to run the Publicity and Decorations Committee."

"You what . . ."

"Layla, is that all right with you?" Elliot asked. She looked around to see a dozen pairs of eyes staring at her.

"Uh . . . sure. That'll be fine." Just wait till I get that man alone, she thought, shooting him a quick frown. He smiled blandly and sat back.

Layla fumed silently during the remainder of the meeting. What in the world was the man thinking about?

How dare he volunteer her for something without even talking to her about it? And to cochair it with him!

She felt suddenly helpless, as if she'd completely lost control of the situation. Dealing with Paul was like trying to hold back floodwaters from a riverbank with her bare hands. In the past twenty-four hours, her life had become crazily entwined with his, and she wasn't sure she liked it.

But beneath the wariness and the irritation another emotion blossomed and struggled to break free.

Excitement.

Dangerous, frightening and incredibly enticing. The idea of spending time with Paul Tressler was like stepping onto a Ferris wheel when you were leery of heights and hoping the thrill of the ride was worth the payment of fear.

Excitement. Layla could feel its beckoning lure as clearly as she felt her lungs breathing air.

By the time the last of the committees had been assigned, an hour had passed and Layla had gotten her emotions under control. She'd stay calm and cool. There was no reason to panic; neighbors worked on projects together all the time. And as for Tank, she'd ask Paul precisely what his conditions of employment were and then she'd ask him how the hell to cope with that darned dog.

But before she could ask him anything, his beeper went off.

Paul plucked the beeper out of his pocket, stared at the digital display for a moment and then headed toward the door. "I've got to get to the office," he called over his shoulder to Layla. "I'll come by your house before work tomorrow. We can talk about your problem then."

Layla sank lower in her chair; half the people in the hall were staring at her. She was going to kill Paul Tressler.

At seven-thirty the next morning, Paul walked up the stairs to Layla's porch. He was dead tired, but she'd aroused his curiosity and he wanted to see her. Yawning, he jabbed the doorbell and then wearily leaned against the frame. Maybe she'd make him some breakfast?

But when Layla opened the door, she wasn't wearing a hospitable smile. She looked frantic.

"Good morning," he said pleasantly.

"You've got to do something," Layla wailed. "He hasn't moved." She grabbed Paul's arm and pulled him none too gently into the house. "You should have warned me. This is getting eerie. No. It's not eerie, it's downright scary."

"What are you talking about . . . ?"

"I should never have agreed to this. . . ." She dragged him through the living room and into the kitchen.

"Now hold on a minute." Paul managed to free his arm. He put his hands on his hips and stared down at her. "Just calm down and tell me what's going on."

"That." She pointed toward the refrigerator.

Stanley was sitting in front of it.

"What?" Paul asked, clearly befuddled.

"That. The only time that wretched dog moves is when I feed him or let him outside to do his business. The rest of the time he sits smack in front of my refrigerator."

Paul sighed theatrically. "Is that all? You're upset because the dog camps in front of your fridge?"

Put like that, it did sound ridiculous. But she wasn't going to give up the offensive so easily. He should have warned her that the animal wasn't right in the head. And there was still the little matter of making her cochair of a committee. "Isn't that enough? I'll admit I don't know much about dogs, but he's been sitting there for almost two days. That's hardly normal behavior."

"It is for him. Joe used to feed him every time he went to the refrigerator. Since you've cut back his rations, I guess he thinks he's got to sit there all the time."

That took the wind out of her sails. "Oh. Well, uh, how do I get him to stop? I mean it's pretty difficult to cook or anything with eighty pounds of dog under my feet every time I try to open the door."

Paul ran a hand through his hair and closed his eyes briefly. For the first time, she noticed how tired he looked.

"You don't get him to stop," he replied. "But he'll eventually learn you're not going to feed him and get bored."

Paul *sounded* tired, too, she thought. "You look like you haven't slept all night."

"I didn't," he replied. He stifled a yawn. "I had to do emergency surgery."

"Was that why your beeper went off? What happened?"

"The Harrisons' labrador got hit by a car. It was a hit-and-run," he said with a disgusted shake of his head. "The poor thing was pretty mangled. MaryBeth was frantic—she's the one who found him. His leg was broken and he had internal bleeding."

"Is he going to be all right?"

"Yes, at least I think so. He came out of the anesthetic early this morning and MaryBeth came over to sit with him. If he does all right today, I'll let her take him home tonight."

"God, you must be exhausted." She winced guiltily. "And I jumped on you the minute you walked in. Would you like some coffee?"

"I'd love some coffee."

"Why don't you wait in the living room," she suggested. "My couch is a lot more comfortable than these chairs."

"That sounds good." Paul wandered into the living room. As he went toward the couch, the bookcase caught his eye. Curious, he stopped and scanned the titles.

His eyebrows rose in fascination. *Recreate Your Self-Esteem, Imaging for Everyone, Positive Affirmations, The Goddess Inside You,* and there was a nifty hot pink paperback intriguingly titled, *Inventing Yourself.*

Amazed, Paul studied the row upon row of self-help books. There were three shelves of the darned things. He'd never seen so many in one bookcase. Kneeling down, he trailed his fingers along the paperbacks as he shook his head, wondering what it meant, what it said about her. He knew that these sorts of books routinely made the bestseller lists and that they tended to be very popular with women, but the only place he'd ever seen so many of them in one place was a bookstore.

The clink of china from the kitchen had him hastily getting to his feet and heading for the couch. But as he heard Layla's soft footsteps coming down the hall, he couldn't help but be even more curious about this woman. She had enough self-improvement books to fill half the shelves at the Riker's Pass Library. Instinctively he realized he'd just learned something important about Layla. Only he couldn't figure out what it was.

"Sorry that took so long," Layla apologized as she sat the tray on the coffee table. "But I thought you might be hungry, too, and I wanted to warm these rolls."

"I am hungry," he admitted, trying not to drool over the luscious cinnamon rolls. "And he thinks he is, too."

"Oh, my goodness," she exclaimed. "Stanley's moved."

The dog had followed her into the living room. He sat down in front of the coffee table and gazed longingly at the plate of pastry.

"Yeah," Paul snorted in derision. "I guess it takes food to get his butt to budge. That's one of the things I wanted to talk to you about."

"Feeding Stanley?" Layla stared at him in surprise. "But you've already told me and I don't overfeed him." She glanced at Stanley and then determinedly tried to ignore the dog's pathetic expression.

"I'm sure you don't," he said. He suspected Layla was the type who followed instructions to the letter. "But considering the shape he's in, we're going to have to do a little more than just cut back on his food. His whole psyche's out of kilter. He's forgotten how to be a dog. This mutt needs some heavy-duty exercise."

"I tried taking him for a walk," she explained, somewhat defensively. "But after a few feet, he just sits down. Maybe he's too old, or he has arthritis or something."

"Too old! Stanley? He's five. That's not old." Paul leaned forward and picked up a roll. "And I gave him a thorough examination. He doesn't have arthritis. He's just lazy and bored. All he and Joe ever did was eat. Stanley needs some stimulation in his life."

"So what should I do?"

Paul stared at her thoughtfully. He had a hidden agenda here, but it was important to sound spontaneous. He wanted time with Layla. Time to get to know her, time to be with her, time to see if his attraction to this woman was nothing more than an overactive libido. "I've got an idea. Why don't we take Stanley for a hike tomorrow? You know, make him stay outside for a few hours, let him do some serious walking, chase a few butterflies, act like a dog. We could take a picnic and go up to Clifton's Peak. That's an easy trail. And tomorrow's Sunday, you don't have to open the store.''

She automatically started to say no, but at the last second, she changed her mind. For some reason, she couldn't bring herself to refuse. This man made her curious. What did he want from her? Or more importantly, what did she want from him?

''Well, I suppose we could do that,'' she said. ''But, uh, don't you have other things you'd rather be doing? After all, Sunday's your day off, too. Just because I'm having problems with my dog—'' she was amazed she'd actually begun to think of Stanley as hers ''—is no reason for you to give up your free time.''

''Don't worry about it. I'll enjoy the exercise.'' He smiled faintly and sat back. ''And it'll give us a chance to start making plans.''

''Making plans?'' Layla eyed him warily. Exactly what did he have in mind?

''For the Centennial.''

''Oh, yes,'' she said, her voice faintly laced with sarcasm. ''You did volunteer me for that, didn't you?''

Her sarcasm was completely lost on Paul. He yawned again, reached for his cup, drained it and rose to his feet.

''Uh-huh. You said Velma wanted you to stay involved.'' He began a long, slow stretch, groaning in pleasure as the tight muscles and knotted tendons expanded and relaxed.

Layla stared at him.

"Sorry," he said apologetically, "But I'm half-dead. I'll pick you up at eleven tomorrow. Don't worry about the food, I'll take care of it."

With difficulty, she dragged her gaze away from his body. That slow, sinuous stretch of his almost hypnotized her. Her nerve endings leaped to the edge of her skin and her pulse rate jumped into double time.

Layla got a hold of herself, silently vowing to pick up that book on women's sexuality she'd seen advertised. Female sensuality was supposed to peak in a woman's mid-thirties, but she was beginning to think she must be hitting it early. God knew, *this* wasn't normal behavior for her. "That's fine."

Layla panted as she climbed the last few feet toward the summit of Clifton's Peak. Though the air was crisp and cool, she could feel perspiration trickling down her back.

"This is the spot," Paul said as she reached him. "I told you it would be perfect." He dropped Stanley's leash and the dog flopped down.

Collapsing beside the animal, Layla smiled wryly. "He doesn't exactly look like he's eager to chase any butterflies."

Paul laughed and spread out the blanket he'd carried up from the truck. He put the picnic hamper on the edge and then sat down himself. "He will be. Just give him a minute to catch his wind." He gazed around the summit. "What do you think of the view?"

"It's beautiful." Below she could see the town, looking now like a children's set of building blocks nestled in a tiny clearing among the trees. Behind her, a large meadow strewn with oaks, pines and grasses spread out to the base of the huge barren mountain that was part of the coastal range.

Birds sang, the wind whistled faintly in the trees and her own breathing echoed harshly in her ears. She scooted over and settled herself comfortably on the quilt.

"Are you hungry yet?" Paul asked in a soft, husky voice.

His question startled her. She'd been staring at the view, her face turned partially away from him. Looking around, she found his eyes locked on her mouth.

After a moment, he raised his gaze to meet hers. Her breath caught in her throat. Paul's eyes were warm, sensual and faintly mysterious. The way he looked at her set off an explosion of contradictory feelings inside her.

Once again she felt as if she was losing control. She was simultaneously cautious and wary, attracted and scared. What did this man want from her?

Flustered, she dropped her gaze and stared at the patterns of the faded patchwork quilt. "Not yet," she murmured. "Why don't we talk first?"

"Ah, yes. I knew there was something on your mind." He leaned back on one elbow, stretching his long denim-clad legs out on the blanket. "Go ahead. I'm all ears."

"What kind of work do you have Tank doing?" She looked away as she asked the question. She had no right to question him and she knew it, but she couldn't help herself. Someone had to watch out for Tank Mullins.

"That's a strange question?" His voice hardened. "Has Tank been complaining already?"

"No." She turned to look at him. Paul's eyes were narrowed speculatively. "He just said the work was dirty."

"Cleaning cages usually is."

"You have him cleaning cages?"

"Yes." He sat up. "I'm a vet. What did you think I'd have him do? Administer anesthetic?"

"No," she replied hastily. "I was just curious, that's all."

"Really?" He looked skeptical. "Or were you trying to make sure I wasn't riding roughshod over your fair-haired baby?"

"That's a nasty thing to say. And he isn't my fair-haired baby," she shot back irritably. "But it seems to me that everyone in this town, and that includes you, doesn't want to see him get a decent break. I know what he did was wrong, but for God's sake, everyone deserves a second chance."

"Or a third or a fourth or a fifth." He laughed cynically. "Tank's had chances. Lots of them. But after that stunt with MaryBeth, some of us just plain don't trust him."

"Well, I *do* trust him." Aware that she was dangerously close to losing her temper, she got a grip on herself. Giving in to any extremes of emotion around this man could be dangerous. She knew it. "Look, I wasn't trying to imply you're some kind of Simon Legree and I know you're doing me a big favor, but please, ease up on him a little."

"I haven't done anything to the kid," Paul protested.

"You think he hasn't realized that you don't trust him?"

"Of course he realizes it, but once trust has been violated, it's got to be reearned. Tank knows that."

"But he didn't violate *your* trust...."

"Yes, he did."

"How?" she demanded. "When?"

"The night Tank left MaryBeth unconscious on the front seat of her daddy's car." Paul sighed. "I was the one that talked Bud and Susan into letting her go out with Tank. Like you, I used to be one of the kid's defenders in this town."

Layla stared at him in surprise.

"So you see, I feel more than a little responsible for what happened. If I'd stayed out of it, if I'd kept my mouth shut, my goddaughter wouldn't have almost ended up dead."

"I thought you said she wasn't badly hurt," Layla mumbled.

"That's not the point. I trusted Tank and I talked my friends into trusting him, too. He violated that trust. As far as I'm concerned, he's not just on probation with the state of California, he's on probation with me, too."

She didn't know what to say. Paul had a legitimate reason for his attitude to Tank, but on the other hand, she was convinced there was more to the story than any of them knew.

"Look," Paul said after a few moments. "Let's not argue about Tank. I've given you my word I'm not treating him unfairly and you'll just have to trust *me* on it."

She stared at him and their gazes locked. His eyes were compelling, willing her to put her faith in him and take his word at face value.

"All right," she said softly. "I'll trust you on this."

Surprisingly enough, she was telling the truth. She did trust Paul. Against his better judgment, he'd hired Tank and given him another chance. And somehow, she knew that if he said he'd treat the boy fairly, he meant it.

Paul cocked his head to one side, his expression curious. "Why are you doing this?"

"Doing what?"

"Taking Tank under your wing. What is he to you? It's not like you've known him all your life."

His question took her off guard. Without thinking she blurted out, "Because someone once helped *me*. Someone once took my side against..." Her voice trailed off as she realized how much she was revealing, how much of herself she was exposing. "It's not important. Anyway, you've agreed to be fair to him and I know you will. Let's talk about something else. How's MaryBeth's dog?"

For a moment he was tempted to press her. But something in the overly bright way she'd changed the subject made him back off. Yet he was more curious than ever. Who had taken her side and more importantly, against whom?

"The dog's doing fine. They were able to take him home last night. But the animal was very lucky. If MaryBeth hadn't found him, he'd probably have lain on the road all night. There isn't much traffic out that way."

She nodded. Neither of them spoke for a moment. Then Paul reached for the picnic hamper. Stanley moved for the first time since sitting down.

After eating a huge lunch of roast beef sandwiches, cole slaw and potato chips, Layla lay back against the blanket and stared up at the sky.

"Can I ask you something?" Paul said softly.

"What?" She closed her eyes.

"Why do you have all those books?"

She didn't have to ask which books. Embarrassed, she kept her eyes closed. "You must be talking about my self-improvement books."

"Yes. Uh, you seem to have a lot of them." Paul spoke in the same soothing tone he used when giving a puppy its first distemper shot.

"I do." She didn't open her eyes. "I like to read."

He cleared his throat. "I like to read, too," he said, "but what I really meant was why those kinds of books? Are you interested in psychology or something?"

"A little." Abruptly she opened her eyes and sat up.

"So you don't read them for yourself—" He broke off as he realized how badly he was handling this conversation. But he couldn't help himself; he really wanted to know why a beautiful young woman had enough self-improvement books to stock a library. It was more than just a hobby for her. "You just read them because you find them ... intriguing, is that it?"

"No." She sighed audibly and he cringed. "I read them for the same reason everyone else does. Self-improvement."

"What do you need to improve?" he asked, giving her a slow, sexy grin. "From here it looks like you're just about perfect."

She smiled at the compliment and then lifted one shoulder in a negligent shrug. "Thanks. But everyone can use a little help. I happen to like making myself better."

Flattening her hands against her thighs, she inhaled the clean mountain air. Talking to Paul wasn't difficult at all. She sensed that he was genuinely curious and there was one part of her that wanted to give him fair warning.

If he was looking for perfection, he'd better look elsewhere. Smiling brilliantly, she looked him directly in the eyes. "You could almost say I was a self-made woman."

Chapter Four

Beneath the flippancy of her words, Paul could sense an undercurrent of truth. Noting that her smile didn't quite reach her eyes, he watched her for a moment. Taking care to keep his tone casual, he said, "That's an intriguing statement. Do you mind telling me what it means?"

She hesitated before answering. "Just that like a lot of people, I've had to work hard to overcome a certain amount of destructive and negative garbage that was drilled into me as a child," she replied reluctantly. "Most of us can use a little help in building our self-esteem or learning to handle life better."

"I see." He didn't but he could hardly admit that to Layla. The number of books she owned suggested she was doing more than getting a few pointers on building a stronger self-image. "So, you've gotten a lot out of them?"

She shrugged and absently reached over to pet Stanley. "I suppose you could say that. Actually sometimes I almost feel like I've invented myself. People might make fun of self-help books, but if I hadn't made a conscious effort to overcome my upbringing, I'd be a totally different person today. Those books helped."

A dozen different questions flashed through Paul's mind and he tried to think of a tactful way to keep her talking. He wanted to understand. There were hidden depths and secrets to Layla. She reminded him of a Chinese puzzle box he'd had as a boy; the minute he'd figured out one layer, another more difficult piece popped into its place.

But before he could ask her another question, she turned to him and said, "Look, I don't want to talk about me anymore, that's boring. Let's talk about the Centennial Celebration. We've got a lot of planning to do. The opening dance is only a month away."

Layla closed her mouth tighter than a clam. She was desperate to change the subject. She wasn't used to opening up so much and Paul's probing was starting to rattle her. He was too easy to talk to; there was something about him that made you want to share confidences. But she'd already told him too much. If she wasn't careful, she'd be spilling the story of her life in a couple of minutes.

But what few miserable secrets she had, she preferred to keep to herself.

Paul shifted onto one elbow and gave her a deceptively lazy smile. He noticed the stubborn set of her jaw and the now-rigid way she held herself. Only a fool would ignore body language like that, and he was no fool. As much as she fascinated him, he knew he wasn't going to learn any more about her today. Her strained smile and the way she was concentrating on petting Stanley indicated she was embarrassed to have told him so much.

But Paul was a patient man. One day she'd trust him enough to tell him everything he wanted to know. He wondered why that had suddenly become so important to him, then he shrugged the question off. It didn't matter. She'd become important to him.

"Actually I don't think we're going to have time to do much of anything except make a run for the truck." He pointed up at the sky. "Storm clouds."

"Oh, no," she protested, frowning at the clouds. "Where did those come from. We haven't talked about the Centennial at all." As she spoke she gathered their things. Stanley, who hadn't been able to con either of them out of so much as one bite of lunch, gazed at her hopefully as she stuffed a roast beef sandwich back into the basket.

Paul began to help. Ignoring the dog's pathetic expression, he clipped on the leash, rose to his feet and tugged Stanley off the blanket.

"That's no problem," he said casually. "Why don't you come to my place for dinner tomorrow night? I'm not on call and we'd have plenty of time to make some preliminary decisions. We do need to get a move on things."

Before she realized what she was doing, she heard herself say, "Yes."

The storm clouds were real. She and Paul made it to the safety of his truck before it started to pour. The rain continued for the rest of the day and through the night. It was still bucketing down when she opened the store.

There was little traffic on the main street and even less traffic in her store. Layla shrugged and glanced at the clock. It was past ten and so far this morning she'd had one customer.

She sighed and leaned on the top of the counter. Usually she liked rain, but today some bright, cheery sunshine would be welcome. At least it would lift her spirits. Tonight she had to go to Paul's for dinner and after everything she'd told him yesterday, she wasn't looking forward to seeing him again. She still couldn't believe how she'd opened up. It was embarrassing.

From the back of the store, she heard a muffled grunt as Tank set a box onto the floor. Layla turned her head and watched as he sliced open the top of the cardboard. He stooped and began unloading cans of stewed tomatoes onto the bottom shelf.

She straightened and slowly walked down the aisle. She'd put this off long enough. After the things Paul had told her she had to talk to the boy.

Inwardly she cringed as she realized what she was thinking. She was going to take advantage of her position as Tank's employer and invade his privacy. The thought brought back several painful memories. Memories of times when she'd had to face a harsh and disapproving father, memories of answering questions that shouldn't have been asked in the first place. Memories of another day and another time and place.

It had rained then, too. She closed her eyes as her father's enraged face flashed into sharp, painful focus. She could still hear his voice as he'd screamed that she was nothing but a little tramp, nothing more than a no-count white trash slut who didn't care who she was seen with.

Layla stopped in the middle of the store and forced the image out of her mind. A bitter laugh welled up in her throat. The only crime she'd been guilty of was holding the hand of a thirteen-year-old boy as she walked home from the library.

But this is different, she told herself as she started moving again, this is for Tank's own good. Oh, yeah, whispered a sly voice from the back of her mind, that's what your father told himself, too. Her footsteps slowed as uncertainty flooded her.

Maybe Tank's life wasn't any of her business. Maybe she'd do more harm than good. Hadn't she interfered enough?

Then she remembered Miss Pine. Layla continued down the aisle.

Tank looked up as he heard her approach. "How's Stanley doing? Did that hike perk him up any?"

"Not that I could tell," she answered. "He collapsed as soon as we got home. But at least he's moved out from in front of my refrigerator." She'd shared her woes about Stanley with Tank and he actually found the story funny.

"When are you going to bring him in? I'd like to meet him." He put the last can on the shelf and rose to his feet. "Maybe I could take him for a walk or something. It's not like I have much else to do with my free time and I like dogs."

This was the opening Layla had been waiting for. "Then I guess it's lucky that Dr. Tressler hired you. Does he let you spend much time with animals that come into the clinic?"

"No," Tank replied with a shake of his head. "So far the only things he's let me do is clean cages and scrub floors." He glanced down at the empty cardboard box. "I don't think he trusts me."

Layla could see what that admission cost the boy. She hated making him feel worse, but if she was going to help him, she had to get him to confide in her. The irony didn't escape her. She hated opening up but she was willing to pry into his life.

"Does he have a reason for not trusting you?" she asked softly. "From what I know of Dr. Tressler, he's not a hard man."

Tank looked up and met her eyes. "Yes. He's got a reason. At least he thinks he does. But he's dead wrong about me and the only way I can prove it is by being the best darned employee he ever had."

Puzzled, Layla stared at him. But before she asked what he meant, the bell over the front door rang. "We'll talk later," she said before she hurried to the front.

When she saw who was standing on the other side of the register, Layla sent up a short, silent prayer of thanks that Tank was in the back. The last thing she needed was for Paul to walk in and find MaryBeth Harrison anywhere near their mutual employee.

"Hello, MaryBeth," she said brightly. "What are you doing out of school today? The teachers go on strike?"

Covertly she studied the teenager. MaryBeth Harrison was perfect. Tall, blond and already beautiful, she exuded the kind of all-American good looks usually seen on the front covers of glossy magazines.

"No." MaryBeth's straight white teeth flashed as she laughed. "It's Senior Ditch Day. Mom and I are cleaning out all the closets so she sent me in to pick up a box of those lavender sachets you carry." She flicked a blond curl over her shoulder and casually looked around.

"The sachets are over there." Layla pointed to a shelf near the front door. She studied the girl as she walked away. From what Paul had said about his goddaughter, she was a prom queen, cheerleader, straight A student and the most popular girl on campus.

Then why, Layla wondered, is she spending Senior Ditch Day cleaning out closets with her mother instead of going roller-skating or mall-hopping with her friends?

"This should be enough." MaryBeth sat half a dozen sachets on the counter. As she shoved them forward Layla's nose wrinkled. The girl's heavy perfume clashed violently with the delicate lavender.

"Anything else for you?"

"No." MaryBeth pulled a packet of breath mints out of her jeans and popped one into her mouth. "Is Tank around?"

Layla's fingers paused on the cash register. She wasn't sure how to answer. "Uh, he's busy right now."

Unfortunately Tank chose that moment to appear. He had another large cardboard box hoisted onto his shoulder. As he rounded the aisle and spied MaryBeth, he stopped in his tracks.

"Hello, Tank."

"Hi." His face turned bright red, and his gaze dropped as he hurried past the cash register and over to the half-empty shelf where he set the box on the floor.

"How have you been?" MaryBeth fumbled in her pocket for another breath mint.

"Fine." He didn't look up but kept his attention firmly glued to slitting open the cardboard.

Layla watched the two in fascination. MaryBeth appeared as cool as a cucumber and Tank looked as if he wished the earth would open up and swallow him. Trying to help, she said, "That'll be six dollars and seventy-five cents."

Without taking her gaze off Tank, the girl fumbled in her purse and handed a ten-dollar bill across the counter.

"You know, Tank," MaryBeth said softly. "There's a potluck dinner at the church youth group on Tuesday night. We'd love to have you come."

"Can't." He began shoving boxes onto the shelf. "I'm going to Layla's to meet her dog. After that, I promised to take my aunt grocery shopping."

It was a good thing MaryBeth's attention was riveted on Tank, because otherwise she'd have seen the surprised look on Layla's face.

"That's too bad," MaryBeth said. "I hadn't realized your social life was so busy." She turned her back on Tank and drummed her fingers on the countertop.

Layla put the sachets into a bag. She felt sorry for MaryBeth, who was probably embarrassed. Tank's excuses were lame, but she could easily understand his reluctance to accept the invitation. If he went anywhere near the pretty teenager, Paul would probably fire him.

But one question nagged at the back of her mind. If Tank had abandoned MaryBeth in a wrecked car, why was she in here trying to cozy up to him?

As MaryBeth marched out of the store, she noticed that Tank was staring fixedly at the girl's back. But his expression was peculiar, his eyes intense. It took a moment for Layla to understand what it was she saw in the boy's face and when she did, she was surprised.

Tank was watching MaryBeth as if he didn't trust her an inch. She saw his gaze follow her through the front window of the store, his eyes narrowing suspiciously as she got behind the wheel of her car and drove off.

But Layla's chance to talk to Tank evaporated as the rain suddenly stopped and from out of nowhere a horde of customers materialized.

Layla climbed the four steps that led to Paul's red-tiled porch, rang the doorbell and waited. From inside the double doors, she could hear barking. She'd been edgy all afternoon and when she'd found herself dithering for thirty minutes over what dress to wear, she had finally gotten disgusted at herself. Her reaction to what should be nothing more than a casual business meeting touched a raw nerve. In self-defense she had discarded the planned dress and wore a sweater and a pair of jeans instead.

She smiled to hear Paul's voice ordering his dogs back. A second later the door swung open.

"Hi," Paul said. He reached over, grabbed her hand and tugged her inside. "Ignore the menagerie, they won't hurt you but they might try to love you to death."

"My goodness," she said, reaching down and trying to pet three dogs simultaneously. "You do have a lot of them."

Paul had been looking forward to this evening all afternoon. He leaned back against the door and watched her as she made friends with his dogs. Her hair was down and swinging freely to her shoulders, and she was wearing that sexy green sweater that drove him wild. Even her smile seemed different, less reserved than usual.

Laughing, she straightened and said, "Are they always this enthusiastic?"

"Pretty much." Paul pushed away from the door and led the way into the living room. "By the way, how's Stanley?"

"He's fine. He's finally stopping camping in front of the refrigerator and he met me at the door this evening when I got home. His tail was wagging. I consider that a major step forward in our relationship...." Her voice faltered as they stepped into the living room and her attention was caught by a bookcase at the far end.

Most of the shelves were filled with row upon row of distinctly familiar yellow magazines. "Are those *National Geographics?*"

"Yes. I've collected them for years."

He watched her curiously as she crossed the room and pulled one of the magazines off the top shelf. "This is great. It's a nineteen seventy-one." She looked up and smiled sheepishly. "I'm sorry, I hope you don't mind me getting it down like that, but I've always loved this magazine. Especially the older issues."

"I don't mind at all, help yourself." Paul watched as she leafed through the magazine, an expression of utter delight on her face. His insides tightened. Every time he was with her, he discovered something else they shared in common.

He sensed she was a kindred spirit. She hadn't even noticed his lack of furniture. He heard her sigh as she carefully put the magazine back, then she bent down and looked at the old books on the last shelf.

His attention was immediately drawn to the enticingly rounded shape of her bottom. His gaze drifted up to her small waist, and the slender curve of her spine. She was so petite, so womanly. Despite the differences in their size, he just knew her body was made to fit perfectly to his. He could imagine the softness of her skin, the feel of her shape, the . . .

"My goodness," Layla exclaimed, jumping up and waving the book in the air. "Where did you get this? This is fantastic! Do you have the whole collection?"

"Uh, which one is it?" He paced across the room and took the book from her fingers. Still lost in his fantasy, he stared at the volume blankly.

"It's a Horatio Alger book," Layla explained. She thought for a moment he wasn't listening. Paul looked very distracted. "Didn't you know you had it?"

With difficulty, he forced his imagination under control. "Sure. I just couldn't see which book it was from across the room."

"Well, do you?"

"Do I what?"

"Have the whole set?" Layla shook her head. "Paul, is something wrong? You seem awfully preoccupied tonight."

He could hardly admit the only thing bothering him was her tantalizing body. Then he realized that wasn't quite true, either. He was physically attracted all right, but his feelings toward her went deeper than that. The more he knew her, the more he liked her. Beneath that cool facade of hers, he'd discovered a tenderhearted woman who was a soft touch for fat dogs and delinquent teenagers.

"Sorry." He smiled apologetically. "I was just thinking about a surgery I did this afternoon." He glanced at the book in his hand. "And I'm also sorry to say that I don't have a complete set of these, but I wish I did."

"Oh." She was genuinely disappointed. "That's too bad."

He put the book on the end table. "Come on, let's eat and then I'll give you a complete tour of the house."

As Layla followed him down the hall toward the kitchen, she noticed the walls on both sides of the passageway were covered with family photographs. She swiveled her head, trying to get a better look, but Paul was walking too fast and she didn't have a chance to satisfy her curiosity.

The kitchen was beautiful. A cool but welcoming room with dark blue ceramic tile counters and a Spanish-red tile floor. Next to the breakfast bar there was a bulletin board covered with notes, phone numbers and candid snapshots of people she didn't recognize.

"Is there anything I can do to help?" she asked.

He waved her toward an elegantly set table in the center of the room. "No, just make yourself comfortable." He opened the oven and pulled out a covered casserole. "There isn't much to do. I'll only be a minute."

He smiled as he sat the steaming dish in the center of the table. "I hope you're hungry."

Her mouth watered as he lifted the lid. "It smells wonderful, what is it?"

"Chili relleno casserole," he replied, reaching for the wine. He poured them both a glass of chardonnay and then filled their plates with generous portions of the spicy cheese and green chili concoction.

Layla waited until he sat down before picking up her fork. She took a bite and her eyes widened in delight. "This is fantastic. You're some cook!"

"I didn't make it," he admitted ruefully. "My housekeeper took pity on you when she heard you were coming for dinner. My repertoire is basically limited to frozen dinners and scrambled eggs, although I do know how to barbecue a steak."

"You live on frozen food and eggs!"

"Why does that surprise you?" Paul asked.

"Because, well—" She hesitated for a moment. "One of the things I've learned about living on my own is to try to take care of myself and that includes decent food. I guess I'm just surprised that you don't mind eating that stuff all the time. I mean, you live alone, too."

"I haven't always lived by myself." He watched her carefully, hoping she'd be curious enough to ask the obvious questions.

"Oh," Layla replied slowly, "I see." She toyed with the stem of her wineglass. Finally she said, "Did you used to have a roommate?"

Paul stifled a grin. "No. I was married."

"Oh."

"My wife did the cooking."

"Oh."

"Have you ever been married?" He was fairly certain she hadn't, but it never hurt to ask.

"No, no," she replied quickly. "I never even got close." The minute the words were out, she felt like kicking herself. She sounded like a pathetic old maid. "So how long were you married?"

"Five years. Kimberly and I married when I was a senior in college but it didn't last. She's a nice lady, but we were both too young and we wanted different things in life. I wanted to stay here in Riker's Pass, while she was more the city type. So we put our mistake behind us and got on with our lives." He grinned suddenly. "But the experience didn't sour me on matrimony. I think it's a great institution."

Layla dropped her gaze to her plate. She had no idea why she was surprised to find he'd been married. In this day and age, it was rare to meet an attractive man Paul's age who wasn't divorced. Yet he wasn't bitter and he spoke nicely about his former wife, which she found admirable.

"Have you ever been tempted?"

Her head snapped up. "To what?"

"Get married."

"Oh, that." She shrugged. "No, I've been too busy." The conversation made her uncomfortable. Paul was too good at getting her to talk, too good at getting her to reveal her secrets and her fears. Her inadequacies. She took another bite of the casserole and racked her brain for something to say that would change the direction of the conversation.

Then she remembered why she was here. "Paul, would you have any objection to using some of your collection for the Centennial?"

He frowned as he realized she'd neatly changed the subject. "How do you mean?"

"Well, for example, your Horatio Alger books." She leaned toward him, her eyes shining as the idea crystallized in her mind. "We could use them to decorate the school gym for the opening dance. I could bring down my butter churn and we could scatter around some of your old *National Geographics* and rummage up some old school desks." Excited now, she spoke even faster. "That's a lot more interesting than just sticking up some balloons and paper streamers. We could try to make the gym reminiscent of an old one-room schoolhouse from a hundred years ago."

Paul gave in gracefully. He'd rather be discussing more personal matters, but he knew he should be grateful for what progress he'd made. "That's an idea. And using genuine period pieces would give the Centennial an authentic touch. But do you think we could find enough stuff from that era?"

"Sure we could. Just between the two of us we've got plenty to start with. And I'm sure if we asked other people, we'd find all kinds of old things we could use."

Paul was delighted by Layla's enthusiasm and he found himself wholeheartedly falling in with her plans. By the end of dinner they'd come up with half a dozen other ideas as well. And all of them ensured he'd get to spend lots of time with Miss Layla Odell.

"How about some coffee?" he asked with a grin. "Even I don't mess that up. I can show you the rest of the house while it's brewing."

Layla laughed easily and rose to her feet. While he made the coffee she peeked at his bulletin board. "Are these pictures of your family?"

"Yes, the one in the corner is my younger brother and the other two were taken last Thanksgiving. My mom and dad are sitting behind the turkey."

She stared at the snapshots, noting the resemblance between Paul and his brother.

"Come on." He took her hand. "It's time for the grand tour."

The dogs besieged them as they went out onto the patio, where Paul had a pool and hot tub. "You must spend a fortune on food," Layla exclaimed. "How many animals do you have?"

"Six. There's two cats around here somewhere, too."

She felt guilty as she remembered the way poor Stanley had stared at her so mournfully when she'd left.

"Paul," she asked as they went back into the kitchen. "Do animals get lonely?"

"Sure. Why do you ask?"

She sighed. "I was just thinking about Stanley. He was stuck all by himself today and then I went out tonight, too."

"Next time," he said easily, "bring him with you."

"You mean you wouldn't mind? But wouldn't your dogs get upset, you know, fight with him or something?" She shook her head. "I don't think Stanley would do very well in a fight."

He started to laugh but caught himself when he saw how serious she looked. "Don't worry about it. When you bring Stanley over, we'll make my dogs stay outside."

It didn't occur to her to question his basic assumption—that she'd be spending a lot of time at his house. Instead, she merely said, "I don't know. I'm used to him, but to be perfectly honest, he, uh, doesn't smell very nice. I haven't given him a bath yet, I mean . . ."

"You coward," Paul teased. "You just haven't wanted to handle that big mutt all by yourself." He sighed melodramatically. "Okay, you've talked me into it. Tomorrow night I'll come by and we can both give him a bath. How's that."

For a moment she didn't know what to say. She hadn't been hinting, yet he'd volunteered. Layla wasn't about to look a gift horse in the mouth. "Well." She smiled broadly. "If it's no trouble."

"Of course not," he said, heading down the hall, "as long as you promise to feed me afterward, it's no trouble at all."

Knowing he'd just conned her into agreeing to fix him dinner, she laughed.

The tour continued through the den, formal dining room, and upstairs bedrooms. There were family photos stuck everywhere. Finally they ended up in the master bedroom. Layla's throat went dry as she stood in the doorway. Paul stood right behind her. Though he wasn't touching her, she could feel the heat of his body searing her back.

The room was spartan. There was a dark mahogany chest of drawers, a matching bedside table with a phone on it and a king-size bed covered with a heavy red bedspread.

"It's very nice," she murmured. The sight of his bedroom seemed to have glued her tongue to the roof of her mouth.

That bed. There was something starkly sensual in the sparse, masculine lines of the wood, something sexy in the deep red of the bedspread, something that made her absolutely certain that a night in that bed would be the experience of a lifetime.

Shocked by her thoughts, Layla hastily stepped back and bumped into Paul. His arms closed around her waist. "Is there something wrong?"

"No, no, of course not." She tried to move away from him but his arms tightened around her. "It's just that it's getting late."

He turned her to face him. For a moment they stared at each other and then he slowly lowered his mouth to hers.

She closed her eyes at the brush of his lips. The kiss was gentle, with the merest hint of pressure. She edged closer to him and the next thing she knew, his mouth was slanting across hers with restrained passion.

She'd been kissed before, but never like this. His mouth was warm and moist and incredibly insistent. So insistent she found herself opening her lips to the exploratory probing of his tongue. His hands stroked slowly up and down her spine as he explored the inside of her mouth. She couldn't breathe, she couldn't think, she could only feel a shocking desire that sparked from the tip of his tongue to deep inside her body.

Paul hadn't meant to move so quickly. But her response sent his good intentions flying out the window. The urge to hold her closer, to mold her body to his and feel the way they meshed so perfectly together was overwhelming. His hands moved of their own accord, strok-

ing over the softness of her sweater and down onto the
rounded curve of her backside. He felt her stiffen.

Forcing his mouth away from hers, he released her and
stepped back.

They were both breathing heavily. He was aroused and
tense. Her eyes were glassy and stunned. Several moments passed. Then he said, "I'm sorry. I didn't mean to
come on so strong."

Layla mentally shook herself. She'd never experienced anything like this before but she was pretty sure she
knew what it was. Passion. Desire. Lust. The words raced
through her mind, sending her emotions into a frenzy.

Paul could see the confusion in her eyes and it tore at
his insides. She looked terrified by the way she'd responded to him. "You're right," he said softly. "It is
getting late."

Relieved and vaguely disappointed, Layla followed him
to the front door. Paul walked her out to her car.

As he held the car door open, she racked her brain for
something to say. "Your home is beautiful. Thanks for
showing it to me."

"My pleasure."

"Uh, I'd better get going." She forced a laugh. "I
don't want Stanley getting worried."

"Yeah." He made no move to close the door.

"Well, it's a great house..." Groping for something
else to say, she asked him something that had crossed her
mind earlier. "But isn't it awfully big for just one person?"

He bent down until his face was inches from hers. "I
want to get married again one day. And I wanted a big
house so I could fill it with babies."

Chapter Five

Layla pulled out onto the county road, her head still reeling from Paul's unexpected announcement. You did ask, she chided herself wryly, but how was she supposed to know he'd come back with such an outrageous statement? Men didn't say things like that, did they?

I could fill it with babies.... His words echoed in her head as she drove. Was he trying to tell her something? Was he warning her that he intended to get serious? No, she decided. He was being facetious. Then she remembered all the family photographs stuck in every nook and cranny of his house.

Family was obviously important to him. Very important.

Layla stopped speculating and concentrated on the winding highway. She wasn't sure how she felt about Paul. She knew one thing, though. It might be better if their friendship was strictly casual.

But that kiss. That long, sensuous kiss. She braked as she came to a sharp curve in the road. And the way she'd responded. Maybe she couldn't remain causal about him. At least not if he kept kissing her like that.

Paul was downright lethal. Any man that could make a woman ignite the way she had should come with a warning label.

Or maybe she was giving him more credit than he deserved. Her dating had been very limited and she was inexperienced. Perhaps she'd reached the point in her life where she was ready for an adult relationship.

A physical relationship.

The human psyche was very complex, capable of sending signals in mysterious and convoluted ways. Maybe her subconscious was trying to tell her something.

It would be a lot easier if a big sign blinked on behind your eyes, she thought morosely as she slowed the car to turn into her driveway. Then you wouldn't have to spend half your life playing guessing games with yourself.

She shivered as she stepped out into the cold air and hurried into the house. Stanley met her at the door. Tail wagging, he butted his big head against her knees. Layla was touched.

"Hello, boy," she crooned, bending down to pet him. "Did you miss me? I sure missed you. The next time I go to Paul's, you get to come, too."

The dog trailed at her heels as she went into the kitchen to make a cup of tea. She had a lot to think about. Tonight had made her realize she needed to make some decisions about what kind of friendship she wanted with Paul.

Entering the kitchen, she automatically checked Stanley's food dish. Empty, of course, but then it was usually empty thirty seconds after she filled it. She went to the back door and pulled it open. "Come on, boy, out you go."

Stanley stared at her for a moment and then reluctantly trudged out into the chilly night air. She put the kettle on as she waited for the dog to return.

She pulled a cup and saucer out of the cupboard, wondering how Paul felt about her. Even a novice like her could tell he was interested.

But how interested? Exactly what did he have in mind? Friendship? An affair? What?

She knew he wasn't the kind to play around and he didn't have a string of women from here to San Diego. She was as certain of that as she was that the sun would rise the next day.

Or was she? Could you ever really be certain about anyone?

Not really. But people did drop clues. And Paul hadn't given her any of those pompous speeches that some men gave you on the very first date. The ones about needing their space or wanting to find themselves before they made a commitment. Even with her limited experience, she'd known that was a line that usually just meant they were out for what they could get. The few times she'd heard that spiel, she'd found it funny.

But Paul wasn't like that. The indications she'd seen of his character weren't in the least negative. Just the opposite, he appeared to be kindhearted, willing to make commitments, straightforward and honest. Perfectly willing to answer her questions. He wasn't playing games.

Or was he? Layla hated being so suspicious, but she couldn't seem to help herself. She had a feeling there was a lot at stake here.

There was a creak as the dog wedged himself through the partially opened door. Sighing, she got up and went to the refrigerator. Stanley watched her hopefully. His ears perked up when she pulled out the milk and she took pity on him.

"Okay," she muttered, pouring a small amount into his dish. "You can have a drop. It's low fat and I bet you're sick of this diet. A little cheating every once in a while won't kill you."

The kettle whistled. "You know, Stanley," she continued as she poured the boiling water into her cup. Talking to the dog was a habit she'd started when he'd been camped in her kitchen. "Paul seems to be a nice person. But then again, it's so hard to be sure."

Picking up her tea, she sat down at the table. "I'll bet my father acted real nice while he was dating my mother, and look how miserable she ended up being."

Stanley waddled over and sat down on her foot. Layla didn't mind; his big body was comforting and warm.

"That's the real problem, you see," she continued. "How do you know what someone's true character is? How do you know if you can trust them? Paul seems like he's easygoing and tolerant, but look at the way he turned against Tank."

She broke off and stared into space. In all fairness, she wasn't sure she could fault Paul for his treatment of Tank. Despite his reservations, he had, after all, hired him.

"I guess I'm just scared," she said. The dog cocked his head to one side. "I know Tank made a bad mistake, but I've got to tell you, it bothers me that Paul was so reluctant to give him another chance." She took a sip of tea. "What if I get involved with him and then I make a mistake."

Her gaze focused on the opposite wall as she remembered the sick feeling she used to get in the pit of her stomach when she'd made a mistake in front of her father. No matter how hard she used to try, no matter what she did, she was always doing something wrong.

Messing up. Making a mistake.

Hoping to make him proud, she'd entered the school spelling bee. But when she'd shown him her third-place ribbon, he'd been furious that she hadn't won.

Layla shook herself back to the present. She smiled wryly as she gazed into Stanley's sympathetic brown eyes. "You see, Stanley. You just never know. Will I have to jump through hoops to get back in Paul's good graces if I do something he doesn't like?"

The idea terrified her. She'd spent too many years jumping through hoops as a child. Layla was determined never to have to do it again. No one was worth that.

The following evening, Layla popped a chicken casserole into the oven and then double-checked the table setting. Paul was due any minute and she didn't want to have to worry about dinner details while she was bathing Stanley.

The doorbell chimed. She hurried to the front door, flung it open and blinked in surprise.

Tank grinned uneasily. "I thought I'd meet your dog. It's okay, isn't it? Uh, I mentioned yesterday that I might come by."

"Of course it's okay," Layla assured him, opening the door wider and ushering him inside. She'd assumed he was only using her as an excuse to refuse MaryBeth's invitation to that church function. "He's right in here."

Tank followed her into the kitchen. His thin face broke into a wide grin as Stanley trundled over to greet him. "Wow," he exclaimed, dropping to his knees and running his hand over the dog's broad back. "You were right, he is fat."

The animal didn't mind the insult. Layla grinned. From the way Stanley was rubbing his head against Tank's knees, it looked like a case of love at first sight.

"He's getting thinner," she said. "But I suspect he thinks that dieting is for the birds. He's taken to giving me the evil eye every time I walk past his food dish. Do you want a cup of coffee?"

"Sure." Rising to his feet, Tank started toward the table and then hesitated when he saw it was set for company. "Uh, I didn't mean to barge in on you. It looks like you've got plans. Maybe I should take off."

"No, no. It's only Paul," Layla replied quickly, "and he isn't due for a few minutes yet. We've got plenty of time to visit."

"Okay," he agreed eagerly. "If you're sure."

His quick acceptance of her invitation told her something else. Something she hadn't really thought about before. Tank was lonely.

She poured two cups of coffee. "Let's take our coffee into the living room. I'm glad you dropped by, I'd like to talk to you."

Layla didn't want Tank to leave yet. She'd been worrying about him all day and now was a good chance to finish the conversation they'd started yesterday.

She picked up the mugs and pushed open the door. Tank and Stanley trotted along behind her.

"Uh..." The boy perched awkwardly on the edge of the couch. "What did you want to talk about?"

Layla set their cups down and took a deep breath. "I want to ask you something. But before I do, I want you to know that I've thought long and hard about whether or not I have any right to butt into your business."

He eyed her warily but didn't say anything.

"I've come to the conclusion that I do have a right to interfere," Layla continued gently, "mainly because I care about you and I want to see that you have a chance to make something of your life."

Tank's face turned red. "I know that. You hired me when no one else would." He looked down at the floor and then back up at her. "I also know Dr. Tressler would never have taken me on if you hadn't talked him into it. Go ahead, ask me anything you want. I'd never lie to you."

"Good." She flattened her hands on her thighs. This was the hard part. "I have to know. Do you drink?"

He didn't answer for a moment. Finally he said. "No."

Layla's stomach tightened. She knew Paul wouldn't have condemned Tank just because the boy had made one mistake—no matter how big a one. She wanted to trust them both, yet their stories seemed in conflict.

"At least, I don't anymore." Tank's voice was a faint whisper in the quiet room. He reached down and scratched Stanley behind the ears.

"What does that mean?"

"It means I got drunk once, but I swear, that was the only time. I hate alcohol. I can't stand what it did to my father."

"Then why did you do it even once?" She stared at him curiously, trying to gauge whether or not he was telling her the truth.

A sad, cynical smile crossed his thin face. "Because of my father."

She shook her head. "I don't understand?"

Tank sighed. "I wanted to show the old man what he looked like, how disgusting he was. What he was doing to me." He broke off and slumped against the cushions. "God, he made me sick."

His face hardened in a mask of rage and shame and bitter memories. Layla's heart swelled with sympathy. She knew what it was like to want to respect and love your father and she also knew what it was like when that turned out to be impossible.

"Do you want to tell me about it?" she asked sympathetically.

He shrugged and stared at a point over her shoulder. "It was about a week before he died. I was fourteen at the time. He'd lost his job, of course, and we were on the verge of being evicted from that dump we lived in. I remember coming home from school and walking into that filthy house. There the old man was, sitting at the kitchen table, surrounded by dirty dishes and empty booze bottles."

Tank broke off and cleared his throat before continuing. "He'd promised me he'd go out job hunting. He'd promised me he'd find something so we could pay the rent and keep a roof over our heads. But he didn't. And when I saw him just sitting there, something snapped inside me. I was scared to death we were going to lose the only home we had and he was pouring Scotch down his throat like there was no tomorrow. It made me mad. Madder than I've ever been in my whole life. So I figured, why not? Why not show him how he's wrecking both our lives, why not drown my sorrows the way he did."

"And that's what you did."

"Yeah, I knew where he kept his stash." He laughed harshly. "I took his last bottle and headed into town, drinking as I went. By the time I hit Main Street, I was flying higher than a kite. I wasn't scared anymore, either. When you're drunk you don't worry about where you're going to live or where your next meal's coming from."

Layla could see the pain in his eyes. But she said nothing.

"He must have realized I'd taken his last bottle, because he came after me. That's when the trouble started."

"Didn't anyone in town try to help you? For God's sake, you were a fourteen-year-old kid stumbling drunk in the center of town."

"Yeah." Tank sighed. "Your aunt Velma drug me into the back of her store. She propped me up on a crate and then went to get Paul. But Dad had followed me into town, and he saw Velma take me inside. When I saw him coming up the aisle toward me, I had enough brains to take off. He chased me to Dr. Tressler's. The gate was open and I tried to hide back of his office. I was crouching behind the circus calliope when he found me."

"What happened then?" she asked hesitantly.

"He yanked me to my feet and started to beat the hell out of me. I screamed and I guess Dr. Tressler must have heard us, because he came charging in and pulled my old man off. But my father had used his fists and I didn't remember much after that. I must have blacked out, because the next thing I knew, I was in the hospital and the old man was in jail."

"How long did your father stay in jail?"

"Only overnight." Tank sneered. "One of his drinking buddies bailed him out. He tried to see me, but my shoulder was dislocated and the nursing staff wouldn't let him come near me. They'd heard what had happened. By the time I was able to leave, Dad had gone on one drunk too many and crashed his truck into a tree. I never saw him again.''

She felt like crying. No child should ever have to bear such a burden. She knew how Tank felt. Their experiences had been different, yet in one sense, they'd been the same. No matter how abusive or cold or uncaring a parent was, there was always that one tiny part of a child that kept hoping for a miracle, that kept hoping that one day things would be better.

''Oh God,'' Layla said softly, staring at Tank's bowed head. ''I'm sorry.''

He continued to pet the dog. She could see him blinking his eyes furiously in an effort to fight off tears. After a moment, he cleared his throat again and raised his chin. He looked her directly in the eyes. ''I swear to you, Layla,'' he said solemnly. ''When I heard my father was dead, I swore I'd never take another drink as long as I lived. And I haven't. No matter what they say here in town.''

Layla believed him. Yet, if Tank wasn't responsible, that still didn't explain what had *really* happened that night MaryBeth's car was crashed. She stared at him, wondering if she should just flat out ask, but then she decided not to. One of these days Tank would tell her the truth. And it was suddenly important to her that he be the one to bring the subject up. Layla wanted Tank to trust her enough to tell her what had really happened, but she was also wise enough to let him do it in his own good time.

There was a knock on the front door. ''That's probably Paul.'' She rose to her feet and hurried across the room.

"Hi. Come on in," she said, motioning him inside.

"It's cold out there tonight," Paul said as he shrugged out of his jacket. "I brought along some extra flea shampoo—" He broke off as he spied Tank sitting on the couch. His smile vanished. "Hello, Tank. What are you doing here?"

The boy flushed and then hastily scrambled to his feet. "I, uh..."

"I invited Tank over to meet Stanley."

Paul turned his gaze to Layla. "I see."

The room was suddenly filled with tension and Layla didn't like it one bit. Why should Paul care that Tank had dropped by? From the tense set of his jaw and the rigid way he held himself, it was damned obvious he did care.

She stiffened in resentment as Tank edged past a frowning Paul and headed for the door. Stanley was right at his heels.

The boy was her guest and this was her house. Paul had no right to act like such a jerk. As soon as they were alone, she'd damned well tell him that, too!

"I've got to get going," Tank called from the doorway. "Night, Layla. See you tomorrow." He bent down and gave the dog one last pat. "See you at work, Dr. Tressler."

Then he was gone.

Paul stopped glaring at the door and turned to Layla. "You adopting him now?"

She crossed her arms over her chest. "No. I told you. He came by to meet Stanley. And even if I was, it wouldn't be any of your business. Tank's not just my employee, he's my friend."

"Oh, really." His eyebrows rose skeptically. "Well, then I hope you're careful. With friends like Tank you won't need any enemies."

"For goodness' sake," she said angrily, disgusted by his attitude. "What do you expect the kid to do, knock me unconscious and steal the silverware? It seems to me that poor child needs all the friends he can get. Now that he's been branded as public enemy number one, no one wants to come near him."

Paul forced himself to resist the urge to argue the point further. He didn't want to alienate Layla, nor did he want her thinking he was a heartless monster. On the other hand, he didn't trust Tank Mullins. The boy had already left one young woman unconscious in the front seat of a car, even if Layla was refusing to admit it.

Paul forced a smile to his lips. "You're right. I'm sorry. This is a ridiculous argument. It's none of my business who you have over to your house."

He was still holding his jacket, and he reached inside the pocket and drew out a plastic bottle. "Here," he said, holding it toward her. "Consider this a peace offering."

"What is it?" she asked warily.

"Flea shampoo."

She stared at him for a second and then smiled uneasily. His answering smile was equally strained.

"How can I resist a present like that," she finally said, reaching for the bottle. Their fingers brushed as her hand closed around the plastic. The touch was brief, lasting only an instant, but in that fraction of a second, she could feel his warmth and energy.

The effect startled her, coming as it did after their argument, so she yanked the bottle away and quickly began scanning the label. "Let's get started then."

He nodded, his expression bland and unreadable. She wondered whether or not he was really sorry for snapping at her about Tank or whether he just wanted some peace and quiet.

"I've got everything set up in the garage," she explained, moving toward the kitchen. "There's a hot water hookup out there."

A few minutes later they were standing next to an old galvanized washtub that Layla had found in the back of the store.

Paul hooked the hose up to the faucet. "Is the other end in the tub?"

"Yes."

He turned on the tap and a moment later the silence in the garage was broken by the splash of water onto the metal bottom of the tub. Paul sighed. He felt as though he was back to square one. Hell, he thought morosely, why didn't I keep my mouth shut? Why didn't I just let the kid leave and keep my nasty comments to myself?

He'd finally realized that for reasons of her own, Layla was using his distrust of Tank Mullins to rebuild the walls between the two of them. But why? Why try so hard to keep him at arm's length? Why jump down his throat every time he showed the least little concern about Tank? Didn't she realize he was worried about her safety? Didn't she understand that the boy just might be dangerous? He knew damned good and well that she understood his motives.

Then why was she acting cold and hostile just because he hadn't liked the thought of the kid hanging around her house. Hell, she hadn't even looked at him in the past five minutes.

If she didn't like him, why didn't she just tell him to take a hike?

"Maybe I'd better go and get Stanley," Layla said to Paul's back.

He nodded without turning around.

Disappointed at the way the evening was turning out and not knowing how to salvage it, she turned on her heel to get Stanley. She found him hiding behind the couch. It took her ten minutes to coax, tug and drag him into the garage.

"I think he knows what we're going to do," she said breathlessly as she pulled him by the collar toward the tub. Stanley stiffened his legs. "He's not being very co-operative."

Paul turned at the sound of her voice, and had to grin at the spectacle. Layla's hair was messed, her face was red and her neatly tucked-in blouse had come out of the waistband of her jeans. The dog was rigidly resisting her every inch of the way.

"Come on, boy." He picked up the dog and hauled him to the tub. "In you go."

Stanley stood stock-still for a long moment, then he gave a low, keening moan and shivered.

They both laughed and the tension suddenly evaporated as quickly as it had come. Dropping to her knees, Layla patted the dog's head. "Now, now, it'll be all right. We're just going to clean you up. You'll feel better afterward, Stanley. Honest, we're going to kill all those nasty old fleas."

"Wet him down," Paul instructed as he picked up the bottle of shampoo, unscrewed the lid and poured a generous measure into the palm of his hand. He waited until Layla had splashed water onto the dog's back and then he reached over and began slowly massaging the shampoo into the fur. Stanley whimpered pathetically.

"It'll be over soon, sweetheart," Layla crooned, patting his big head.

"Oh, for God's sake," Paul muttered, "it's only a bath. We're not hurting him."

"But he's scared."

"He's a ham." He worked the lather into Stanley's hind legs. "And he's milking it for all it's worth. This dog is no dummy. He loves the attention, and he loves you making over him like he was a helpless baby."

"I guess everyone loves attention," she said with a chuckle. Reaching down she began to briskly scrub at Stanley's forepaws. A moment later she glanced sideways at Paul. He had the same grin on his face that he'd had when she was trying to get Stanley into the garage. "What's so funny?" she asked suspiciously.

"You. For someone who wasn't even sure she liked dogs a week ago, you're clucking over this hound like a mother hen. I think that's pretty funny. Here, scrub him like this." He reached down and placed his fingers directly over hers and then scooted around until their bodies were side by side. "You need to learn how to bathe him correctly."

That was a lie. Any moron could figure out how to scrub a dog. But he didn't care. He wanted to be close to her, physically close. He wanted to use their bodies to close the emotional distance that had sprung up between them tonight. He wanted to smash her resistance to him and let her know with touch and smell and intimacy that she could trust him. That he would never hurt her. Not in any way.

And she was letting him. Dear God, she was letting him.

The feel of her flesh nestled close against his side was driving him to distraction; he could smell the herbal scent of her hair and feel the softness of her breast pressing into his arm. The clasp of their entwined hands over the dog's wet, soapy fur was unbelievably erotic.

Slowly, gently, he moved their hands up and down Stanley's chest in long, heavy strokes. The motion tugged her closer, so that now her thigh brushed rhythmically against the denim of his jeans. His body reacted. Desire, hot and potent, coiled into a rapidly hardening knot between his legs.

Layla took a silent, deep breath of air. His nearness made her head spin, she could feel her blood racing and it suddenly got difficult to concentrate on what she was doing.

She was racked by conflicting urges. Being this close to him, this close to any man, was foreign to her. She had always made it a point to keep her distance. Yet now she was overwhelmed by the desire to nestle closer and explore the strange feelings this man had the power to generate.

Fascinated, she watched their entwined hands move up and down on the dog. "Like this," she croaked, her voice strained.

"Yes," he said softly, his breath feathering against the sensitive skin of her neck. The urge to bury his mouth in the hollow of her neck was strong and it took every drop of discipline he possessed to stay in control.

"Exactly like this." Paul brought their hands up and around to rub the lather into Stanley's back. He shifted so that she was now tucked between his legs, her back against his chest. It was torture. It was the sweetest torment.

With every shift of her hips, she brushed against that already sensitized part of him and he had to grit his teeth to keep from groaning at the pleasure of it. For a moment he wondered if she was doing it deliberately and playing the tease. But a glance at her face quickly dispelled that notion.

He reached around her shoulders with his free arm, clasped her other hand and plunged it into the soapy water and onto Stanley's back. She was completely caged within his arms.

"That's good," he encouraged, desperately trying to keep his mind on washing the damned dog. "Rub him firmly, yet gently. Always act confident. Dogs operate on their instincts. If they sense you're nervous, they'll react that way, too."

Layla helplessly gave into the magic spell Paul wove. She could feel the warmth of his chest against her back, feel the brush of his thighs against her legs. Her skin felt alive and incredibly sensitized. Even through the layers of cloth separating their flesh, at every contact point between their bodies her nerve endings quivered in sensual awareness.

"That's it, that's it." Paul repeated as her strokes got surer and more confident. "Let him know you're in charge. Let him know he can trust you."

Trust. That one word broke the magic spell. Layla tensed. The air of intimacy surrounding them was suddenly threatening. The situation was too erotic, too overpowering and too frightening. Her hands stilled and she awkwardly leaned away from him.

"What's wrong?" he asked softly.

"Uh, nothing. But shouldn't we start rinsing him now?"

Paul had to fight back a jolt of pure frustration. He had no idea why she withdrew like this, but he knew enough to back off.

Striving to keep his movements casual, he disengaged their fingers and rose lithely to his feet. Layla quickly followed suit.

For the next five minutes, they both kept their attention strictly on Stanley, who, as soon as he was dried off with a big fluffy towel, immediately began shaking water all over the place. He then bounced crazily around their feet like a puppy.

Layla shook her head. "Look at him. A few minutes ago he was acting like one of the condemned and now he's happier than I've ever seen him."

"Of course he's happy. You've shown him you care." He smiled enigmatically.

"Why don't you come on into the house," Layla said. "You're probably hungry and the food should be ready."

Paul nodded thoughtfully but made no move to leave the garage. "You don't have to, you know."

"Have to what?"

"Feed me. If you'd rather I left, just say so. I'll understand."

Chapter Six

Layla went still. His sensitivity surprised her. Could the man read minds? Did he realize she'd spent the past twenty-four hours in a state of siege, vacillating between giving in to her attraction for him or finding a reason to end it before she got hurt. "Why would you think I wanted you to leave?"

He smiled gently, his eyes filled with understanding. "Because we started the evening off on the wrong foot when I walked in and snipped at you about Tank. And because I think I make you nervous."

Her comfort zone was completely shattered. He was perceptive. Very perceptive. Too perceptive. She knew she hadn't been that obvious and their differences over Tank was an old argument. But despite the awkwardness, despite her anxiety, she was more frightened of him leaving than staying.

"Don't be silly, I invited you for dinner." She lifted her chin. "And you don't make me nervous." Turning on her heel she marched out of the garage.

Stanley trotted after Layla. So did Paul.

In the kitchen, she hurriedly put the finishing touches on the table. Relief hit her when she heard Paul's footsteps as he and the dog came across the back porch.

"Can you pour the wine?" she called without looking up. "It's in the fridge."

"Sure."

She heard him open the refrigerator. Her heart was pounding against her ribs, and she wondered why she hadn't let him leave. He was right, he did make her nervous. But he also touched something else inside her. Something she couldn't quite find a name for, but which was even stronger than her fear of getting close to another person. Something that was more than just attraction. Something that was becoming so real, that no matter what her apprehension or her mistrust, she couldn't turn her back on it.

A few moments later they were seated across from each other at the table. Paul slowly sipped his wine, his expression thoughtful as he watched her serve a delicious smelling chicken and dumpling concoction onto their plates.

He didn't know what to make of her anymore. When they'd been washing the dog he'd felt they were on the same wavelength, intimate, and communicating without words. But then she'd stiffened and pulled away. Her withdrawal had been subtle, but he'd felt it nonetheless. And it wasn't because he was coming on too strong; he'd made sure he kept himself under control. Then why had she jerked away from him as if he were radioactive? Why had she shut him out? But she hadn't jumped at the chance to get rid of him. Maybe he was wrong, maybe she'd pulled away because she really wanted to rinse the dog.

"This looks great," he said. "I'm glad I stayed."

Layla looked up and met his gaze. "So am I," she admitted honestly. Then she gave him an impish grin. "I'd get as fat as Stanley if I had to eat all this food by myself."

Paul chuckled and put down his glass. He decided to ask her straight out. The excuses he used to see Layla because of her dog were wearing thin. A five-year-old could figure out that diets, dog baths and hikes weren't a routine part of a vet's service. But more importantly, he wanted to know how she felt about him. He couldn't stand the suspense any longer.

"Are you seeing anyone?" Paul was fairly certain she wasn't.

Layla stared at him. The blunt question should have surprised her, but it didn't. Then she realized it was completely in keeping with what she was learning about his character. "Are you asking me if I'm dating anyone at the moment?"

He nodded and took a bite of chicken. He couldn't taste it.

"No."

"Good."

That did surprise her. She went still, her fork halfway to her mouth. She'd been edgy before, now her blood pressure skyrocketed. But it wasn't fear that had her pulse soaring, it was excitement.

"I don't know why you look so surprised," he said when she continued to stare at him. "Surely you've figured out that I'm more than casually interested in you." He put his fork down and leaned across the table. "And

I was hoping you felt the same way about me. Am I wrong?"

She couldn't think of how to answer him. She *was* interested. Very interested. No man had ever affected her the way he did. No man had ever made her body react with just a brush of his flesh against hers or a touch of his hand. No man had ever made her *want* the way he did. But she was scared.

No man had ever gotten this close before, either. She'd never let them.

"Well," he prompted. "Was I wrong? Do you like me or are you just being polite because you owe me?"

That brought her back to earth quick enough. "I *owe* you? Are you referring to Tank?"

"Uh-huh."

"Now just a minute here, it seems to me I did you a pretty big favor, too." She glanced meaningfully at Stanley, who was curled up on her rug, his gaze glued to the table. "But while we're on the subject of Tank, I do have a few things I'd like to say. First of all—"

"Hold on," he interrupted, raising his hand. "I'm not letting you off the hook that easily. We can talk about Tank later. I've got a few things to say along those lines myself. But we were discussing us and I want an answer. Do you or do you not like me?"

He almost cringed at his choice of words. Hell, he sounded like a teenager with his first crush. But what other words were there? He could hardly ask if she was in love with him. It was a bit too soon for either of them to be thinking in those kind of terms, no matter how attracted he was.

"Of course I like you," she protested. "I don't routinely knock myself out making chicken and dumplings for casual acquaintances. I skinned chicken and chopped onions for two hours today."

He grinned. "How much?"

"How much?" She gazed at him in exasperation. "How much what, for goodness' sake?"

"How much do you like me?" He hated ambiguity and his choice of words, limited as they were, covered a lot of territory. Paul wanted things crystal clear between them.

"*Like* can mean a lot of things. Am I just a nice neighbor, or do you see me as good old Doc Tressler who drops by to help you wash your dog, or—" he paused and drew in a long, deep breath "—do you see me as a man you're romantically involved with?"

Dumbfounded, she stared at him. "What do you want? A rating on a scale of one to ten?"

"That would be nice, but you're evading the question."

"You tell me how much you like me first," she challenged, getting into the spirit. "That's the gentlemanly thing to do."

"All right." He crossed his arms over his chest. "I'll admit I want a romantic relationship with you."

Layla was suddenly horrified by what she'd done. The situation was quickly getting out of control. But it was too late to stop now.

"First, I'm physically very attracted to you," he enumerated calmly, not looking in the least embarrassed. "And from the way you responded when I kissed you, I suspect you're equally attracted. Secondly, I admire the fact that you're willing to work hard to make a success of your business. Unlike a lot of people, you don't seem to feel that the world owes you a living. And thirdly, I admire your character. Your willingness to take on Tank and Stanley is proof that your heart's in the right place.

And of course, I'm delighted by the fact that we have so much in common. Very few women are as into old books and furniture as much as I am." He leaned back and smiled expectantly. "Now it's your turn."

Good Lord, Layla thought frantically, what on earth did he want her to say? And more importantly, how much did she want to admit? She didn't want to have to tell him how much she was coming to care about him. That was skirting too close to a commitment for her. But on the other hand, she didn't want him to think she didn't give a hoot about him, either.

Layla willed her reeling emotions into some semblance of order. Paul looked as if he was prepared to sit at her dining table all night unless she answered him. "First of all, you're right. I am attracted to you. But..."

"Let's hold the 'buts' till later."

"All right," she agreed grudgingly. "Secondly, I also admire your character. But I have to confess I do have some doubts..."

"We'll get to the 'doubts' later, too," he interjected smoothly. "Let's not muddy the waters with side issues yet."

Her head was spinning but she didn't seem to have much choice except to go on. "Thirdly, like you, I'm, I'm..." Oh Lord, she thought helplessly as he continued to watch her with that eager expression on his face, surely he didn't expect her to say she wanted to hop into bed with him. "I'm very interested in having a...a..."

"Affair?" He supplied helpfully. Then he grinned as she turned a bright pink.

"A relationship," she corrected, reaching for her wineglass. "And it is nice that we share the same hobby."

"That'll do for starters." He smiled in satisfaction and leaned back in the chair. "But I do have to give you a word of warning. I won't stand for you trifling with my affections."

Layla choked.

Paul reached over and clapped her lightly on the back. "Are you all right?" he asked in concern.

Nodding vigorously, she managed to say, "Trifling with your affections! Where did you come up with that little gem?"

He pretended to look hurt. "Perhaps my choice of words is a tad old-fashioned. But I think it expresses my meaning fairly clearly."

"It does?" She was puzzled. Surely he wasn't serious. No one in this day and age talked like that.

Paul watched her confused expression carefully. He'd deliberately used a silly expression to lighten things up, but he was dead serious. Sighing theatrically, he said. "Okay, I'll spell it out for you. I'm not interested in some modern open arrangement where we play games with each other. I'm too damned old for that."

Layla frowned, not sure she understood him exactly. "What does that mean?"

"It means that I think we both want an honest, meaningful relationship with a high degree of integrity."

"Oh."

He gave her a wary look and then continued. "I want to get to know you. I want you to get to know me and I want us to be prepared to handle any and all problems that crop up like two adults. It means . . ."

"I think I get your point," she interrupted dryly.

They stared at each other for a long moment and then both of them burst out laughing.

"This is ludicrous," Layla said. "Trifling with your affections," she mimicked. "You sound like an old bachelor from a really bad Victorian melodrama. How could I possibly play with your affections, when we've never even had a real date.''

"That's easily remedied." He picked up his fork and stuffed another bite of food into his mouth. "Spend Saturday with me. We can go to Balboa Park. There's a great restaurant I'd like to take you to over on the coast. We can spend the whole day getting rid of all your 'buts' and 'doubts.'''

Layla's head was spinning. She couldn't pinpoint precisely how he'd managed to move things so quickly, but strangely enough she wasn't unduly concerned by it. "That sounds nice. I've never been to Balboa Park. But what's wrong with discussing all my 'buts' and 'doubts' right now?"

He shook his head. "No, I don't think so. We've already had one minor skirmish tonight and I don't want to press my luck. I just want to sit here, talk to you and enjoy this great meal. Can you get someone to mind the store on Saturday?"

She nodded. A warm, cozy contentment was filling her and she didn't want to give the feeling up. It was too rare. For once, Layla refused to listen to that little voice in the back of her head, the one that always nagged her to be careful. She didn't want to be careful, she didn't want to be cautious, she wanted to enjoy herself. "Yes. Tank can take over for me. He can use the extra hours."

Paul frowned, opened his mouth to protest and then quickly snapped it shut again. Luckily Layla had looked away and hadn't seen the disapproving expression on his face. He decided he'd pushed his luck enough for one night. The less said on the subject of Tank Mullins, the better.

"Tell me," he said a little later, after they'd finished the chicken and were waiting for the coffee to finish perking. "What did you do before you came to Riker's Pass?"

"I worked in Los Angeles." Layla got up and went to the counter. "I was an accounting supervisor for a cement company."

"You're from L.A.?"

"No. I'm from a small town near Cleveland, Ohio."

"How long have you been in California?"

She shrugged and poured the coffee into two mugs. "About seven years. I was offered a chance to move from the Cleveland branch office to the head office in Pasadena. It was a promotion so I jumped at it."

She picked the mugs up. "Let's move into the living room."

Paul glanced at the table as he rose to his feet. "What about the dishes?"

"You're a guest." She shouldered open the kitchen door. "I'll get those later."

In the living room, she put the mugs on the coffee table, then looked over her shoulder. Paul was standing by her bookcase, staring at the photograph of Miss Pine.

He looked up and caught her glance. "Is this your mother?"

"No." She came to stand next to him. "That's a good friend. Her name was Violet Pine."

"Was?"

"She died a few years ago." She was suddenly very, very apprehensive. The enormity of what she'd agreed to earlier was hitting her with the force of an eight point two earthquake. Paul would now start asking her questions. He'd want to know everything about her. And she wasn't sure she was ready to share that much of herself with him. Not just yet. She walked back to the couch. "Have you lived here all your life?"

He gave her a long, steady stare, sensing that she wanted to talk about anything except herself. Sighing inwardly, he walked the few feet separating them and sat down next to her, close enough that their legs brushed. She shifted slightly but Paul didn't let that bother him.

"I've lived in the San Diego area all of my life," he said. "My folks still live over on the coast in Encinitas. That's one of the reasons I opened my practice up here. It's only a ninety minute drive. I'm close enough so that we can see each other whenever we want, but far enough away so that we don't live in each other's pockets." He raised his cup and took a quick sip. "How about you? Does your family mind you being so far from home?"

He felt her tense.

"There's just my father left," Layla answered cautiously, "and my stepmother. My mother died years ago. My father's pretty busy with his own life now that he's retired. He's been taking night classes at the state college and he's gotten into gardening, too."

Layla didn't add that she hadn't seen her father since coming to California. There was no point. She suddenly knew with utter certainty that Paul would never understand. How could he? You could see how close he was to his family just by listening to the way he talked about them.

"I bet he misses you," Paul said.

She eased away from him, putting several inches between their bodies and he saw her hands knot into fists. He frowned slightly, knowing that she was withdrawing again and not knowing why. But this time, he wasn't going to let her get away with it.

He slipped his arm around her shoulder and pulled her back against his side. If she couldn't bring herself to talk to him yet, he'd take matters into his own hands. There was more than one way to communicate.

Layla's eyes widened slightly, but she didn't move away.

Encouraged, he flattened his palm and began slowly massaging her upper arm. He wanted to be close to her again, the way they had been for those few moments in the kitchen when he'd riled her into opening up to him.

Through the cotton of her blouse, he could feel the warmth of her skin against his fingers. Leaning forward, he placed his coffee mug on the table, then plucked Layla's out of her hand and set it beside his.

She stared at him, her eyes filled with something that could be want or need or just plain old curiosity. Paul didn't care. He only knew that she wasn't pushing him away.

Turning, he put his other arm around her and caged her against the couch. Lowering his head, he brushed his lips against hers, pulled back and stared at her flushed face.

Layla gazed deeply into his warm gray eyes. There was a tender, patient, waiting quality in his expression, as though he were silently asking her permission to continue.

Shyly she smiled, telling him without words to kiss her. He took her mouth again. Only this time he slanted his lips across hers and probed gently with his tongue until she opened up and let him inside.

She moaned when he began a slow, thorough exploration of the mysterious cavern of her mouth. He swept inside, increasing the pressure until his tongue boldly tangled with hers.

Layla was stunned. The kiss was hot and sweet and sensuous and she felt it in every cell of her body.

He kept kissing her, his mouth moving hungrily on hers until without thinking, she twined her arms around his neck and arched her body against the hard wall of his chest.

Paul's hands moved from her shoulders to her back, stroking sensuously up and down the line of her spine. He pushed his hand beneath the soft fabric of her loose blouse until his palms contacted bare skin.

She felt so good, so warm, so right in his arms. Their mouths worked feverishly, tasting and teasing in a delightful intimacy that left him hungry for more. He wanted to get closer, tighter, deeper. His fingers skimmed up her back until they found and unsnapped the catch of her bra. Leaning back, he edged his hand around her ribs and cupped her breast. She gasped but he didn't release her mouth. Instead, he deepened the kiss as his thumb captured her nipple and he circled the soft peak in a slow, languorous stroke. A thrill of fierce satisfaction shot through him as he felt her spring to life against the warmth of his hand.

He was quickly caught up in a passion so intense it was almost painful. Her mouth was addictive, her skin soft and silky and her body was molding to his as if it had been tailor-made for a perfect fit. Somehow they'd shifted on the couch and she was lying half sprawled beneath him.

Layla was lost. She'd never known that physical desire could happen this quickly, this unexpectedly. She only knew she never wanted him to stop kissing her, to stop touching her. Her body had a will all its own. Suddenly she wasn't herself anymore. She was a twisting, writhing stranger who wanted nothing more than to be crushed beneath Paul's hard, male body. Every nerve in her body was straining for connection, appeasement, fulfillment and she wanted to satisfy the wildfire urges raging through her blood.

She moaned in disappointment as Paul broke the kiss. But then she felt his lips nibbling at the sensitive skin of her neck and the moan turned into a hiss of pleasure as the unfamiliar caress sent a shiver coursing along her flesh.

Unbuttoning her shirt, he gently removed it and her bra. Then he lifted his head and looked at her. Their eyes met and he was humbled by the expression of passion and trust he saw mirrored in her gaze. He swallowed and looked down at her half-naked body. Her breasts were lovely—small but perfect ivory mounds with delicate pink tips the color of rose petals.

"You're beautiful," he muttered, his voice husky.

He kissed her again and slipped his arm behind her back as he shifted, wedging himself between her legs. She could feel the bold bulge of his manhood against her thigh, then she couldn't think at all as his mouth worked its way down her neck to her breast.

Paul was so hard he ached. He wanted to touch her and taste her and drive her as wild as she was driving him. He'd meant to stop after the kiss; he'd meant to pull away and just talk some more. But the moment she'd opened her lips for him, the moment he'd felt her body melting against him, his good intentions had flown.

He cupped her breast in his hand and closed his lips over the tip. Slowly, gently, he drew her deep inside and sucked, feeling the pebbly flesh roll beautifully against his tongue. His hand stroked down the satin smoothness of her belly until he reached the zipper of her jeans.

Unconsciously Layla moved her leg and he groaned as her denim-clad thigh rubbed against his hardness. Even through the tough fabric of his jeans, the pleasure was intense.

He quickly worked her zipper down and slipped his hand inside. Layla whimpered and clutched him tighter. Dazed by the intense urges racking her body, she gave herself completely into his keeping.

Then his hand brushed against the soft curls at the top of her thighs, and she stiffened. But he was too far gone to notice. He moved his mouth to her other breast, pulled the nipple inside and tenderly drew on it as his hand cupped the soft mound between her legs. Layla jerked as one unfamiliar but intensely pleasurable sensation after another racked her body. His mouth and hands were doing incredible things to her, things she'd never imagined before. She bit down on her lips to hold back a gasp as his fingers found the tiny center of her feminine desire.

She shuddered and her knees closed as he began to fondle and stroke her. Suddenly she was overwhelmed by what she was doing, by what she was letting him do. She panicked, and pulled away, flattening herself against the back of the couch.

Paul froze. He raised his head and stared at her, wondering what was going on. Her face was pale, her eyes confused and frightened.

"What's wrong?" he asked, his voice hoarse.

She dragged a deep breath into her lungs. "Nothing, but this is happening too fast. I think we'd better stop." She dropped her gaze and stared at the top button of his shirt. "I shouldn't have let things go this far. I didn't mean to get so carried away."

He was intensely frustrated. His body was screaming for release and he didn't understand her reaction. For crying out loud, she was a twenty-nine-year-old woman, not some sixteen-year-old virgin who'd never been kissed.

And though he respected a woman's right to say no,
Layla's abrupt change of heart was extremely confusing.
It wasn't as if they were strangers; it wasn't as if she
hadn't been actively participating every step of the way.

But when she finally lifted her chin and looked at him,
he could see that the confusion and panic in her eyes were
still there. His irritation vanished. When he did make love
to her, he wanted her looking at him the way she had been
a few minutes ago. With passion and trust.

"You didn't do it by yourself," he soothed. "I got
pretty carried away, too." He sat up and she immediately scrambled away from him, her face going scarlet as
she realized she was half-dressed. Frantically she turned
away and began pulling on her bra and shirt. But a second later, she felt Paul's hands on her shoulders. He
tugged her around to face him.

"Let me." He brushed her shaking fingers aside and
gently, but firmly fastened her clothes. Placing one finger under her chin, he turned her face up to his and
lightly dropped a kiss on her nose. "Don't be embarrassed, not with me. We weren't doing anything wrong.
We were making love. I'm sorry if I moved too fast, but
the truth is, I've been wanting you since the moment I
first laid eyes on you."

She felt foolish. She couldn't say she'd wanted him, too
because the truth was, she'd never expected to experience the passion he'd shown her. She hadn't known it was
possible. But now she *had* experienced it, her common
sense seemed to have completely deserted her. All she
could think to do was repeat what he'd said. "Since you
first saw me?"

He smiled. "Yes. The minute I saw you standing on
the porch of the Emporium I knew I wanted to get to
know you better. Intimately, in fact. But you were pretty

good at avoiding me." He cocked his head to one side. "Did you do that deliberately?"

"Avoid you?" Layla's brows came together in a puzzled frown. Had she? She didn't honestly know. "No, at least not consciously."

"Unconsciously then?"

"Well..." She hesitated for a moment. "Maybe. I think I knew I could be attracted to you."

"So you treated me like I had the bubonic plague," he said curiously. "That doesn't make any sense."

"It does to me." She bit her lip and looked away. This was agonizing, but he deserved the truth. "I'm not very good with men," she admitted. "Oh, I've dated some, but I'm not adept at handling relationships. When I began to notice you, I just sort of figured it would be easier to keep my distance."

"But why? I made it pretty obvious from the first time I walked into your store and introduced myself that I was interested."

She stared at him helplessly. How could you tell a man you were scared. That the thought of craving someone's love and approval was tantamount to a living death. That if you let yourself get close, there was always the chance that you'd be repeating the patterns you'd worked so hard to overcome. Before you knew it, you'd be wondering if what you did met with his approval. Before you knew it, you'd be terrified to open your mouth in front of his friends in case you said the wrong thing. Before you knew it, you'd be jumping through hoops over and over again to prove your own worth.

Layla knew most men weren't like her father, but the pattern had been set long ago and she wasn't sure she was capable of breaking it.

"Answer me, Layla," Paul demanded softly.

"I guess it's because I was scared that if we started dating and it didn't work out, things would get awkward. After all, we are neighbors and this is a small town." She shrugged. "I didn't want people gossiping about me, so it seemed wiser to keep my distance."

Paul knew she was lying. "People are probably gossiping now. Does that bother you?"

She shook her head. "No, I've decided not to worry about it."

An uneasy silence fell between them. He didn't know what to think. She was obviously not going to tell him any more. But Paul wanted to make sure she understood exactly how he felt.

There was something strong linking the two of them. Something so intense that when he'd touched her his feelings had taken him by surprise and shattered his emotional and physical control. And he was wise enough to know that emotions that powerful had to be good.

Probably the best thing that had ever happened to either of them.

"Well," he said softly, his voice loaded with meaning. "You may have kept your distance for a few months, but things have changed now." He rose to his feet and stared down at her.

Layla scrambled to her feet.

He reached over and pulled her against him. Lowering his head, he kissed her long and passionately. When he drew away, she was gazing at him with stunned surprise.

"And believe me, sweetheart," he said, releasing her and moving toward the door. "Now that we've come this far, I don't intend to let you get away."

Chapter Seven

Layla stood stock-still, staring at the closed door. She remained there for several moments, lost in her thoughts as the implications of his parting words sank in.

She jumped as a cold, wet nose nudged her hand. "Oh, sorry boy," she murmured to Stanley, "I'll bet you want to go out." He wagged his tail.

She let the dog out the back and started cleaning the kitchen. As she carried their dirty plates to the sink, she caught her reflection in the toaster on the counter. Layla paused and stared at herself. She was shaken by an eerie sense of déjà vu because the face that gazed back at her belonged to someone else. It belonged to Elaine Odell.

People had often commented on how much she looked like her mother, but tonight was the first time she'd ever seen the resemblance. And it made her distinctly uneasy.

Because the eyes that bored into hers were filled with anxiety and apprehension. Just the way her mother's had been.

Sighing, she put the dishes in the sink and leaned against the counter. No wonder her mother had died so young. The doctors had called it a heart attack, but Layla was convinced the poor woman had worried herself to death. She'd spent her life constantly placating her husband. Constantly fetching and carrying and making sure his neat, narrow little world stayed just the way he liked it. And had the man ever been grateful, had he ever treated his wife with courtesy or love or respect?

Hell, no!

No matter what her mother did, her father was never satisfied, never content. Not with either of them.

As a child, she'd frequently asked why her father was so harsh, why he never smiled. Elaine always gave her the same answer. She'd smile sadly and say, "Because that's just the way he is." She said it as if it were one of the Ten Commandments, or a law of the universe that could never be changed.

For years, Layla had imagined that somewhere out in the depths of space, there were billions and billions of neatly laid squares of stone stretching farther than the eye could see. They were endless, they were infinite and they were immutable. There was one for everyone. For every soul who had come before her and for every soul who would come after her.

And the stone with your name on it was your fate. Your destiny. Your pattern.

There was no escape. There was no changing it. The basic weave of your existence, the basic building blocks of what you *were*, were written on that stone and etched forever in granite.

And her mother's pattern had been one of sacrifice and privation. She fell in love and lost herself. Lost the girl who'd once been captain of the debate team and editor of the school yearbook. Once married, she'd devoted her whole life to winning her husband's love and approval.

And despite Miss Pine, despite dozens of self-help books and positive affirmations, Layla was scared the resemblance to her mother was more than skin-deep. She was terrified that once she gave her heart, she'd lose everything else: her self-respect, her ambitions, her future. Once she loved someone, everything else in her life would become unimportant. That's how it had been for her mother.

After marrying, the woman had given up her whole life to become a doormat. Layla was scared she'd do the same thing. For she knew she hadn't changed anything basic about the writing on her stone, she'd only obscured the words with a covering of dust.

But Paul wasn't her father.

He wasn't like any man she'd ever known. He was different. Special. He had the power to coax a shocking response from her. A response that would be branded into her brain forever.

Stanley woofed and she let him back in. Frowning, she locked the door and decided to leave the dishes until the morning. Flicking off the lights, she went to her bed.

But the last thing that went through her mind before she fell asleep was that it didn't make any difference whether or not Paul was like Daniel Odell. She was like her mother.

By morning, Layla had willed her fanciful notions under some semblance of control. Paul had asked her for a date, not her hand in marriage. It was way too premature to worry about anything other than having a good time when he took her to Balboa Park.

On Saturday Paul picked her up promptly at eight o'clock. As she climbed into his truck, he leaned over and surprised her with a swift kiss.

She drew back, startled by the casual caress. But Paul didn't appear to notice her reaction. He'd turned his head, and was watching through the back window as he backed out onto the road.

"This has been one helluva of a week," he announced as they sped down the mountain toward the highway. "I wanted to call or drop by, but I didn't have a chance. Every animal in Riker's Pass either went into labor or needed emergency surgery."

"That's okay," she replied. "You don't owe me any explanations." She glanced out the window and gazed at the rows of avocado trees lining the side of the hill. She hoped he got the message. Neither of them should have to account for their time to the other. "I've been busy, too."

"Did you miss me?"

Her head snapped around and she stared at his profile. His gaze was fixed on the road, but she could see a teasing grin on his face. Her serious mood vanished and she laughed. Paul was good at making her laugh. "Does your ego need stroking this morning? It's only been a couple of days since we saw each other."

"My ego always needs stroking. Doesn't everyone's?"

"Mine doesn't." She gave him a smug smile.

"Liar." Paul grinned in satisfaction as the first moments of tension were successfully dealt with. The past few days had been hard. He'd had plenty of emergencies, that was true, but he could have called or even gone by to see her. He'd wanted to badly enough. He'd been so hungry for the sight of her that a couple of times he'd stationed himself at his office window just to see her open the store in the mornings. But he'd sensed she needed some time to herself.

The depth of their passion that night had surprised him, and he was smart enough to realize if he'd been that stunned, she must be absolutely poleaxed.

They laughed and teased each other as they continued their descent off the mountain. By the time they reached San Diego, Layla was thoroughly enjoying herself. Riding in Paul's pickup truck was fun, the sky clear, the sun shining and there was a cool, brisk ocean breeze that guaranteed they wouldn't be broiled to a crisp as they toured the park.

Paul reached over and patted her knee. "You think Tank will be all right at the store today?"

She gazed at the large, tanned hand resting on her thigh. He seemed to feel no compunction about touching her. There was no hesitancy, no awkwardness in his casual caresses. She decided that would take some getting used to, but on the whole, she rather liked it.

"He'll be fine," Layla replied. "He's a very bright young man." She spoke with more confidence than she felt, because she didn't want Paul to know she had any qualms about trusting Tank. "And he was thrilled to get the extra hours. He's saving for college, you know."

"College," Paul repeated cynically.

"Yes. And I'm encouraging him." Layla turned in her seat and fixed Paul with a steady stare. "And you should, too."

He shrugged. "Well, at least if he goes off to school it'll get him out of town and away from MaryBeth."

"What do you mean, 'get him away from Mary-Beth'!" Layla was offended on Tank's behalf. "I'll have you know, your little goddaughter is the one who's chasing him, not the other way around."

He glanced at her skeptically. "Did Tank tell you that?"

"No. I saw it with my own eyes. MaryBeth came into the store this week and tried to talk Tank into going to some kind of youth thing at her church. So don't you go accusing Tank of chasing after her. He's innocent of that particular crime."

His mouth settled into a flat, grim line. He didn't want to rake up this old argument. Layla had made it clear she wasn't going to listen to any criticism of Tank. "MaryBeth was just being nice. She's a real sweetheart, she's always going out of her way for other people. She probably still feels sorry for him. But I wouldn't repeat that to anyone else. If her parents find out she's still trying to help him, they'll have a fit."

"MaryBeth's been trying to help Tank? How?"

"By being his friend. As you once pointed out to me, he doesn't have many. But frankly, I'd just as soon she stay the hell away from him. He drinks and he's unstable, and he's already hurt her once."

Layla balled her hands into fists. She wanted to scream that she was sure Tank didn't drink, that there had to be some explanation for the episode with MaryBeth. But she knew it would be pointless. She was taking the boy on faith, but Paul had no faith in Tank any longer. No matter how long and hard she argued, he wasn't going to change his mind.

"That's ridiculous," she scoffed. "Has he been goofing off on the job? Has he missed any work? Has he come in late or left early?"

"Okay," he admitted grudgingly, "Tank is a good worker. But then again, he has to be. He's practically under a court order to keep his nose clean on the job front. But that doesn't mean he's a suitable friend for an impressionable and naive teenage girl."

Layla stared at him for a moment and then sighed. Even though he saw the boy every day, Paul's attitude to Tank Mullins hadn't changed. She had the feeling it wasn't ever going to, either. "You don't trust him at all, do you?" She turned and stared out the window at the heavy freeway traffic.

"No. But you knew that already. However, just because I don't trust him doesn't mean I treat him unfairly." He glanced at her and saw that she was glaring at him stubbornly. Her expression needled him. "I don't, however, give him the keys to the cash box."

"And you think I'm stupid because I do." She'd not only given him the keys to the cash register, but she'd also given him the keys to her house. Layla didn't know what time she'd be home, so she'd asked Tank to feed Stanley.

He felt petty. "Of course you're not stupid. Your relationship with the kid is obviously different from mine. But you do confuse me."

Startled, Layla's head snapped around. Didn't he understand? He was the one that confused *her*. Ever since she'd stood in his office and negotiated with him about Tank and Stanley, her whole world had been turned upside down. He'd inspired feelings inside her she didn't know she had. Being with him was exciting, exhilarating and disorienting. Sometimes he made her feel as if she'd been beamed into an alien landscape where she stumbled blindly around a mine field of explosive emotions, a place where each and every movement was fraught with risk.

"How do I confuse you?" she asked.

He cast her an enigmatic smile. "Oh, in a whole bunch of ways. We'll talk about it. Soon. But not right now." He pointed straight ahead. "There's the park entrance. Come on, let's go out and enjoy ourselves. Okay?"

Layla wished he'd tell her what he'd meant. But he wasn't going to and she didn't want to push him about it. She didn't have the courage. "All right."

Balboa Park was San Diego's cultural and recreational center. There were over a thousand acres of grassy lawns, garden walks, museums and restaurants.

Paul suggested their first stop be The Museum of Man and they spent what was left of the morning enjoying the anthropology and archaeology exhibits from Indian and Mexican cultures.

As they came out into the sunshine, Layla's stomach growled.

Paul grinned. "You sound hungry. Where do you want to eat."

She chose a restaurant with a beautiful view and they ate on the patio, chatting easily and talking about everything except themselves.

"What do you want to do now," Paul asked once they were back outside. "There's lots to see yet. We can go to the Aero-Space Museum or the Spanish Village Arts and Crafts Center or the Art Institute."

"I'd like to take a walk." She smiled and spun around. "It's so beautiful here and the fresh air feels good."

They spent the next hour strolling around the open spaces of the park. Paul finally stopped under a large tree and plopped down. "Let's rest for a while. I don't know about you, but my feet hurt."

Layla nodded and sat down beside him. She tucked her legs beneath her denim skirt and stared at the peaceful greenery of the park. "What did you mean when you said I confused you?"

He folded his arms behind his head and leaned back against the trunk, his gaze fixed straight ahead. "Ah-ha, so you *were* listening."

"Of course I was listening. As a matter of fact, I believed I asked you at the time what you meant."

"So you did," he replied cryptically. He was stalling. In one sense, he wanted to see if she cared enough to push him. He'd been mildly disappointed when she'd let him change the subject so easily earlier.

"Well?"

"Well what?" He gave her a lazy smile.

She frowned in exasperation. "What did you mean earlier? You didn't make a lot of sense. There's absolutely nothing confusing about me. I'm perfectly simple and straightforward."

"Are you?" He gazed at her thoughtfully.

Layla felt like shaking him. "Yes, damn it. I am. Now are you going to tell me or not."

It was tough, but he managed to keep from smiling. She did care enough to nag. "Of course I'm going to tell you," he said softly. "You're usually so calm and composed I can't resist teasing you."

She made a face at him and he laughed.

"To begin with," he said, "you're not at all simple or straightforward, you're a very complex lady."

"Why do you say that?"

"Well, for some reason, you're willing to trust someone like Tank Mullins while I get the distinct impression you've got me on probation. That's fairly puzzling."

"That's not true," she protested. "And I do trust you."

"Do you?" He looked doubtful. "Sometimes with you I get the feeling you haven't quite made up your mind yet. You're very polite about it, but you do run hot and cold. One minute you're all warm and soft and the next, you're pulling away from me like I've got bad breath."

Layla looked down at her hands. He had her there. "Are you talking about when we almost..." She faltered and tried to think of the right word.

"Made love?"

She nodded but didn't look up. "You've got to admit, you have moved things pretty fast in this relationship. Faster than I'm used to, anyway. I only called a halt because I thought we were moving too quickly, not because I don't trust you."

"So you're saying you do trust me?"

Layla was silent for a long time. Finally she lifted her chin and gave him a long, level stare. "I trust that you're a good person, and that you wouldn't deliberately mislead me or use me. But—" She broke off as she sought for the best way to make him understand.

"Oh, yes," he said softly, "those famous 'buts' of yours." He moved suddenly, shifting away from the tree and crossing his long jean-clad legs. "Tell me, Layla. Tell me what's got you so uptight about me. I'm just a man. A man who wants very much to have you as a part of his life. What's wrong with that? What do you think I'm going to do to you?"

His gaze bored into hers. Eyes of slate gray that should have been cold but weren't. Instead they were soft, compelling and filled with understanding and patience.

Layla couldn't evade his question. He needed to understand why she was so hesitant to make any kind of commitment to him. Not that he'd ask for one, but she suspected that wasn't far off. Paul wasn't looking for a one-night stand or a quick fling. She was suddenly reminded of an old jest that frequently made the rounds during coffee breaks back when she worked in L.A. The joke was if you wanted to get rid of a man all you had to do was say you were looking to quit your job, get married and have six kids. Conventional wisdom dictated that any man hearing that would take off like a shot. But somehow she doubted that was true in Paul's case.

He had "nest builder" written all over him.

She gave him a hesitant smile. "I guess I'm a little uptight because of your attitude to Tank."

Paul's jaw dropped. "Are we back to him again! What does Tank have to do with you trusting me?"

"It's got everything to do with it," she explained. "You were once one of Tank's few supporters in town. But he did something that seemed terrible and, instead of digging deeper into the whole situation, you accepted it at face value. Without trying to find out his side, you tried and convicted him." She sat up straighter. "I know there's more to that story. And if you'd really had any faith in the boy, you'd have known it, too, and kept at him until you uncovered the truth. But you didn't. You just believed the worst. What if we get involved and I do something you think is wrong? Will you stop seeing me? Will you turn against me, too?"

He shook his head in amazement. "That's crazy, Layla. First of all, I'm not against Tank. But the facts speak for themselves and I couldn't ignore the evidence of my own eyes. He did hurt someone I care about. But even then, I hired him, didn't I?"

"Only because that was the only way you could get me to take Stanley off your hands."

He gave her a pitying look. "Layla, half the town owes me favors. I gave you the dog because I wanted you to have some protection out in that isolated house of yours and I thought he'd be good company for you. To be honest, I hired Tank because of you. It was a good excuse to get to know you better. Also, even though I was mad as hell at him, and despite your claim that I tried and convicted him, I wanted to give him one last chance. But that's beside the point." He made an impatient gesture with his hand.

"We're talking about us. You're not on trial with me. For God's sake, I care about you. Why are you so worried about making a mistake? What were you planning on doing, burning down my house?"

"Of course not," she said. "But it's not just that."

"Go on," he urged. "Tell me what's wrong. I thought we agreed the other night to be open and honest with each other."

"Maybe you won't like hearing what I have to say," she warned.

"I'm a big boy, Layla. I think I can handle it. And believe it or not, if there's a major problem between the two of us, I'd just as soon deal with it now as later."

"Paul." She cleared her throat. "I want you to know something about me. Something that's as important to me as being honest seems to be with you. I've worked hard to become well . . . emotionally independent."

"Emotionally independent?" He repeated the phrase as if it was in a foreign language.

"You're a very overwhelming kind of personality," she continued earnestly. "I guess I'm a little frightened that you'll ask more of me than I want to give."

"What the hell does that mean?"

"It means," she said slowly, "that I'm fairly self-contained. That I've learned to rely on my inner resources and not other people. It means that I don't look to anyone else for my happiness, that I take responsibility for my own actions and feelings. It means I don't need other people for my emotional well-being, it means—"

"It means you've been reading too many self-help books," he interjected dryly.

Taken aback, she stared at him openmouthed. "If you're going to be flippant about this, I don't think we can discuss the matter. It happens to be very important to me."

"You're right," Paul said apologetically. "I shouldn't have said that. But have you listened to what you're telling me?"

"Of course I know what I'm saying."

"Do you? I wonder." He rose to his feet and stood staring down at her, a cryptic expression on his face.

Layla stood up, too. Suddenly the day wasn't as bright as it had been, and the air wasn't quite as crisp and refreshing as before. She wished she'd kept her mouth shut. She'd as good as told the man she didn't get emotionally involved.

"Paul, listen. Maybe I didn't explain things very well. I do want to keep seeing you. But it's only fair that I should warn you about how I feel."

He didn't respond for a few moments, he just looked at her with a narrow, assessing gaze that made her uneasy. Finally he took her elbow and started across the grass. "Then it's only fair that I should warn you about how *I* feel."

There was something in the tone of his voice that warned her she wouldn't like what he had to say. But there was really no way to avoid it. After all, she'd started this conversation. But telling him her feelings hadn't been quite as liberating as she'd hoped. As a matter of fact, she felt downright depressed.

"All right," she said, a tad reluctantly. "I suppose turnabout is fair play."

He nodded. "Number one, I think the whole concept of 'emotional independence' is total nonsense." Paul ignored her gasp of outrage. "If you're not connected and dependent on other human beings, then you might as well be dead." He turned her to face him. He spoke quietly, calmly, but his expression, his body and his whole manner indicated he meant every word he said.

"Number two," he continued. "I fully intend to become emotionally dependent on you and number three, I fully intend that you will become emotionally dependent upon me. That's the whole point of a relationship, Layla."

She shook her head. "But that's not what I want."

"How do you know?"

"How do I know?" she repeated, mainly because she didn't have a clue as to how to answer him. "How do I know?"

"You sound like a parrot. Answer the question."

Layla started walking again. Her mind was working frantically, trying to come up with an answer. Explaining her entire life would take too long and she didn't want to do that anyway.

He caught up with her in two strides. "Didn't anyone ever tell you it's rude to walk off in the middle of an important conversation?"

"I wasn't walking off in the middle of anything," she replied. "I was trying to think of how to answer you."

"Ah-ha, then you admit you don't know what you want."

"I'm not admitting anything," she retorted, feeling her temper start to rise. "Of course I know what I want. It's just hard to think of another way to put it into words."

"Nonsense. You didn't have any problem before."

"Well, obviously you didn't like what I said, because you immediately started telling me how wrong I was."

"I didn't say you were wrong, I merely explained how I felt. Then I asked how you knew what you wanted. But so far, you haven't been able to answer that one."

"And I don't intend to, either," Layla snapped.

She glared at him. She was tired of answering his questions. Tired of defending herself. "What is it with you? You sound like a broken record, one question after another. I thought this was supposed to be a date, not an appearance before the Spanish Inquisition."

Paul stared at her solemnly. Beneath the bravado of her words, he could see the confusion and panic in her eyes. He was pushing her and he knew it. And he wasn't sure why.

"Point taken." He grinned sheepishly. "Let's call a truce. You're right, we're supposed to be enjoying ourselves. I'm sorry I pushed you, okay?"

She eyed him warily for a moment and then gave him a strained smile. "Okay. Truce accepted. It has been a nice day and I've had a good time. At least until we started playing twenty questions."

"We won't play it anymore today," he promised. "Come on, if we hurry, we can see the Arts and Crafts Village before it closes."

Ten minutes later, they were at the Village, but neither of them was enjoying it. Their tour was perfunctory, with each of them lost in his own thoughts.

Paul was thinking about what she'd said. But more importantly, he kept trying to pinpoint *why* she'd said it. Why she had a need to believe such ridiculous nonsense.

She appeared to be telling him that she intended to live her life emotionally cut off from the rest of the world. But something about it didn't ring true.

He watched her bend and pick up a handmade ceramic jug. Her hair was loose and flowing around her shoulders, she wore a scoop-necked white sweater with pink appliquéd roses around the neck and a flared denim skirt that set off her figure to perfection. Layla was beautiful and soft and ripe for a man's love. Then why was she trying to seal herself behind a wall of steel? Why was she trying to send her emotions into permanent hibernation? It didn't make any sense.

"This is gorgeous." She held up the piece of pottery so he could examine it. "I think I'll buy it. It would look perfect on my kitchen table."

"Let me get it for you."

Layla shook her head. "No. Thanks anyway. But I can't let you do that."

He watched her take the jug and head for the cash register inside the store. She was running scared and she had reason to be. He'd meant every word he'd said. He did intend to become emotionally dependent on her as well as physically and mentally, too. And he damned well intended she would feel the same way about him. Paul frowned. But first he had to figure out why she was so skittish. Why she was so adamant about keeping him at a distance.

Layla came back, smiling and holding her bag up. "I think you'd better get me out of here before I go broke. This stuff is beautiful, but it isn't cheap."

"We should be leaving anyway. Our dinner reservations are for six and it'll take an hour to get there."

They drove up Highway 101 to Solano Beach and had dinner. Paul managed to keep the conversation lighthearted and casual. By the time they climbed into his truck for the drive back to Riker's Pass, Layla was yawning.

"Why don't you take a nap," he suggested, leaning over and snapping in her seat belt. "You look tired."

"Oh, but I need to keep you company." She yawned again. "It's a long drive back."

"Don't worry about it." He turned on the radio, filling the cab of the truck with soft, mellow music. A few moments later he glanced over and saw her slumped down in the seat, sound asleep.

Paul sighed. Once again he considered the puzzle of Layla Jane Odell. One minute she was soft and warm and reacting delightfully to his overtures, and the next she was tossing up roadblocks and hiding behind walls.

He thought of her willingness to champion Tank Mullins and her obvious devotion to that fat mutt Stanley. Any woman who reacted that way to those two wasn't as cut off from the world as she liked to pretend. Any woman who would take a misguided delinquent under her wing was reaching out for human contact in the riskiest of ways. Then why was she holding him at bay? He considered the matter as he sped down the freeway.

Paul thought of her reluctance to discuss her past or her family. He'd gotten maybe less than three minutes conversation on that topic, and that was peculiar, too.

As these things whirled in his head, he suddenly thought of Rhea, his shy mixed breed dog. He'd found her half-starved in an empty shack not far from his house.

Rhea had been abandoned, dirty and starved not only for food but also for affection. But when he first tried to help her, she wouldn't take either. It had taken him days to get the dog to trust him enough so that she'd even eat

NO RISK, NO OBLIGATION TO BUY…NOW OR EVER!

GUARANTEED

PLAY "ROLL A DOUBLE" AND GET AS MANY AS FIVE GIFTS!

HERE'S HOW TO PLAY:

1. Peel off label from front cover. Place it in space provided at right. With a coin, carefully scratch off the silver dice. This makes you eligible to receive two or more free books, and possibly another gift, depending on what is revealed beneath the scratch-off area.

2. You'll receive brand-new Silhouette Special Edition® novels. When you return this card, we'll rush you the books and gift you qualify for ABSOLUTELY FREE!

3. Then, if we don't hear from you, every month, we'll send you 6 additional novels to read and enjoy. You can return them and owe nothing, but if you decide to keep them, you'll pay only $2.96 per book—a saving of 43¢ each off the cover price.

4. When you subscribe to the Silhouette Reader Service™, you'll also get our newsletter, as well as additional free gifts from time to time.

5. You must be completely satisfied. You may cancel at any time simply by sending us a note or a shipping statement marked "cancel" or by returning any shipment to us at our expense.

The Austrian crystal sparkles like a diamond! And it's carefully set in a romantic "Key to Your Heart" pendant on a generous 18" chain. The entire necklace is yours free as added thanks for giving our Reader Service a try!

YES! I have placed my label from the front cover into the space provided above and scratched off the silver dice. Please rush me the free books and gift that I am entitled to. I understand that I am under no obligation to purchase any books, as explained on the opposite page.

NAME _____

ADDRESS _____ APT. _____

CITY _____ STATE _____ ZIP CODE _____

CLAIM CHART

🎲🎲	**4 FREE BOOKS PLUS FREE "KEY TO YOUR HEART" NECKLACE**
🎲🎲	**3 FREE BOOKS**
🎲🎲	**2 FREE BOOKS**

CLAIM NO.37-829

Offer limited to one per household and not valid to current Silhouette Special Edition® subscribers. All orders subject to approval. ©1990 Harlequin Enterprises Limited

PRINTED IN U.S.A.

DETACH AND MAIL CARD TODAY!

SILHOUETTE "NO RISK" GUARANTEE

- You're not required to buy a single book—ever!
- You must be completely satisfied or you may cancel at any time simply by sending us a note or shipping statement marked "cancel" or by returning any shipment to us at our cost. Either way, you will receive no more books; you'll have no obligation to buy.
- The free books and gift you claimed on this "Roll A Double" offer remain yours to keep no matter what you decide.

If offer card is missing, please write to: Silhouette Reader Service, 3010 Walden Ave., P.O. Box 1867, Buffalo, NY 14269-1867

DETACH AND MAIL CARD TODAY!

BUSINESS REPLY MAIL
FIRST CLASS MAIL   PERMIT NO. 717   BUFFALO, NY

POSTAGE WILL BE PAID BY ADDRESSEE

SILHOUETTE READER SERVICE
3010 WALDEN AVE
PO BOX 1867
BUFFALO NY 14240-9952

NO POSTAGE
NECESSARY
IF MAILED
IN THE
UNITED STATES

in his presence. He'd had to leave her food on the porch and then walk away before she'd come near it. He remembered the feeling of triumph when she'd finally eaten the food while he was still within her range of vision.

After that it had taken several days of coaxing before she'd come close enough to let him pet her. And the damnedest thing was, the dog *wanted* affection. Rhea's tail would go a mile a minute, but the second he went toward her, she'd start to back up. Almost as though she were afraid to believe it was true. Finally one day he'd coaxed her into his truck and taken her home. She'd been there ever since. But of all his animals, she was the only one who didn't take his affection and love for granted. Even now, she hung back, waiting until the other dogs had bounced all over him. Only then would she shyly approach, only then would she let him pet her and croon over her and tell her what a wonderful dog she was.

Paul shook his head, wondering how his mind had wandered. Then it hit him and he swore softly, savagely into the darkness.

He looked over at the sleeping beauty in his truck with a mixture of compassion and empathy. Layla was like Rhea. Hungry for affection but not trusting herself or the world enough to go after it.

A burst of hot, potent anger flooded his system. Like Rhea, someone had hurt her. Badly. He vowed right there and then that no one would ever hurt her again.

Chapter Eight

Layla awoke Sunday morning with a feeling of deep contentment. Yawning, she pulled a robe over her white flannel nightgown and went into the kitchen. Stanley greeted her by butting his head against her knees. She patted him absently and let him out the back door. Still half-asleep, she stumbled toward the cupboard, a soft smile curving her lips as she remembered how gently Paul had awakened her last night when he brought her home. He'd held her close for a few moments in the truck before walking her inside. Then he'd pulled her into his arms and kissed her passionately. She hadn't protested, though perhaps she should have, considering the uneasy state of their relationship. But being in his embrace had felt so right. So perfect.

Stanley woofed softly and she let him in. Stretching, Layla pulled down a can of coffee. "Hey, ouch," she yelped, glaring at her dog. "Don't scratch my foot like that, I don't have any shoes on and those claws of yours are sharp."

He looked at her unrepentantly, then trotted over to his food dish and gazed at her.

Layla put the coffee down. "Okay, Stanley, I get the message." She got a bag of dog food out of the pantry and poured it carefully into a large plastic measuring cup. After she'd dumped a generous portion into his food dish, he stared at his rations pathetically and finally started to eat.

"I know, boy," she murmured, stroking his broad back. "You think I'm downright stingy. But take my word for it, this diet is for your own good. You're nowhere near as fat as you used to be." He ignored her.

Layla reached for the coffee and popped off the plastic lid. She frowned when she saw the can was empty. "Oh, no," she moaned. "This can't be right. I distinctly remember that I had enough left for this morning."

Shaking her head, she put the can down and snatched up the teakettle. "I tell you, Stanley, I must be losing my mind. Either that or Paul's got me so rattled I can't think straight."

Yet somehow that didn't ring true. Layla plopped down at the kitchen table. There had been at least two scoops left. She was sure of it. But who would come into her kitchen and steal something that ridiculous? Tank had her house keys, but it seemed odd that he'd brew a pot of coffee just for the few minutes it would take to feed Stanley. She pushed the mystery to the back of her mind. Tank had probably been tired and thirsty, no doubt he just made himself at home. She'd ask him about it when she saw him tomorrow.

Layla drank a cup of tea, took a shower and then settled down on the couch with the Sunday newspaper. She gave the telephone one quick, guilty glance. She hadn't spoken to her father and stepmother in weeks and she supposed she should give them a call. But she didn't feel like it. Besides, she told herself, she'd sent them a letter last month; they probably weren't expecting to hear from her yet.

But she knew she was rationalizing. Ginnie, her stepmother, was always prodding her to stay closer in touch. Layla smiled wryly. It was a wonder she and her father communicated at all. She supposed it was their middle-class values that kept them from drifting completely apart. Even after she'd moved in with Miss Pine when she was fourteen, she still hadn't been able to cut him totally out of her life.

Sighing, she picked up the paper again, quieting her conscience with a silent promise to call them early this evening. Talking to her father wasn't nearly as bad as it used to be. Since his remarriage, he was almost downright human.

She opened the paper and started reading the front page, but none of the articles held her attention for more than a few seconds. Paul kept intruding on her thoughts. She kept remembering everything he'd said to her yesterday.

They were poles apart in their attitude toward relationships, and that should have scared the dickens out of her, but it didn't. She wondered why? He certainly wasn't shy about trying to get his own way. He'd told her straight out precisely what his intentions were.

Layla finally put the paper down and gazed across the room at her bookcase. She smiled wryly. Maybe all those books had done more good than she'd thought. Maybe she wasn't quite as scared by the idea of commitment as she used to be. Commitment? She sat bolt upright. What was she thinking of! Technically she'd only had one date with the man.

Stanley, who had taken to following her around the house, got up off the rug and nudged her with his head.

"It's okay, sweetheart," she murmured, stroking his fur. "Go back and lie down. I'm just a little edgy today. Everything's all right."

The phone rang. Hastily, she leaped to her feet, dodged Stanley and grabbed it. "Hello."

"Hi, sweetheart." The endearment rolled off Paul's tongue with ease. "Did you sleep well?"

"Yes. All that walking we did yesterday tired me out. I slept like a log."

"Good, then you'll have plenty of energy to get some work done. I'm stuck here for the afternoon, I'm on call. So why don't you pack up that lazy dog and come over? We can go over the Centennial plans."

Her vow not to be a fool evaporated. "That sounds fine. Give me half an hour."

Layla sat on Paul's patio with her back to the sun. She tapped her pencil against the glass top of the table. "I still think we ought to at least try to find those old school desks, they've got to be somewhere."

"I've already talked to Elliot Thaxton, he's on the Board of Education. He says no one has any idea where that stuff ended up."

"But it would make the gym look so good, there's got to be someone who remembers what happened to everything from the school," she said stubbornly. "What about one of the old teachers?"

"Layla, they tore down the original schoolhouse in 1924. Even if we found someone who used to work there, she'd probably be so senile by now that she couldn't tell you what day it was, let alone what happened to a few old desks and chairs seventy odd years ago.''

''I guess you're right,'' she replied doubtfully. She turned her head and gazed down at Stanley, who was sprawled across her foot.

Paul studied her profile. She was such a serious little thing. He was delighted that she'd come over. After yesterday, he was afraid she might be running scared, that he'd come on too strong. He'd been playing it by ear, one part of him thinking that he couldn't stand being less than honest with her, while another part was screaming at him to slow down, to give her some time and space. Yet he had a feeling that if he let the pressure up a minute, she'd retreat. And he didn't want that. He didn't want her backing off to a safe distance. He wanted her excited and trusting and as totally involved in this relationship as he was.

''Why don't you come down to the yard behind my office sometime soon?'' Paul asked. ''I don't have any old-fashioned school desks, but there's probably lots of other old things we could use for the dance.''

''Like what?''

He shrugged. ''I'm not exactly sure, I've forgotten half the stuff that's stored out there, but it's worth a shot.''

''Hmm. That's a good idea.'' She smiled enthusiastically. ''When?''

''How about next Wednesday after five? No, make that Thursday. I'm having dinner at my parents' on Wednesday. Blankenship's on call for emergencies starting then. We could go out and grab a bite to eat after I give you the grand tour?''

She was disappointed he hadn't suggested Monday, or even Tuesday. ''Sure, that'll be fine.'' She gazed at him curiously. "Your family's very important to you, aren't they?"

Paul looked surprised by the question. "I see someone from the clan at least once a week."

"Once a week?" she echoed. "Is that some kind of rule in your family?"

"No." He laughed. "It's my own rule." But then his smile faded as he saw how serious she looked. "My family means a lot to me and I like to see them as often as I can."

"I see." She glanced down at her notebook. "You're obviously a very dutiful son. I'm sure that must make your parents very happy."

"That's not why I do it," he explained somberly. "You see, I don't take my family for granted. I don't assume I'll have them around forever. I learned that the hard way."

Apprehension flooded Layla. This sounded serious and she wasn't sure she wanted to hear it. Sharing confidences was a two-way street and if he told her about his family, he'd have every right to expect the same from her.

She gave a weak laugh and raised her eyes to meet his. "I wasn't trying to pry."

"Pry all you want," he said swiftly, sensing her withdrawal. "I certainly intend to."

She gave him an exasperated frown. But he just grinned at her. Why did he have to be so honest? Because she knew he meant every word. He would pry and snoop and probably have her spilling her guts if she wasn't careful. But she had to admit, she was interested. "Okay, you've done it. I'm hooked. What happened twenty years ago?"

Paul took a sip of his iced tea. "It's very simple. I thought my family were all dead. All three of them." He gazed off and stared at the mountains in the distance.

"Oh, no, what happened?"

"A car wreck. It happened during my first year of college. I was up at UC Davis, that's in northern California. This god-awful storm blew in from the Pacific, it hit the whole state. It was about midnight when the call came. I picked up the phone and a deputy sheriff told me my family had been in a serious three-car pileup on the freeway. But before I could ask any details, before I knew whether they were dead or alive, the damned phone went dead." Paul closed his eyes for a moment. "It was ten hours before I was able to get through. But that was the longest night of my life. It made me realize how important the people you love really are."

"How bad was the accident?" Layla asked softly.

"Just about everyone had a few broken bones, and my younger brother had a concussion. But we were very lucky. No one was killed. Anyway, I learned a lesson I'll never forget."

His eyes were fixed on her. Uncomfortable, Layla dropped her gaze and stared at her pencil. He was waiting for her to echo his sentiments. Of course she was glad his relatives hadn't been seriously hurt or killed. But that didn't mean they shared the same views on familial bliss.

"So are we on for Thursday night?"

She looked up and found him staring at her quizzically. His expression reminded her to be careful. They might have many things in common, but on the most important issues, they were light-years apart.

She smiled hesitantly. "I don't know, Paul. Maybe we should take a little break and see how we feel. We've spent practically this whole weekend together and we don't want to jump into anything too fast—"

"Fast?" he interrupted. "You've got to be kidding. We're talking about searching through my antiques followed by a chili dog! Besides, what's wrong with moving things along? We don't need a break, we're not a couple of kids. We've known each other for months."

Paul wanted to demolish her excuses before she could talk herself into saying no. He suddenly knew that her reluctance had nothing to do with him and everything to do with what went on in that mysterious head of hers. "Yesterday you said you wanted to keep seeing me," he reminded her forcefully. "Were you lying?"

"No," she protested. "Of course not."

"Then it's settled. For goodness' sake, don't look so worried. A meal at a coffee shop isn't going to threaten your precious emotional independence."

"That really bothers you, doesn't it?"

"It would bother anyone," he replied bluntly. "What is it exactly that you're looking for, anyway? Companionship with no strings attached, and maybe some sex thrown in on the side?"

Embarrassed, she glared at him and said the first thing that came into her head. "Isn't that what most men are looking for?"

"Don't be so sexist," he countered. "Contrary to all that junk you read in women's magazines, most men aren't heartless monsters lying in wait to seduce and abandon innocent virgins. They're human beings, with the same needs and wants as the rest of the human race."

Layla knew she was being ridiculous. Her knowledge of what most men wanted could be written on the head of a pin. And even if it were true, Paul wasn't most men. He was different. "Don't you think this is a pretty silly discussion?" she said quietly, determined not to be drawn into another confrontation. "What are we arguing about anyway? We've both made our positions perfectly clear."

"And that's the whole problem."

"Problem?"

"Your position. It stinks." He ignored her outraged gasp at his bluntness. He wanted to shock her into really listening to him. "I don't know why you think you've got to protect yourself from the rest of the world. Maybe you've got your reasons and maybe one of these days you'll trust me enough to share them. But I do know that living the way you seem to want to isn't living at all."

"You have no right to say that," she snapped. "You don't know me well enough to make that kind of judgment." Layla felt cornered and trapped. He was trying to get her to admit she was wrong and she couldn't do that. She wouldn't do that.

"Oh, yes, I do. I know you a lot better than you think."

"Just who the hell do you think you are?" Layla was incensed. She leaped to her feet and whirled toward the sliding glass door.

But Paul was too quick for her. He grabbed her shoulders and spun her around to face him before she'd taken two steps. "Never mind who I think I am," he told her flatly. "But how you choose to live your life affects me and that gives me all the rights I need."

"No, it doesn't. Just because we've gone out with each other a few times..."

"We haven't *just* gone out," he said, shaking his head. "We're involved and you know it. What do you think's going on here. What do you think we are, a couple of acquaintances who wave to each other from across the street. It's more than just that. You owe me something."

"I don't owe you anything." She tried to jerk away, but he wouldn't let her.

"Oh, yes, you do. You owe me the chance to get inside that head of yours and try to make sense out of things so we have a decent shot at something good together." He tightened his fingers on her shoulders. "And *you* know what we have together is good. Damned good. You've known it since the first time I kissed you and it scares the hell out of you! The kind of passion that flares up between us isn't plain old garden variety lust, it's different. It's special. I won't let you pretend otherwise."

For a moment she was too stunned to move. Her anger died, leaving behind a quiet confusion. Paul's gray eyes bored into hers, forcing her to hold his gaze, forcing her to see the truth. He cared. About her. "What makes you so sure? How can you be so certain about us? About how you feel? About me?"

"Because I've never felt like this before and I don't think you have, either. I can tell that you care, that you really want to let me get past those walls you've built," he said earnestly, relaxing the grip on her shoulders, "but I think you're scared and there's no reason to be. I'd never, ever, hurt you."

Layla stared at him. He was right. She was scared. No, that wasn't quite true, she was terrified. If she refused to let him get close, she might be giving up her last chance for a man's love. But what if in the process of getting close to him, she lost herself. If she *did* trust him, she might be in for more heartbreak than she'd ever imagined. It was a big risk.

Layla chewed on her lower lip. Finally she said, "You're very perceptive. But if you knew more about me, you'd understand how hard it is for me to trust people."

"Then make me understand," he whispered passionately. "Tell me about you. Tell me what makes you want to seal your emotions behind a wall when anyone with half a brain can see you were born to give and receive love.''

Paul was tempted to tell her about Rhea but he caught himself in time. Layla might not appreciate being compared to a stray dog. Instead, he pulled her closer to him.

Layla squirmed in his embrace. "It's hard," she whispered.

There was a low, guttural growl and they both looked down at the same time. Stanley snarled up at Paul and then butted his head between their legs.

"Good Lord, look at that," Paul said, clearly surprised. "That damned dog thinks I'm manhandling you." He released Layla and went down on one knee. "It's okay, boy. It's okay. You're a good dog but I wasn't trying to hurt your lady. I like her, too."

Stanley stared at him suspiciously, grunted and waddled over to the front door. He sank down and gave Layla a long, pointed stare. She and Paul burst out laughing. "I think he's hinting. The poor dog wants to take me home," she said.

Paul stood up and cupped her face in his hands. "Not yet." He stared directly into her eyes. "Are you mad at me? You know, for being so pushy."

"No," she admitted honestly. "I'd like to be, but I can't."

"Good." He expelled the breath he'd been holding. "Then will you spend next weekend with me? We can go to my parents' beach house in Del Mar."

She swallowed. She wanted to say yes, but she couldn't force the word out of her mouth. "I've got to work on Saturday."

He brushed his lips against hers. "Let Tank do it. You said he was saving for college."

"Well . . ." She wanted him to talk her into it.

Paul kissed her again, and this time he increased the pressure until she opened and let him slip his tongue inside.

For a moment, she stood passive and he took the opportunity to woo her with his mouth. His tongue skimmed against hers with delicate, featherlike strokes and then quickly retreated. Once, twice, three times and then she was kissing him back.

She wound her arms around his neck and he drew her closer, cradling her against his body as he made sweet, languid love to her mouth.

Rational thought disappeared for Layla. One tiny taste of him had her hungry and wanting more. She could feel his arms tightening around her and his big, warm hands moving slowly up and down her back. She sighed against his mouth as he eased his lips away. Mesmerized by the hot, sensual pleasure flooding her, she closed her eyes and let her head tip back against his arm.

Paul kissed her exposed neck, working his way down her flesh to the throbbing pulse point of her throat. She made a small sound that was part whimper, part moan, and nestled closer. His blood pressure skyrocketed at the feel of breasts splayed against his chest and her soft femininity cupping the hardness between his thighs. But he held himself rigidly in check.

This was for her. A few moments of intimacy and touching, with no fear and no expectations. The last time he'd held her in his arms this way, he'd let his desire overcome him and she'd panicked. As much as he wanted to make love to her, he wanted her trust more.

She trembled and tangled her fingers in the silky hair at the back of his neck. He lifted his head and gazed into her face. Her eyes were closed, her lips were wet and her breathing was shallow and rapid. When she opened her eyes, he saw no wariness or apprehension.

Instead, she looked dazed with passion, a little confused by the abrupt ceasing of the lovemaking and almost a little…irritated. Pleased at the effect, Paul smiled. "You're wondering why I stopped, aren't you?" He lifted a finger and stroked the now-pink blush in her cheeks.

She nodded.

"I didn't want to," he explained in a husky whisper. His hands slipped down and cupped her bottom, bringing her flush against the now-straining bulge of his jeans. He heard her sharply indrawn breath and saw her cheeks blush an even deeper pink as she felt the extent of his arousal.

"You can feel the effect you have on me," he said meaningfully. "I'd like nothing more than to pull you down on the floor and make long, passionate love to you all afternoon. But this isn't the time, and I think we both know it."

"But next weekend will be the time?" she asked gravely. "Why?"

"Because you'll have had a few more days to think about us. And that's important. When we make love, I want it to be because we both want to, because we've both committed to a course of action from which there's no retreat."

She stared at him. Paul was putting his cards on the table and the message was crystal clear. If she spent the weekend with him, she was committing to more than just a physical relationship. If that was all he'd wanted, he'd have seduced her now.

The idea should have had her running for the door, but it didn't. The urge to say yes was strong, too strong to resist. The tiny voice in the back of her mind, the one that always warned her to watch her step and take care, was suddenly mute. "I'd like that. But I'll have to make sure Tank can work for me. I can't close the store."

Paul released her and stepped back. Holding her so intimately was putting a real strain on his good intentions. A man could only take so much. "Can you talk to Tank tonight?"

"What's the hurry? Can't I do it tomorrow?"

He shook his head. "I'd prefer we get everything confirmed tonight. The Harrisons wanted me to bring you by for dinner next weekend. If we're going to be able to get away I'll have to cancel out."

"You accepted a dinner invitation for us? Wouldn't it be rude to back out?"

He was pleased she didn't seem angry that he had automatically accepted without consulting her. But she did seem a tad annoyed that he was going to change the plans. "I left it up in the air. Bud and Susan won't mind."

"All right," she said doubtfully, "they're your friends. I just hate the thought of ruining someone else's plans."

"Don't worry about it." He grinned. "They'll understand. But I do want you to get to know them. They're good friends. Susan and I went to high school together."

The mention of the Harrisons reminded her of MaryBeth and Tank. "Why didn't they approve of Tank? I mean before he got in so much trouble. You told me you had to talk them into letting her go out with him. Why was that? Was it because he was the son of the town drunk?"

Paul looked startled by the question. "No," he replied. "But Tank was never exactly what you'd call a model citizen, and you can't blame Bud and Susan for wanting the best for their daughter."

"I'm not blaming anyone," she said. "I'm just curious. After all, the one thing Tank did have going for him was his grades. He's always been a straight *A* student and he and MaryBeth were good friends."

"I wouldn't say they were *good* friends," Paul answered, shrugging. "Tank tutored MaryBeth in algebra for a while. That's all."

"He was her tutor? But I thought she was an *A* student, too?" Something didn't add up here. Layla had seen the way MaryBeth had looked at Tank.

"She is. But even the brightest kids sometimes need help and she had some trouble in math. In that subject, Tank is a certifiable genius and he tutored her. It was no big deal, at least not for MaryBeth. But then he took advantage of the situation and conned her into a date."

"He didn't con her into anything." Layla put her hands on her hips.

"Hey." Paul grinned. "Lighten up, we've already done one round today. Isn't that enough? Tank is staying away from her and that's all I care about."

"Well, I care about Tank," she muttered.

Paul's beeper went off.

He turned it off and reached for the telephone. Within seconds she realized there was an emergency.

As Paul took the details, Layla went out onto the patio for her purse. Stanley came trotting up as she stepped back into the living room. He then proceeded to run between her and the front door repeatedly as she waited for Paul to finish the call. On his third pass, Layla bent down and hissed, "Knock it off, Stanley. I know you want to go home, but this is getting embarrassing." She glanced at Paul as she heard him put the phone down. He was grinning at her.

"I've got to go. One of Ted Allison's mares is in trouble." He leaped up and snatched his keys off the end table. "If I get the chance, I'll call you tonight to see if everything's set with Tank."

Layla hustled to the front door. Stanley was already there.

On the way home, she decided to stop by the store and pick up the account books. She pulled into the small deserted area behind the store, switched off the ignition and opened the door.

She glanced hesitantly around, then looked at the dog. "Okay, Stanley," she said, getting out of the car and then stepping quickly back so he wouldn't bowl her over. "You can come in with me. You're hardly a killer guard dog, but it's eerie down here with everything closed."

Inside, Layla quickly looked around, then smiled as she realized Tank had left everything in order. She picked up the books and turned to call her dog. She sighed; he was standing in front of the candy display, his tongue hanging out.

"Oh, give it up, Stanley," she chided. "We've got to get home and I've already slipped you too many treats this week. Come on."

The dog cast one last mournful look at the case and then obediently trailed after her.

She pulled the heavy back door closed, then jammed in the key while balancing the ledgers in her other hand. But she couldn't get the old lock to turn. "Damn," she muttered. She put the books on the ground and, using both hands, got the door solidly locked. As she bent down to pick up the ledger, she noticed a shaft of sunlight reflecting brightly off a bottle that was sticking out of the trash.

Layla wasn't sure what instinct made her take a closer look, but when she did, her stomach twisted. She picked it up and stared at the label. It could have been dropped by some passerby, but she doubted it. There were only two people who ever came back here. Herself and Tank. Shaking her head, she tossed the bottle back into the can and heard the unmistakable sound of breaking glass. When she peeked over the rim, she felt like swearing.

There were two more bottles. One of them was now shattered.

Layla got a grip on herself. This was hardly evidence. Tank had given her his word. Just because no one else was ever back here and he'd been alone all day Saturday was no reason to convict him.

Then why, she wondered, were there three empty vodka bottles in her trash can?

Chapter Nine

By the time Layla arrived home and picked up the phone to call Tank, she'd decided not to mention the vodka bottles. She couldn't bring herself to say anything on such flimsy evidence. That would be tantamount to an out-and-out accusation.

Even though Riker's Pass didn't have an abundance of drunks stumbling around at night looking for trash cans to dump their empties into, that didn't mean someone else couldn't have put those bottles there. If you trusted someone, you had faith in them. And she'd made up her mind that she was going to give Tank Mullins the benefit of the doubt.

Just the way Miss Pine had believed in her.

Tank answered on the third ring. She quickly asked if he'd be available to run the store the following weekend.

"Sure," he said enthusiastically, "Saturday was a piece of cake. I had a great time and the extra money's nice, too." He paused. "Uh, where are you going? If you don't mind my asking, that is. I'm, uh, wondering if you want me to stop by your house and feed Stanley, too?"

Touched by his thoughtful offer, she smiled. "Of course I don't mind you asking, I'd have told you anyway. I've got to leave a number with you in case of an emergency. And it's really sweet of you to volunteer to feed my dog. I'll pay you extra— I should give you something for doing it for me yesterday."

"Nah, you don't have to pay me. I told you, I like dogs, and we can't have one here because my aunt's allergic to them." He hesitated and then added quietly, "Besides, I owe you one. You've done me plenty of favors."

"All right," she murmured, understanding how important it was for him to be able to do this for her. She hesitated for a moment, trying to think of a tactful way to tell a seventeen-year-old boy you were spending the weekend with your lover. Lover? She cringed as another problem popped into her mind.

"Layla, are you there?"

"Oh, sorry, I was just, uh, trying to move Stanley off my foot." Stanley walked over and put his head in her lap when he heard his name. "But back to the reason for this call. I'll be at Del Mar. Paul's invited me to his family's beach house for the weekend."

That didn't sound too bad, she thought quickly. Without actually lying she'd made it sound somewhat respectable. Maybe he would assume the entire Tressler family would be there. She hoped so.

"Hey, neat," Tank replied enthusiastically. "Del Mar's a nifty town. You should try to get to La Jolla, too. There's a whole bunch of terrific shops and art galleries.

It's a university town, so there's always something interesting happening."

He then launched into an excited description of every possible thing one could do in a Southern California beach community.

Layla listened patiently, knowing that the boy didn't often get a chance to really talk to anyone. She found it sad that a person with all Tank's wonderful qualities was so lonely. But he was. She'd noticed he snatched any and all opportunities for a little human contact. No wonder he'd enjoyed working behind the register on Saturday. He got to talk to people.

Her gaze drifted around the room and stopped at her cup from this morning. She frowned, remembering the missing scoops of coffee.

When Tank finally ran out of steam, she hesitated before saying, "Tank, I've got to ask you something."

"Sure. What?"

Suddenly asking him if he'd brewed a pot of coffee sounded ridiculous. So instead, she asked. "Have you seen anyone hanging around the back of the store?"

There was a long pause. Layla tensed apprehensively. Why was he taking so long to answer her? "Tank?"

"Uh, I'm just trying to think."

His voice sounded different. Guarded. Layla's spirits plummeted. "What's there to think about?" she asked impatiently. "Either you've seen someone or you haven't."

"Well, I thought I heard someone back there on Saturday," he said, his tone still cautious. "But by the time I got finished ringing up Mrs. Detweiler and I had a chance to look around, whoever it was was gone. But I think someone was dumping something in our trash can. That's what it sounded like anyway. But I was keeping an eye on the place. I just didn't want to leave a customer standing there while I ran outside and chased them off, could I?''

His answer eased her doubts. The bottles weren't his! If they had been, he'd have denied hearing anything, he'd have asked her what she was talking about and played dumb. Wouldn't he?

"No, no," she assured him quickly. "You did the right thing. I've thought I've heard someone back there a time or two myself."

"Yeah, looks like someone might be dumping garbage in our cans. Kinda weird, if you ask me. But don't worry, I'll keep a close eye out on Saturday, Layla. You can count on me."

"I know that, Tank," she said seriously. "You've always done a good job for me. I'll see you tomorrow morning. Good night."

For the next few days, Layla was busy and she didn't see Paul. But he called every night and they talked about everything from the Centennial Dance, less than two weeks away, to their plans for the weekend.

By Thursday, Layla had made up her mind to tell Paul the truth when he took her out for dinner. After all, if the man was going to spend the weekend with her, he had a right to know. But she didn't get a chance to tell him anything. On Thursday afternoon he called to cancel their date.

Darn, she thought, glaring at the receiver as she put it down. Tonight would have been a perfect opportunity.

"Is something wrong?" Tank asked, jarring her out of her reverie.

"Oh, no," she asked hastily, giving him a smile. "I'm just disappointed that Paul had to back out of our date.

He's way behind schedule. You're probably going to be busy over there this afternoon. It sounds like every animal in north San Diego county is sick."

Del Mar was a charming town nestled on the coast north of San Diego. The Tressler beach house was a small, wood-frame bungalow located at the end of a tiny street that ended at the sand.

"It's nothing fancy," Paul explained, shouldering open the front door and pushing inside. He dropped their bags on the floor and turned to smile at Layla. "But it has all the necessary amenities and it's comfortable."

"It's lovely," she said hastily, casting a quick look around.

Paul stifled a sigh. Layla was as nervous as a kitten on its second visit to his office. The first time didn't count. Most animals had no idea they were about to get a bunch of shots, but on their next visit, they knew what to expect and they acted accordingly. Nervous, scared, and ready to jump at the least little thing. Layla had acted like that since he'd picked her up this evening. "Why don't you have a look around while I get dinner on the table?"

He put the brown paper bag containing the Chinese food they'd picked up on the way into town on the table and gave her a reassuring smile. "There's no rush to do anything. You can unpack later."

She nodded dumbly, not trusting herself to speak. The tour didn't take long. There was only a small living room with a dining room leading off it, a kitchen, an old-fashioned bathroom and two bedrooms. But only one bedroom was made up. She gulped and quickly shut the door at the sight of the double bed. She was being ridiculous and she knew it. But the situation was embarrassing. As she went back to the dining room, she told herself to just get it over with and tell him. It was really no big deal; he'd understand.

"Mmm." She sniffed appreciatively and forced a bright smile as she joined him at the table. "That looks good. I'm starving."

Paul dropped a set of chopsticks by each plate and grinned. "I hope you don't object to the paper plates and eating right out of the cartons, but I didn't think we wanted to spend our evening doing dishes."

"Suits me fine," she replied, sitting down. She picked up her chopsticks and gazed at them curiously. "Do you know how to use these things?"

"Sure, like this." He plucked the chopsticks out of her hand and positioned them between his fingers. Deftly he tapped the two pieces together a couple of times. "See, it's easy."

"I don't know," she said, reaching for them. She imitated his fingers and tried bringing the ends together the way he'd shown her. But after three attempts, the only thing she'd managed to do was drop one of the sticks. Twice.

"I hope you've got a fork around here somewhere," she muttered as she attempted it a fourth time. "Otherwise, I'm going to starve to death."

Paul laughed and got her a fork and they worked their way through kung-pao chicken and moo goo gai pan. By the time they were cleaning up the empty cartons and finishing off the last of the wine, she'd almost forgotten her earlier tension. He was good at making her relax.

"How about a walk on the beach before we turn in?" Paul asked.

The casual question brought back all her apprehension.

She took a deep breath and tried to force herself back to calmness. But it was impossible. Butterflies were now dancing in her stomach. "I'd like that. I've never walked on a beach at night."

As they strolled along the hard-packed sand, his arms around her shoulders, she told herself her nervousness was natural. Anyone would feel tense. But still she didn't tell him. And then it was too late, he was taking her hand and guiding her back to the house. Back to the bedroom.

Paul closed the back door and turned to face her. He smiled gently. She stared back at him and he could see her throat working as she swallowed.

Layla was as jumpy as a Chihuahua in a pen full of pit bulls. There was no help for it, he was going to have to ask. "Is something wrong?"

This was the opening she'd waited for. Her mouth went dry. "Of course not," Layla answered quickly. Too quickly. "Uh, I'm just a little nervous."

The moment the words were out she felt like kicking herself. Why hadn't she told him? This was absurd. She was being ridiculous. There was no reason to be so embarrassed. It wasn't as though she was admitting to being an ax murderess or a serial killer, for God's sake. She took another deep breath.

"Hey," he said softly, before she had a chance to speak. "That's all right. You're not the only one around here who's uptight. I am, too. It's only natural...we're about to become lovers."

Paul pulled her into his arms and kissed her. God, he wanted her so much he was being eaten alive. But he wanted her to want him, to come to him without fear and worry etching her face. There *was* passion in her, he knew. He'd been scared before when he'd held her in his arms. "Do you want to use the bathroom first?"

Layla nodded, accepting the reprieve gratefully. If he was admitting to a case of nerves, who knew how he'd react when he found out about her. She pulled away and headed for the bathroom, picking up her small overnight case on the way.

Her hands trembled as she shut the bathroom door. But she wasn't going to back out now. She wanted to make love with Paul. She wanted it more than anything. She'd just have to trust that he'd know what to do when the time came.

A few minutes later, she opened the bedroom door and saw him lying on the bed.

Paul got to his feet and came toward her, his eyes locked on her scantily clad body. The air felt chilly on her skin and she shivered.

He stopped in front of her. She wore a cream-colored satin nightgown with a deep scoop neck and tiny straps. It ended at midthigh, giving him a tantalizing view of her smooth legs. With every breath she took, the slinky material dipped and swelled against the mound of her breasts and he could see the outline of her nipples against the thin fabric.

He felt the blood quickening in his veins as he reacted to the erotic sight of her standing half-naked less than six inches away. Paul took a deep, steadying breath. "I've got to take a quick shower."

After he'd disappeared, Layla forced herself to the bed. She lifted the covers and climbed between the sheets. Perhaps this would have been easier if they'd undressed each other, she thought. Maybe that would have made it less nerve-racking.

Paul must have taken the fastest shower on record, because it seemed only seconds had gone by before she heard the door open. Then he was standing next to the bed, a towel wrapped around his waist. He studied her gravely for a moment, reached over and switched off the lamp before dropping the towel.

Layla's heart leaped into her throat as she felt the puff of air as the covers were drawn back and the bed dipped beneath his weight.

In the darkness, he pulled her into his arms. She went rigid as their naked flesh touched.

"Relax," he soothed. "Just relax. It's going to be so good between us, sweetheart. We've got all night. We'll take it slow and easy, all right."

She was so stiff he thought she'd shatter. And he didn't want that. Oh, he wanted her to shatter all right, but from passion, not from nerves. He drew himself up on his elbow and slanted his mouth across hers. She parted her lips, but her body remained rigid.

With his other hand, he cupped her breast. If anything, she went even stiffer. He deepened the kiss, toying with her tongue while his thumb rubbed lightly across her nipple. He heard her draw a ragged breath and then she tore her mouth away and turned her head.

He went still as he realized something was seriously wrong, that it had been wrong all evening. Layla wasn't just having a bad case of new-lover jitters. "What's wrong?"

In answer she rolled away from him and curled herself into a tight ball on the edge of the bed.

Puzzled, he touched her shoulder. "Layla, for God's sake, what's wrong?

Silence.

"Tell me." He clasped her arm and pulled her onto her back so he could see her face. In the faint moonlight coming through the windows, he could see the tears in her eyes. "Don't cry," he said in confusion. "Whatever's the matter, we can work it out."

She sniffed and hastily brushed an escaping tear off her cheek. "I'm sorry, Paul."

Unable to stand the concern on his face, she looked away. But Paul wouldn't let her retreat an inch. He grasped her chin. "You haven't done anything to be sorry about," he said softly. "And neither have I. Just tell me what's the matter."

She shook her head.

"I'll be gentle," he promised. "I know how to make love to a woman."

And that's the whole problem, she thought morosely. She didn't know how to make love to a man.

"Are you afraid of getting pregnant?" he continued patiently. "Don't be, I'll make sure it doesn't happen."

She took a deep breath. "I'm embarrassed."

"Embarrassed?" he repeated. "Why?"

Layla shuddered. She knew he was a good man; she wouldn't be here with him otherwise. But this was so hard. "I've never done this before," she said in a shaky voice. "I don't know how." Humiliation washed over her and she shut her eyes.

He was silent for what seemed an eternity. Finally he said, "You're a virgin." His voice was hushed.

"Yes."

Paul could feel the tension emanating from her. How he reacted could make or break their entire relationship. He knew that. She was wound as tightly as a spring under pressure. Making love to her when she was this tense would be miserable for both of them. On the other hand, he didn't want her thinking that her inexperience turned him off. Because that certainly wasn't true. He wanted her. Badly. He could feel her skin along every centimeter of his body. Her flesh was warm, soft and fragrant. His desire to make love to Layla battled with his conscience. His conscience won.

"Paul." Her voice was a faint whisper in the shadows.

"It's all right, honey," he soothed, forcing his body away from hers. "There's no reason to be embarrassed. Virginity isn't something to be ashamed of. I'm honored that you care enough about me to want to make love. But we don't have to do it tonight. We've got all weekend, we can be patient with each other."

"Are you saying you want to wait?" The relief in her voice was obvious. "But you're, you're..."

"Aroused," he finished for her. He touched her shoulder with gentle fingers. "Of course I am. I want you. But I can wait until you're ready. And that's not going to be tonight. You're too wound up. When we do make love, I want you to want me so much you're willing to trust me completely."

Layla propped herself on her elbow and watched him. "It's not a matter of trust," she said quietly. "It's just first-time nerves." She sighed. "But you're right, I can't seem to relax."

Wisely Paul didn't try to correct her. If she wanted to believe trust had nothing to do with it, he wouldn't be able to convince her otherwise.

He smiled at her. "Let's just get some sleep, okay? Like I said, we've got the whole weekend. I can wait."

With that, he pulled her down and drew her body close. Rolling his eyes heavenward, he sent up a short, fervent prayer asking for strength. The sweet herbal scent of her hair filled his nostrils, his skin tingled where their bare flesh touched and his hands were itching to stroke the soft slopes and angles of her body. Her breasts flattened against his chest as she dragged in a long, relaxing breath and then her hips cuddled directly into his groin. He gritted his teeth. This was going to be one helluva long night.

Paul drifted slowly awake. He went still as he realized the warm softness nestling in his hand was Layla's breast. Her hips were intimately pressed against his early-morning arousal and their legs were so entwined he didn't know where he began and she ended.

Raising his head slightly, he studied the woman sleeping in his arms. Her eyes were closed, her breathing was slow and regular and her lips were curved in a trusting smile.

Last night, she'd been so tense she couldn't have responded to him if he'd been Casanova, Don Juan and Rudolph Valentino all rolled into one. But maybe she could this morning.

He knew she was passionate and he knew she wanted him. The other times he'd touched her, she'd gone up in flames when he kissed and fondled her. She hadn't been faking her response. He didn't believe that for a moment. Then why, he wondered, had she been so edgy?

He gazed at the far wall as he went over and over everything that she'd said last night. For several minutes he dissected every little thing either of them had said or done before they got into bed. The only thing that stuck out in his mind was the way she'd been embarrassed to admit she was a virgin.

Paul frowned and cast her a worried glance. Could that have been it? No. Impossible. But maybe, just maybe that was a big part of her stress. Maybe she'd felt humiliated. Perhaps she'd come to see her virginity as a symbol of her failure in relationships with men. Paul sighed, that was really stretching, but it was the best explanation he could think of.

Experimentally he rubbed his thumb across her nipple and knew a swift satisfaction as the peak hardened. She gave a low, sensual moan that encouraged him to touch her again. He was rewarded this time by a small, sexy stretch that thrust her breast deeper into his palm. Unable to resist, he lowered his head and kissed her neck while his other hand stroked the silky skin of her thigh.

Layla whimpered. Still asleep, she rolled over onto her back, forcing his hand to the inside of her leg. He blinked in surprise. Her eyes were tightly closed, but there was a half smile on her face, and her breathing was low and shallow. She looked sleepy and passionate and ready.

His qualms about making love to her disappeared. He massaged the softness of her inner thigh for a few seconds, noting how the action made her legs move restlessly. Taking care not to jostle her, he shifted and reached for the straps on her shoulders. He lowered her nightgown to her waist, and his breath caught as her small, perfectly-formed, pink-tipped breasts came into view.

She was beautiful. Slowly, gently, he leaned over and nuzzled her chest. She shifted languidly, encouraging him. Her scent intoxicated him, the feel of her skin against his tongue only made him hungrier, more ravenous. He kissed his way to her nipple and flicked it lightly with his tongue. She moaned.

Layla woke slowly as the dreamlike sensations invaded her consciousness and focused into a demanding plea. Her eyes half opened to see Paul's dark head bent over her breast. She gasped as his warm, wet tongue

connected with her nipple and sent a hot shaft of pleasure deep into her womb. Her hands came up and she
gripped him around the waist.

Paul stopped and raised his head, his eyes silently asking permission to continue. In answer she lifted her hips
and pushed her gown down her legs.

He smiled, a sleepy, pleased male smile that sent her
pulse into high gear. She forgot she was a virgin, she forgot that the night before she'd been too tense to respond. She forgot everything as his big hand cupped her
breast and drew her deep inside the moistness of his
mouth. His other hand smoothed down the skin of her
stomach, skimmed the nest of curls and then cupped her
gently. Her breath stopped.

But her body didn't.

Seeking something she couldn't yet identify, she arched
into his warmth. The sensations caused by his stroking
fingers made her head swim and she cried out at the
pleasure.

"That's it," he coaxed, raising his head and staring
into her eyes. "That's what I want. You. Hot, aroused
and wanting me as much as I want you." He bent and
took her mouth. The kiss was wild, urgent.

Paul steeled his body into control. He knew what he
had to do. He wanted her at a fever pitch, he wanted her
damp and slick and ready for him. Because if she wasn't,
it would hurt. And he was determined that she would remember making love with him as pleasure, not pain.

He gently massaged the tender spot between her legs
until he felt the dampness that signaled her body's response. He kissed her again, his mouth slanting across
hers and his tongue slipping inside where it began dupli-
cating the slow stroking of his hand. She writhed beneath him and with every lift of her hips, she brushed

against his hard arousal and almost blasted his good intentions to hell and back.

Her whimpers increased as he quickened the pace of his strokes, but he didn't take his mouth off hers. His tongue was sliding furiously against hers and she was answering in kind. He shifted suddenly onto his side and brought his free hand up to tease her nipple.

Layla broke the kiss and tossed her head wildly on the pillow as the ecstatic feelings flooded her senses in a wild rush. Her skin was raw, her nerve endings electrified to a fever pitch and there was an unfamiliar pulsing ache deep inside.

"Paul," she gasped, not caring that her voice sounded thin and reedy and desperate. She only cared about one thing. Having Paul inside her and ending this glorious torment. "Make love to me. Now."

"Soon, sweetheart. I promise, it'll be soon." Paul was in agony. The urge to bury himself deeply inside her was overwhelming, but he held back. Just a few more moments. She was excited and aroused and almost ready.

She clutched at him. "Don't wait. Oh, please. Now."

He parted her carefully and slipped his finger inside her. She pushed up against his hand and moaned.

The feel of her soft, wet sheath pushed him over the edge. Paul used his free hand to reach for the foil packet he'd placed on the bedside table the night before.

A moment later, he tossed back the covers and moved quickly between her thighs. "Open your legs," he instructed as he felt her tense. She kept her eyes tightly closed but did as he asked. He knew some of the fire had died, so instead of pushing inside her, as he longed to do, he reached down and wedged his hand between their bodies, his fingers lightly fondling her core. She moaned as another set of pulsations racked her body.

Unconsciously, she opened her legs further and her hands clutched at the strong muscles of his back. He tantalized her body for what seemed an eternity, stoking her fires until she was straining against him and trying to bring him inside. He waited until she arched high, then he carefully eased inside.

Her eyes flew open.

"Do you want me to stop?" he asked hoarsely, praying she wouldn't.

She shook her head and tilted her hips. The movement pushed him deeper. Paul clenched his teeth against the urge to move.

"No, no, don't stop," she panted. He hoped it was passion and not pain that made her breathe so erratically.

"I don't want to hurt you."

"You won't." She smiled then, a wise, ancient and very feminine smile that sent a shock wave of tenderness through him.

Slowly, carefully, he eased deeper inside her. When he was fully embedded he stopped again and took her lips. They kissed long enough for her body to adjust to the invasion. When Paul felt the first, tentative movement of her hips, he began to move as well.

He kept his thrusts slow and shallow, his gaze locked onto her face to ensure she wasn't in pain. But as she rose to meet him, he saw her eyes widen in passion and heard her breathing turn harsh and shallow just as he felt her womanhood pulling him deeper inside.

Layla let her instincts take over. With every stroke Paul took her higher and higher. She clutched at him and held fast as the sensations contracted into an almost painful knot at the center of her being. The pleasure came in wave upon wave, tying her tighter and tighter until she didn't think she could stand it.

She felt his hands slip under her hips and he held her rigidly against him as he surged again and again into her body. Each thrust sent a shock wave of tension coiling into her center. She held him closer, harder as she felt a series of tiny convulsions start low in her belly and then break free. When she didn't think she could stand the pleasure a second longer, the pressure snapped and splintered her into a million pieces.

Paul went taut as she cried out his name when she climaxed.

Chapter Ten

Paul's gaze locked on her face. In awe, he watched her expressive features mirror the tumultuous pleasure coursing through his body. He knew a possessive satisfaction as he saw her eyes glaze in surprised delight, saw her lips curve in a wide smile and heard her breathy gasps of release. She was beautiful in her passion and the memory would be forever engraved on his mind.

Her reaction excited him. His need for completion escalated to unbelievable heights and he couldn't hold back a second longer. He shuddered, thrusting fast and deep as he hurtled over the edge, letting the pent-up pressure explode into a scorching fulfillment that seemed to last forever. By the time the last tremor died, he slumped on top of her, drained.

For both of them, the world spun crazily as they struggled to catch their breath. Paul felt her shift against his rib cage. Fearing he was crushing her, he rolled to the side, still holding her against him.

His need to touch her hadn't diminished. He smoothed his palm up her side, caressing her delicate frame in long, lazy strokes. He felt her sigh as he buried his face in her silky hair and inhaled her unique fragrance as though it was his birthright. She moaned softly in the back of her throat as he stroked and fondled her.

He grinned, his lips brushing her neck as the decidedly feminine sound coupled with the sexy little wiggle of her hips told him without words that she'd found satisfaction in his arms. "Layla," he whispered. "Are you all right?"

She nodded, not sure she was yet capable of a coherent answer. Opening her eyes, she stared at the sunlight striking the far wall. She didn't know what to say or what to feel. Her confusion was overwhelming. She wanted to run and hide. She never wanted to let him go. She wanted this moment to last forever.

Making love with Paul had shaken the foundations on which she'd lived. She felt as if the walls of her life had been blasted with dynamite or smashed with a sledgehammer.

Disoriented, she could do nothing but sag against his comforting warmth as complex but conflicting messages whirled frantically in her brain.

Her skin felt new and unbearably sensitive, as though she'd lost a protective layer of cells. The unfamiliar earthy smell of their lovemaking hovered in the air, mixing with his clean, male scent and heightening her turmoil.

But despite the chaotic emotions battling for control, she was drawn to his warmth like a moth to a flame. She was mystified by the sudden but unmistakable sense of oneness she felt with this man. Layla surrendered to the urge to cuddle against his chest and let the heat of his body blanket her in its comforting intimacy.

. Paul didn't press her. He sensed that Layla needed a few moments to pull herself together. For that matter, he thought wryly, so did he.

What had started as a gentle initiation into the joys of physical love had unexpectedly changed and become something much more. He lay beside her, alternately feeling proud and humble. The pride he could understand. What man wouldn't be proud that he'd given pleasure to a woman he cared about the first time she'd ever made love? But the humility?

Paul recognized that Layla had given him more than just her body. Whether she understood it or not, she'd given him her trust. He struggled in silent confusion, trying to make sense out of his feelings. They were a helluva lot more intense than he'd imagined.

"Paul?" Layla said hesitantly. "Was it, uh, okay?"

The plea in her voice tore at his heart. He squeezed her and nuzzled her neck. "Ah, baby, it was better than okay." He sighed as the truth hit him. "It was one of the best experiences of my life."

She sighed happily. Suddenly she didn't want to think and she didn't want to talk. Words might destroy this delicious sense of contentment, of closeness. She wouldn't risk that. The moment was simply too precious to lose.

For another ten minutes they lay entwined on the bed. Then Paul got up and tugged her to her feet.

"What are you doing?" she gasped, snatching at the sheet and trying to cover herself. But she wasn't fast enough and he snagged it out of her fingers and tossed it back onto the bed.

"You can't shower wrapped in a sheet," he announced, ignoring her outrage. Laughing, he grabbed her hand and pulled her down the hall to the bathroom.

"I can take a bath on my own," she yelped as he gently shoved her inside and closed the door.

"Nonsense, California's always short of water. We're supposed to conserve, remember." He wiggled his eyebrows suggestively. "We'll shower together."

"Together! But Paul—" Her words were cut off as he turned and pulled her into his arms.

He smiled tenderly, his eyes searching her face. "Layla, don't be so modest. We're lovers. I only want to look at you. And I want you to look at me. I want us to relax and play, to enjoy every moment we have together. This is no big deal, it's only a shower."

She swallowed and gave him a strained smile. After what they'd shared it was absurd to be modest. Standing naked in front of a man would take some getting used to, but she'd come this far. She'd go the rest of the way. Even if it killed her.

"All right," she answered. She forced an impish grin. "But you've got to promise not to hog all the hot water."

Laughing, he turned on the water and guided her to the tub. Stepping in behind her, he pulled the curtains together, enveloping them in an intimate, steamy cocoon of warmth and wetness.

Despite her resolve, she was suddenly struck with shyness. She turned so that her back was to him and ducked under the cascading water.

Paul sighed theatrically and turned her to face him. She blushed and crisscrossed her arms across her chest. Just as quickly, he reached over and uncrossed them.

"I know this isn't easy for you," he said quietly, watching her carefully. "But I like looking at you. It gives me pleasure. Enormous pleasure. Don't cover yourself, let me see you."

He was pushing her again, but he couldn't help himself. He needed some reassurances. Although the loveliness of her body *was* a joy to behold, one of nature's true works of art, it wasn't just that. He needed to know just how far she'd really come in their relationship. It was one thing to give herself in the heat of passion, but how much did she really trust him? Enough to forget her inhibitions and completely relax with him? Enough to stand naked and vulnerable in front of her lover and have faith that he wouldn't belittle her or hurt her?

"Layla," he prompted, when she didn't answer.

She nodded and then tensed as he slowly lowered his gaze. She could feel herself turning red as he stared at her breasts for what seemed like hours but was in fact only a few moments, before moving lower, down past her stomach to the joining of her legs. He smiled then and lifted his chin. His eyes were warm and filled with satisfaction.

Paul noticed she kept her eyes glued to his face and he wished she'd look at him with the same erotic curiosity with which he'd examined her. But he knew it was too soon to expect her to do that.

"I'm going to wash you," he announced, reaching for the soap. "And you're going to love it." Never taking his gaze off her, he slowly lathered his hands.

Her heartbeat accelerated as he stepped closer, turned her around so that her back was flush against his chest and then gently cupped her breasts.

For a moment, she stood rigidly, not knowing how to respond. But her body knew. His long, tanned fingers slowly massaged the soap into her skin and set a ripple of sensual excitement shooting all the way to her toes.

"Why would you try to hide from me?" he whispered, bringing his lips to the sensitive spot behind her ear and strumming it with his tongue. "You're so incredibly lovely."

"Thank you," she replied.

Paul thought her voice sounded stilted, as though she wasn't used to receiving compliments. He leaned back and glided his hands around to her back. "But then I'm probably not the first man to tell you that, am I."

"Uh, well, I've been told I was pretty before."

His hands stilled for a moment on her shoulders. "Only that you're pretty? Hasn't anyone ever told you you're sweet and kind and very, very loving?"

She shook her head. "No, not that I remember."

He turned her to face him and slipped his arms around her waist. Lowering his head, he took her mouth in a long, wet kiss. She kissed him back and within seconds, he was fully aroused.

Layla's arms circled his neck and she gave a murmur that was part agreement and part protest. She hadn't expected them to make love again so quickly. All the books she'd read on the subject said that most men needed time to recover.

Obviously you couldn't learn everything in books.

He broke the kiss and reached for the soap again. He began to wash her arms and shoulders.

Puzzled, Layla stared at him. "Why did you kiss me like that?"

"Because I wanted to."

Her confusion mounted. She flicked a quick glance down and then hastily looked away. Paul reached over, cupped her chin and kissed her again.

"Oh." She licked her lips after he drew back.

He could tell she was perplexed. Even to someone as innocent as she was, his arousal was patently obvious. No doubt she was wondering why he'd stopped. He waited for her to ask.

But all she did was cock her head to the side and watch him, a half smile playing on her lips. Then she lowered her eyes and looked, really looked at him for the first time. "You're beautiful, too," she murmured.

His chest was broad, muscled and covered with dark hair. She reached over and tangled her fingers in the silky wet curls, brushing his flat nipples with her thumb. Paul sucked in his breath as her hands and her eyes moved down.

Her fingertips glided over his waist and brushed lightly down his hips to his thighs. Like his chest, his legs were long, heavily muscled and hairy. She thought the contrast between their bodies remarkable. She'd never known just how spectacular a naked man could look.

She felt a sudden heady sense of freedom. A liberation that made her giddy. "Turn around. It's my turn to wash you," she said proudly, her eyes dancing with delight. "And you are going to love it."

He did as she asked and she slowly began to wash his back. Paul stood still, enjoying her ministrations. He could feel his pulse gather speed as she touched him, but he forced himself to stand still and let her explore him.

Layla was giving him more than he dreamed. He hadn't expected her to be comfortable enough with him to do more than follow his lead. But he'd been wrong, she was an active participant!

It was torture. It was heaven. As her hands continued their intimate explorations, he wasn't sure how much more he could take. He rolled his eyes and gritted his jaw as he felt her lathering the back of his knees. Who the hell would have thought *that* was an erogenous zone.

But the torment finally ended as she told him to rinse off. After they both rinsed, he turned off the water and steeled himself for more as they got out and snatched up towels. He started to dry her off, and then quickly thought better of it. If he touched her again, or even worse, if she touched him, he'd want to make love again. And she was going to be way too tender for that. A man could only take so much.

As he'd hoped, their showering together eased the inevitable tension of the morning after. After they dressed, he took her out for a huge breakfast in a local coffee shop.

"What do you want to do today?" Paul asked. He drained the last of his coffee and reached for the check.

"You know the place better than I do," Layla replied. "You tell me."

"Well, you're in for a real treat. Between here and Oceanside there are at least a dozen antique stores and junk shops." He gave her a wicked grin. "Wanna go hunting?"

Layla's eyes lit up like Fourth of July sparklers. "Are you kidding! Does the cardinal want to be the pope?"

They spent the day rummaging in trendy antique stores, searching through dusty boxes at secondhand shops and generally trying to restrain each other's enthusiasm.

At a tiny antique shop in Leucadia, Layla spotted a lovely cameo ring. The face on it was almost a twin to her favorite brooch. But when she saw the price tag, she sighed.

Paul walked up behind her and peered over her shoulder as she put the ring back down on the counter. "You like that ring?"

"Who wouldn't? But it's way too expensive, at least for right now." She promised herself she'd check back after Christmas and see if it was still there. "Have you seen anything you like?"

"There's an interesting Tavern table over there." He pointed to the corner. "What do you think? Would it look good in my living room?"

Layla studied it for a moment. "No, not your living room. But it would look great in your kitchen."

"My kitchen?" He looked doubtful. "Hmm. Really? You think so?" He took her arm and they wandered out of the store.

"Sure. That piece of furniture is small and homey looking. Anyone can see that it's a kitchen piece."

"I don't know. It's maple."

"So? The furniture in your living room isn't. That table wouldn't match, it wouldn't blend and the proportions are all wrong."

They argued in a good-natured way as they crossed the gravel parking lot. As they reached his truck, Paul said. "You know, I think you're right. I'm going back to check the price."

"You mean you didn't look?" Layla was amazed.

"I didn't have time. You distracted me."

"I distracted you! Ha, that's a laugh. You're such a collecting junkie, I don't think anything short of an invasion by the pod people could tear you away from something you've got your eye on."

He arched an eyebrow. "Me. A collecting junkie? Now that's rich, coming from a woman I just saw shell out fifty bucks for a pair of rusty old candle holders." He glanced meaningfully at the wrapped package lying on the front seat.

"Those aren't 'rusty old candle holders,'" she protested. "They're pure brass eighteenth-century candlesticks. You just wait till I get them all polished up. You'll be green with envy."

"Yeah, but not as green as those things are."

She rolled her eyes. He grinned unrepentantly and dropped a swift kiss on her nose. "I'll be right back."

When he came back, they continued on Highway 101. They spent the rest of the day arguing good-humoredly over who liked what and whose taste was all in their mouth.

Neither of them felt like going out to dinner, so they stopped for fresh fish and cooked a meal together in the kitchen of the beach house.

After they finished, they sat on the beach and watched the sunset. As bedtime approached, Layla wondered if Paul would make love to her again. She was disappointed when he gently pulled her into his arms and merely held her.

"Paul," she said hesitantly. "Is something wrong?"

"Nope." He pulled the blankets up higher. "Get some sleep, sweetheart, you're bound to be tired. We were on our feet all day." He yawned, dropped a light kiss on her shoulder and then rolled onto his back.

"But—" Her frustration mounted. "But don't you want to, well . . . you know?"

"Make love? I always want to do that. But not tonight."

"Why not?"

"You're too tender."

She blushed in the darkness. True, she was a little sore. But she was willing to suffer. "I'm not *that* tender."

He chuckled and hugged her tight. "Yes, you are," he countered. "Maybe you're not aware of it, but if we tried it, you would hurt. As much as I want you, I'd rather wait until we could both enjoy it."

His concern and thoughtfulness touched her deeply. She sighed and snuggled deeper into the bedclothes. Paul wasn't like anyone she'd ever known. She was at ease with him in a way that was totally new to her.

Layla lifted her chin and looked at him. He was already asleep. She could hear his slow, even breathing in the quiet of the darkened room. For a moment she simply stared at the outline of his profile. What was it about Paul that made her feel so comfortable?

True, he was good-natured. She could tease him and argue with him and say just about anything that came into her head without worrying that he'd take it the wrong way. But she'd known a lot of people like that. That characteristic wasn't particularly unique. True, he wasn't judgmental or overly critical. But so what? Tolerance and understanding weren't all that rare, either. Yet around him, she felt curiously liberated. Free.

Layla closed her eyes and let her mind wander. She wasn't going to figure him out tonight. Maybe she didn't even really want to. The only thing that mattered was the way he made her feel.

They made love on Sunday morning and it was even more wonderful than the first time. After that, they packed their bags, loaded up the truck and went out for breakfast.

Paul wanted to take her for a walk on the beach before they drove back to Riker's Pass. He took her hand as they crossed the sand and headed for the water. Under his other arm, he carried an old blanket.

The day was perfect. The sky was bright blue, the ocean bluer and the white foam of the crashing surf music to her ears. She didn't remember ever being this happy.

"This is a good spot," Paul said. He spread the blanket and then pulled her down next to him. "We can watch the surfers."

"Aren't they cold?" She shivered. Even though it was spring and the sun was bright, there was a strong wind blowing in off the water.

"They've got on wet suits. That helps. Besides, most of these guys are fanatics. If the surf's up, they're here."

"You sound like you know all about it. Do you surf?" She gazed at him quizzically, her eyes roving over his big, powerful body.

"I did when I was in high school, but I haven't in years." He turned, caught the way she was looking at him and grinned. "How about you? What did you like to do when you were growing up?"

Layla's smile froze and their gazes locked. She was tempted to brush the question aside, but the expression on his face stopped her. He was watching her closely, as though her answer were the most important thing in the world.

For once, she didn't want to change the subject. She wanted, no, she corrected silently, she needed for him to know about her. "I didn't have any special hobbies," she answered carefully. "Except reading. Most of my childhood was spent either hiding in my room or at the library. It was a good way of avoiding my father."

Paul kept his expression neutral. He didn't want her to stop now. She'd opened up to him all weekend and he sensed that what she was about to tell him was important. He knew that one wrong move on his part and she would close up tighter than a bank vault door.

"Why did you try to avoid your father?" he asked hesitantly, watching her closely for any signs of withdrawal. "Did he abuse you?"

She shook her head. "No, he never touched me. But he didn't like me very much."

"He didn't *like* you very much? That's a peculiar way to put it."

"Maybe it's peculiar, but it's true. My first memory of the man is him yelling at my mother that I was obviously an idiot."

She fixed her gaze on the ocean. Somehow, telling Paul wasn't nearly as painful as she'd imagined it would be. "I think I was four or five at the time. He'd ordered my mother to teach me the alphabet. When he asked me to recite it, I couldn't keep the letters straight. Naturally he got furious. At both of us. Me, for being stupid and my mother for having given birth to me."

Now she had started talking, the words began to pour out of Layla. "It didn't get much better after that. Nothing I ever did was right. Nothing I ever said was interesting or funny or even worth listening to. I must have been in my early teens when I finally figured out that he just plain didn't like me. I remember asking my mother why he hated me so much." Layla paused and smiled bitterly. "Of course she insisted he didn't hate me, it was just the way he was, the way he was raised. Hard. Cold. Domineering." She shrugged. "Mother might have been right. My grandparents were a prize pair. I don't think I ever saw either of them smile."

It took every ounce of control Paul possessed to handle the anger pulsing through his veins. Forcing his voice to stay calm, he asked, "Why didn't your mother put a stop to it? Surely she could see what was going on. How it was affecting you?"

Layla sighed and kept gazing at the ocean. "She was too weak I guess, probably scared if she gave him any static he'd divorce her."

"That's no excuse."

She turned and gave him a long, thoughtful stare. "Oh, no? It is if you were born dirt-poor and didn't even finish high school. I didn't understand it at the time, and I had a lot of resentment inside me toward Mom. But after she died, and I finally got to meet her side of the family, I realized she was as trapped as I was."

"Being poor's no excuse for letting your kid get emotionally abused." Paul was losing the battle to control his anger.

"You don't understand. My father and his parents both blamed me and my mother for ruining his life. I didn't know until after mom's death, when I was going through her trunk, that she and my father had to get married when she was seventeen and he was nineteen because he got her pregnant. I found their marriage license and my birth certificate. I was born six and a half months after the wedding."

"So what? That happens all the time. It's hardly grounds for considering your life ruined." Paul's hands balled into fists.

"He always wanted a son. My father's family is well-off, there's a lot of farmland in Ohio that belongs to them. I suspect he wanted someone to carry on the family name or something. He was an only child himself." Layla absently trailed her fingers in the sand. "But after she had me, Mom couldn't have any more children. On top of that, he had to quit college and marry my mother after what was probably a one-night stand in the back seat of his car. I don't think he ever cared about her."

She laughed cynically. "But the real killer is that if anyone's life was ruined, it was my mother's."

"Doesn't sound like yours was any picnic, either."

She shook her head. "But that's not the point. I always knew that when I was old enough I could leave. But Mom was trapped."

"She had you," he pointed out softly.

"Yes. She did. But she could have had so much more. I found her high-school annual from her junior year when I was going through that old trunk. She was captain of the debate team and editor of the yearbook. My great-aunt told me if she hadn't had to marry my father, she'd probably have gotten a full scholarship to college." Layla grimaced in disgust. "But instead of doing something with her life, she married him and became a doormat."

"Maybe at the time she thought she loved him."

"I doubt it. But none of it matters now. It's water under the bridge. I'm an adult now and I've worked hard to get over the nonsense he drilled into me."

He thought perhaps she'd worked a little too hard, or maybe she just needed to believe the past didn't have a hold on her anymore. "Do you ever see him?"

"Not often. Actually he's mellowed now that I've moved two thousand miles away. We write each other and I've got a very nice stepmother. I've always wondered how on earth Ginnie can put up with my father. But she's very different from my mother. For one thing, she's got her own career as a pharmacist, so she's not economically dependent on him."

She shook her head again, her expression somber. "It's really awful, isn't it. The way people screw up their lives.

My mother didn't love my father. I think she stayed with him to make sure we'd be taken care of, but if she'd only had the courage to get the hell out, both our lives would have been so different.''

"Your mother must have loved you very much."

"Yes. She did. And it wasn't all bad. When I was in fifth grade my father got promoted to district manager at work. He traveled some after that. That made life a little easier for Mom and me."

Paul was humbled by her honesty. He resisted the urge to pull her into his arms and assure her no one would ever hurt her again. He sensed Layla wasn't ready for that yet.

She was proud and stubborn and desperately independent, too independent sometimes, but he suspected that was the only way she'd been able to survive the nightmare of her childhood. "So how do you feel about your father now?"

"I don't think about him too much," she replied slowly. "I moved out when I was fourteen and we've gotten along much better ever since."

"Fourteen? You were on your own at fourteen!"

"I wasn't really on my own," she replied quickly. "I moved in with a friend."

"And your parents let you?"

"My mother was dead by then and I don't think my father cared one way or the other." She almost told him the reason her father hadn't cared, but she stopped herself in time. Paul didn't need to know every gory detail about her past.

She turned her head and looked at him. His face was thoughtful, almost grave. "It was a long time ago. It doesn't bother me now."

When he continued to look at her, she knew a rising sense of panic. "What's the matter? You're staring at me like I've grown another head."

"Sorry." He gave her a strained smile. "I'm just amazed that you can be so calm about it."

"Like I said, it was a long time ago." She looked back out at the ocean. "It doesn't matter now."

But it did matter. Paul kept that thought to himself as he studied her profile. So many pieces of the puzzle were beginning to fall into place.

He thought he understood now why she was a virgin, why she avoided entanglements and tried to keep to herself. Yet she had let him get close.

Once again, he was assailed by a sense of humility. The lady had taken one helluva big step. For him.

Chapter Eleven

Monday morning, Layla stepped out of the shower just as the phone rang. Hastily wrapping a towel around her, she hurried to the living room. She absently noticed the unopened letter from her father sitting next to the phone as she picked up the receiver. It had been waiting for her when she got home last night, but she'd been too tired to read it. "Hello."

"Good morning, my love," Paul said. "I hope I didn't drag you out of bed."

"You didn't," she replied with a laugh. "You dragged me out of the shower."

"Hmm . . ." He made the sound wicked and sensual. "Too bad I couldn't come over instead of calling. Ah, the wonders of technology, but it's not a substitute for up close and personal, is it?" He sighed dramatically and she laughed.

"But the reason you're hearing my sexy voice," he continued, "instead of enjoying my sexy body, is because I want dibs on tonight before you make other plans."

"I hardly have that active a social life," she replied. "As a matter of fact, you once made a rather pertinent comment on that very subject. Remember when you were trying to convince me that Stanley could keep me company?"

"Ouch," Paul said. There was a definite cringe in his voice. "I'd hoped you'd forgotten that particular ungallant remark."

"In your wildest dreams," she teased. "Women never forget. Anyway, I'm freezing to death here. Why do you need dibs on my evening? Did something come up on the Centennial, or are you just desperate for my companionship?"

"Desperate, naturally," he said smoothly. "And I want you to come over for a barbecue. My folks are coming over from the coast and I want you to meet them. The Harrisons will be here, too."

Her stomach contracted in sudden, overwhelming panic. Paul wanted her to meet his parents! "I don't know," she said apprehensively, trying hard to think up a good reason to refuse. "It is a work night and I left Stanley alone all weekend. I can't leave him by himself again."

"You don't have to stay late," he countered. "It's a work night for all of us so we're going to eat early. And you know you can bring Stanley. I'm a vet, remember? My guests are used to falling over animals to get to my patio."

She hesitated for a few seconds and then gave in. There was no point in overreacting. Besides, it was too early in the morning for her to think up a decent excuse. It was only a casual meal. It wasn't as though they were announcing their engagement or anything. "That sounds nice. What time should we be there?"

"As soon as you close the store, I'll expect you by a quarter to six, all right?"

"See you then."

After she hung up, she stared blindly at the phone. She shivered as a cool draft of air brushed her damp skin and sent goose bumps racing up her arms.

Layla hated family dinners. She'd avoided them like the plague since she was fourteen and had moved in with Miss Pine. There were no uncomfortable silences at her house. Violet Pine had had the good sense to let you read at the table.

She shook her head slowly as the memories came flooding back. She hadn't thought about those awful family meals in years.

Closing her eyes, an image of her and her mother, both of them sitting rigidly at the dining table with her father, flashed into her mind. The recollection was painful. She could see herself, her long blond hair hanging in two straight pigtails down her stiff spine, sitting in the tension-filled silence that constituted the evening meal at the Odell house.

From the time she was in kindergarten, every second at that table was spent concentrating on her manners so she wouldn't incur her father's cold wrath. She was careful never to eat too fast or spill anything. There was never any talking or laughter or how-was-your-day. There was just that dreadful quiet interspersed with the occasional clink of silverware against china.

Of all the memories from her childhood, mealtimes stood out as the worst.

Layla dragged in a long, deep breath and pushed the recollection to the back of her mind. She was being silly. This was different. She was an adult now and this was Paul's family. Not hers. Maybe the evening would even be fun. Maybe.

Layla got dressed and fixed herself a pot of coffee. As she went out to get the morning paper, she spotted her father's letter. Sighing, she dutifully tossed the newspaper onto the couch and picked up the envelope.

As usual, the missive was neatly divided into two parts. Ginnie's half was all breezy gossip and chatty news of her old neighborhood. Her father's half, or as Layla thought of them, the duty pages, were filled with stilted Hope-your-business-is-doing well comments or news about his flower garden. As she read his neat, careful handwriting going on for paragraph after paragraph about his greenhouse fuchsias and prize-winning tulips, she actually smiled. The eloquence with which Daniel Odell described his new hobby was moving. So moving that Layla had the distinct impression she was reading a letter from a stranger.

She frowned as she refolded the letter and stuffed it back into the envelope. Surprising, she thought, what a hobby could do for someone. But then, she reminded herself, she hadn't been around him much since she was fourteen. In fact, most of his letters nowadays were almost chatty. She shook her head. Maybe he'd mellowed more than she thought.

The front door opened as Layla pulled into Paul's driveway and he came out to meet her. Like her, he was dressed casually. He wore a pair of faded jeans that clung to his long legs like a second skin and a white rugby shirt with turquoise stripes.

Smiling and tugging an uncooperative Stanley behind her, she got out of the car. Without a word of greeting, Paul pulled her into his arms and kissed her.

"Well, hello to you, too," she murmured breathlessly when he released her.

"Come on," he said. "The folks are anxious to meet you." He unclipped Stanley's leash, took her arm and led her toward the patio. "The Harrisons won't be here till six."

Once inside, Stanley immediately flopped down by the front door.

Andre Tressler was coming out of the kitchen, a tray of vegetables in his hand. He was as tall as his son, his dark hair streaked with silver. His tanned face was wreathed in a welcoming smile and behind his horn-rimmed glasses, his eyes sparkled with warmth and humor.

"I've been looking forward to meeting you," he said, extending his hand and enveloping hers in a firm handshake. "Paul talks about you all the time."

Layla murmured a vague pleasantry, then turned and smiled at the petite middle-aged woman coming through the sliding glass door. Fanny Tressler had short auburn hair, was still as slim as a young girl and wore a smile as warm as her husband's.

"Hello, Layla, please call me Fanny," she said as Paul introduced them. Without waiting for a reply, she took Layla's arm and started for the patio.

"It's a bit early in the year for barbecuing," Fanny explained as she ushered her toward the glass-topped table, "but the weather's warm enough and with Paul, you know he's always got a supply of steaks in the freezer. Would you like a glass of wine? We've got white or red or there's iced tea if you prefer."

"White wine, please." Layla sat down on the chair and watched Paul and his father move toward the candy-apple-red barbecue.

"Paul tells me you've taken over the general store on Main Street. That's wonderful. He says you're doing very well," Fanny said.

"So far business has been good," Layla took a sip of wine. "And I do enjoy it."

"It must be nice being your own boss."

"Sometimes," Layla agreed. "But sometimes it's a little scary, too. There are moments when I get tired of having to make every little decision, but luckily, that doesn't happen too often. For the most part, I like it. It's very different from what I used to do."

"I gather you used to work in L.A. and that before that you lived in Cleveland," Fanny said. "How do you like California?"

"I love it," Layla replied emphatically. "Especially the weather."

Fanny laughed. The conversation flowed easily between the two women. Paul's mother was an excellent listener, and seemed genuinely interested in everything Layla said.

"Hey, Mom," Paul called, "can you bring out the barbecue sauce? It's on the counter in the kitchen."

Fanny rolled her eyes, got to her feet and disappeared into the kitchen. Layla grinned. So far, the evening wasn't the ordeal she'd feared. But then again, she thought, why should it be? This wasn't her family.

The barking of Paul's dogs announced the arrival of the Harrisons and they all went into the living room to greet the new arrivals.

Stanley, who'd been lying apathetically by the couch ignoring everyone, got to his feet as MaryBeth came through the door behind her mother. He trotted over to the girl.

Layla watched in amazement. Stanley was acting as if he knew MaryBeth. How odd.

"Hello, Stanley," the girl crooned softly, reaching down to stroke his back. The dog butted his head against her knees.

Layla's surprise died. MaryBeth and Stanley obviously did know each other. But how?

"Good God, Paul," Bud Harrison exclaimed. "Someone else dump a stray on you? Where'd that one come from?"

"That one isn't mine," Paul replied, grinning at Stanley's enthusiastic reception of his goddaughter. "He's Layla's."

After the hellos had been exchanged, they all trooped back to the patio. It was easy to see where MaryBeth got her good looks, Layla thought after they were seated around the table again. Susan Harrison was a beautiful woman. There wasn't a hair out of place anywhere on her elegant blond head, her teal-blue pantsuit outlined a perfect figure and her makeup was so understated you could hardly see she was wearing any.

Layla glanced over at the barbecue where Bud Harrison was huddled with Paul and Andre. He was equally well-groomed, though going prematurely bald.

When the steaks were ready they went into the kitchen to eat. The small group chatted amiably as they worked their way through the delicious meal. Layla noticed, though, that MaryBeth didn't join the conversation unless asked a direct question, and that she barely ate a thing.

It was grossly unfair, she thought, watching the pretty teenager pick at her food. At her age she should be able to relax and enjoy her life rather than measure each mouthful she put into her mouth.

At that moment, MaryBeth glanced up and their eyes met. Layla gave her a friendly smile, but the girl didn't respond. She quickly dropped her gaze back to her plate.

Layla stared at her for a moment, wondering what was wrong. Then she knew. MaryBeth was nervous. Tense. Just the way Layla had been herself when she'd sat at the dinner table with her father. MaryBeth's tension acted as a catalyst. Layla's stomach knotted as the old, painful memories set up a chain reaction deep inside. For a moment she panicked, almost overcome by her feelings. But she wouldn't give in to them. She wouldn't. Layla lowered her head and briefly closed her eyes, forcing the bitter recollections and the feelings they generated to the back of her mind.

After dinner, everyone helped clear the table while the coffee was brewing and then they served themselves. Layla grimaced at the black brew in her cup, decided taking it straight would keep her awake and went to the counter for some cream. She shifted around MaryBeth, who was pouring herself a cup and reached for the cream. She noticed that the girl's hands were shaking.

"MaryBeth, honey!" Bud stared at his daughter in surprise. "What are you doing? You don't drink coffee."

"I've got to study for that trigonometry test tonight, Daddy. It's only one cup, but it'll help me stay awake."

"Ah, honey, you need your rest. I don't want you up half the night studying for a darned test. All that caffeine isn't good for you—"

"Oh, let her alone, Bud," Susan interrupted with a note of irritation in her voice. "She's got to make an *A* on that test, or Stanford will never consider her. It won't hurt her to lose a few hours' sleep.''

Layla glanced from MaryBeth's rigid features to see a small frown flash across Fanny's face.

''Hurry up and drink your coffee,'' Susan continued, checking her gold wristwatch. ''Then you go on home and study.'' She turned and smiled at Paul and his parents. ''I didn't want her to come tonight at all. I knew she needed to study for that test. But she got around me like she always does and talked her daddy into it.''

''I wanted to see Mr. and Mrs. Tressler,'' MaryBeth interjected. ''It's not like I get the chance very often.''

''Well, we're awfully glad she came,'' Fanny said firmly, giving the girl a warm smile. ''We don't see enough of you as it is.'' She turned to Susan. ''I think she's working too hard. The poor girl's always studying or involved in some school activity.''

Susan shrugged. ''That's the only way to get into a decent college. Good grades aren't enough anymore. Nowadays you've got to have half a dozen extracurricular activities as well as straight A's. But we're not worried about MaryBeth. She won't fail us. Did I tell you she's applied to Stanford?''

As she sat down beside Paul, Layla darted a quick look at MaryBeth. She was standing rigidly, one hand lifting the cup to her lip and her other balled into a tight fist. She drank the scalding coffee in less than two minutes, said a quick goodbye and then left.

With MaryBeth's departure, Layla's own tension strained to the snapping point. While the girl had been there, she'd been able to fight off the sense of her own inadequacy and isolation by telling herself she was just reacting to MaryBeth. But that wasn't true. From the moment she'd arrived, she'd been fighting the truth, refusing to acknowledge what was right under her nose.

She didn't belong here.

A warm, chatter-filled kitchen was as foreign to her as the surface of the planet Mars. Her sense of isolation didn't come because they were treating her as an outsider. No, just the opposite. They all went to great lengths to include her in the conversation. Paul was making it obvious she was important to him. She could see that.

And it wasn't a matter of making conversation or not knowing her manners. She could talk to a fence post if she had to, and Emily Post had practically been her mother's bible.

Her isolation was personal; it came from deep inside. From her fears. She felt as if she'd been cast adrift from the rest of the human race at birth and given a set of instructions so she could fend for herself. Her connections were incomplete. Damaged. Unlike most children, she'd never learned the emotional skills needed to be comfortable being a part of a group. There had been no touching, no cuddling, no kind words to guide her through the intricate maze of human relationships. Her mother, wrapped up in her own misery and low self-esteem, hadn't been able to give her what she needed. To let her know she had worth.

Sometimes she felt as if she were running in a fog, desperately trying to make contact and connect with other people. But though she could hear their voices no matter how fast she went, no matter how hard she searched, she could never get close enough to touch.

But she'd touched Paul.

Gamely she fought off the panic attack, refusing to give in to the uncertainties trying to gain a foothold in her self-esteem. She belonged here. She was a part of something. She was a part of Paul.

By nine-thirty, the party was breaking up. Layla tried to leave with the Harrisons, but Paul stopped her.

He kept a firm grip on her hand as they walked his parents to the door and said good-night. Layla watched the easy affection as they all hugged and kissed their goodbyes. She was suddenly envious of him. Her mother had been too withdrawn to touch her and her father just plain hadn't wanted to. He hadn't even hugged her after her mother's funeral.

Paul closed the door and then turned to face her. "What's wrong?"

"Wrong?" Layla hastily bent down and patted Stanley on the head. "Nothing. Nothing at all, why do you ask? Do I look like something's wrong?"

He stepped closer and pulled her into his arms. "Not to someone who doesn't know you. But I can tell something's upset you. You haven't said ten words for the past hour."

"Nothing's wrong," she lied. "I'm just tired, that's all."

Paul released her and shoved his hands into the pockets of his jeans. The urge to push Layla into telling him what was upsetting her was strong, but he didn't want to have to push her into anything. He wanted her to confide in him willingly.

He got a grip on his rising anger, knowing its cause and hating it. The evening had begun so well, then all of a sudden, he'd seen a flash of panic in Layla's eyes and watched her close up tighter than a clam. He'd felt her withdrawal as sharply as if she'd stood up and left. But she obviously wasn't going to tell him. "I know something's wrong. Why don't you just tell me what it is, okay?''

"Nothing's wrong," she insisted. "I'm just a little worried about business, that's all."

He lost the battle to control his temper as he listened to her lame excuse. Waiting for her to open up to him was clearly pointless. He grabbed her shoulders.

She gasped and stared up at him in surprise.

"That's baloney and you know it," he told her angrily. "Tell me the truth. You're no more worried about business than I am. Just this weekend you were telling me it was so good you might have to hire another clerk. So come on, spill it."

"Why are you doing this?" she demanded. "Can't you just leave it alone? Do I have to tell you everything?"

"Yes, damn it, you do. We're together, remember? And we agreed to be honest with each other." He shook his head impatiently. "I've got a right to know what's upset you so much you can't even look me in the eye."

Layla stood stock-still, locked in the grip of long repressed anger that erupted with a suddenness that stunned them both. "You want to know what's wrong?" she yelled. "I'll tell you what's wrong. Everything's wrong. You. Me. Your family." She laughed bitterly. "What are you, blind? Couldn't you see what was going on? Couldn't you tell that I don't belong here?"

"You don't belong here?" he repeated, dumbfounded. What was she talking about? The evening had gone fine. His family liked her. "Did someone say something to make you feel that way? Did someone hurt your feelings?"

"No, no," she cried, desperate to make him understand. She pulled away, needing more distance between them. "No one hurt my feelings, no one said anything. That's not what I'm talking about."

"Then what is it?"

Tears filled her eyes as the truth reared its ugly head. She was an emotional cripple. She always would be. No matter how many books she read, no matter how much positive thinking she did, she'd always be herself. A child so unlovable her own father could barely stand the sight of her.

"Layla," Paul prompted softly when she didn't speak. "Talk to me, damn it. I want to get to the bottom of this."

A hysterical giggle rose in her throat but she fought it back. He deserved to know the truth. She forced her eyes up to meet his. "I'll never be able to give you what you need."

He stared at her for several long, heart-stopping moments. "You already have," he announced, his voice calm and sure. "You're everything I've always wanted. Always needed."

"No," she argued, "I'm not. You all terrify me, the way you love and accept each other. My God, it's unbelievable to someone like me."

"Because of the way you were raised?"

She nodded. "You don't understand. We never had one meal with any conversation or laughter or joking. I don't know how to react when someone hugs me. I don't know how to react when someone gives me a compliment. I don't know how to be a *part* of anything. That little tiff between MaryBeth and her mother brought all those feelings back to me. It was like a rerun. Suddenly I was seven years old again and sitting at my father's dinner table, knowing that if I opened my mouth or spilled my milk there'd be hell to pay." She closed her eyes for a moment. "Before I knew it, I was scared to death I'd say something wrong and your family wouldn't like me, either."

"But they do like you," he said softly.

"But that's not the point." She dragged in a deep breath. "Don't you understand? I don't want to feel this way. I've spent years teaching myself not to feel this way. I won't do this to myself. I won't try and try and try to get you to like me and then fail, just like I failed with him." She swiped at an escaping tear and stepped back, away from his seductive warmth. "I've been alone for a long time. And I made a promise to myself years ago. I'm never going to jump through hoops for anyone again. It's just not worth it."

Paul didn't say anything. He couldn't. One part of him wanted to shake her and tell her he bloody well was worth it. *They* were worth it. But he could see her pain was greater than the damage she'd inflicted to his ego.

She stared at him, her arms crossed defensively over her chest. Her eyes blinked in her effort to hold back her tears and her lips trembled.

He hurt for her. He wanted to comfort her, to tell her that she was babbling nonsense and he'd never let anyone cause her a minute's pain for the rest of her life. But he knew she probably wouldn't believe him.

"Are you saying you don't want to see me anymore?" He asked the question calmly, taking care to keep any hint of threat out of his voice.

"No," she said quickly, then hesitated. "No, I'm not saying that." Layla wasn't sure what she was trying to tell him. Now that the storm had passed, she didn't know what to think or feel, either. But even though she was terrified, she knew she didn't want to end their relationship.

"Good." He smiled gently and pulled her close again. "Because if you were saying 'goodbye' I was prepared to stand here all night and argue the point with you." He buried his lips in her hair and tightened his arms around her stiff body.

She relaxed, giving in to the urge to melt against his warmth. "I'm sorry," she murmured. "I'm not making a lot of sense tonight, am I?"

"No," he murmured, "but that's all right. We've got a long way to go with each other. We've got time to work things out." He raised his hands and cupped her face. "You're not on trial. The only thing I expect from you is that you'll be yourself. That's all I want. Just you."

Paul brushed his lips against hers, once, twice and then took her mouth and kissed her. On a breathy sigh, she opened to his insistent pressure. Their tongues teased and coaxed and played out a delicious duel.

Paul carefully settled her against him, his hands moving down to cup her bottom. He wanted to give her comfort and reassurance, to erase the pain this evening had caused her.

But her arms tightened around his neck and her breasts rubbed erotically against his chest as she returned his kisses with a fervor that curled his toes. His fingers squeezed the soft flesh and Layla moaned in the back of her throat as the heady sensations rippled through her.

She needed him. She needed his passion to blot out the pain of failure. She needed his warmth to ward off the cold.

Against her belly, she could feel him hard and pulsing. She thrust her hips, once, twice, and was rewarded by a low, feral groan. He tore his mouth from hers and watched her through narrow, slitted eyes.

"Make love to me," she whispered. "Make love to me now."

"Are you sure?" Paul wanted her in the worst way. His body was aching to possess her, but he wanted her for all the right reasons. He didn't want her thinking she owed him something, or that she'd failed or that sex was a substitute for understanding. But God, if she rubbed herself against him again, he was going to explode.

"I'm sure." She stood on tiptoe and kissed him. "Oh, Paul," she murmured earnestly. "I need you tonight. I need you in a way I've never needed anyone in my life. Please, take me to bed."

Paul smiled gently, slipped his arm around her waist and led her down the hall and into his bedroom. He turned her to face him. His fingers drifted to the bottom of her blouse and he tugged it up and over her head. She stood watching him, her eyes mysterious pools in the dimly lighted bedroom as he quickly undressed her, then tore off his own clothes.

Paul tossed back the covers and looked at her again. Layla smiled and climbed into the bed, her eyes never leaving his. He didn't understand, he didn't know what was going through that complex mind of hers; he only knew that both of them needed the contact of their flesh and the joining of their bodies.

Paul got in beside her and drew her into his arms. She sighed, twined her arms around his neck and kissed him.

His hands stroked slowly, leisurely over her body. Layla nestled closer, closer, always closer, needing his magical touch, his heat. Her fingers drifted over the sculpted muscles of his shoulders and dug hard into the small of his back.

He rolled to the side and began kissing her neck and her shoulders. Then he cupped her breast and drew her deeply into his mouth. He suckled her gently, then flicked the hardened peak with his tongue. She cried out as the erotic sensations blotted out everything but her growing desire. Her hips shifted restlessly and her legs parted as his questing hand touched her intimately. Slowly, gently, he aroused her until she was twisting in passion.

His own desire escalated sharply as he used his lips and tongue and hands to communicate his feelings.

Layla's breath came in ragged gasps. Her hands moved feverishly over his big body, she tugged against him, trying to bring him on top of her. Inside her.

He moved between her legs, paused and reached into the nightstand. A moment later, he stared down into her face as he carefully entered her. Their gazes locked as he embedded himself deeply and began to move.

She cried out as the excitement spiraled with each and every thrust, her hips moving in perfect counterpoint to him. Still staring into her eyes, he went deeper, faster, harder until she was panting and kneading his arms. They soared together, higher and higher—taking and giving and sharing the ecstatic pleasure until it exploded. Layla cried out sharply, her eyes closing as her body shuddered in completion. Paul gazed down at her and felt the fullness of his love for her swamp him as his body joined hers in surrender.

For a few seconds, he was too drained to move, then he quickly realized he was crushing her and rolled to one side.

They lay entwined, their breathing harsh in the quiet room. Neither of them spoke. Layla had let her mind go blank and Paul was deep in his own thoughts.

He was glad they'd made love, and not just because of the physical pleasure they'd just shared. Making love had brought her back to him.

Layla shifted and he pulled her against him, tucking her head under his chin. For once, he was grateful for her silence. He needed to think.

Her reaction to a simple family barbecue had scared him. He didn't want to lose her. He didn't want the demons that drove her to frighten her so badly she'd walk out of his life for good.

There was a scratch on his bedroom door and they both looked up just as Stanley's head poked through.

"Oh, hell," Paul muttered as the dog wedged himself inside and trundled toward the bed. "I didn't shut the door hard enough."

Stanley stared at them like a jealous husband.

The dog looked so disgusted that Layla giggled. "I think he wants to leave." She pushed away from Paul. "I'd better get dressed and get him home."

"Just a minute." He tightened his arms and pulled her back down. "Spend the night with me."

"You want me to stay all night? But I've got to be up early to open the store and there's Stanley, too," she protested. "What'll we do with him? He's used to sleeping with me. I mean, he sleeps in my bedroom."

Paul glanced at the dog, who was now sitting glued to the rug, his brown eyes narrowed suspiciously. "We'll be up in time for you to get to work, I promise. And Stanley can sleep in the living room for one night. It won't kill him."

Layla debated the merits of a nice warm bed against going out into the chilly night to appease her grumpy dog. It was no contest. She wanted to stay with Paul. "Okay, you've talked me into it."

She snuggled down deeper into the covers as Paul got up and put Stanley in the living room. When he returned, he made sure the door was firmly fastened.

Flicking off the lights, he got in beside her. Drawing her close, he yawned. "Don't let me forget," he murmured. "We've got to go through my antiques and find more things to decorate the gym. That dance is less than a week away."

"All right," she muttered sleepily. "It is getting kind of close, but maybe we can wait until the end of the week. I've got to take inventory tomorrow and Wednesday. How about Thursday or Friday?"

Chapter Twelve

Friday afternoon Layla double-checked the lock on the back door before going to Paul's. Though it was just past five, heavy gray clouds darkened the sky and the air had the faint scent of moisture that signaled a coming storm. But she refused to let the dulling twilight dampen her spirits.

She was too happy. She and Paul had been together every evening since Monday night working on the Centennial Dance. They'd not only put together most of the decorations, but they'd also gotten a committee together to help with the work on Saturday. The only thing left to do was find that one perfect nostalgia item that would add the final touch to all their hard work.

But even better than finishing their chores for the dance, Layla liked what had developed between her and Paul. She felt comfortable around him now. Her feelings no longer frightened her. She'd come to realize that this man would never hurt her, this man would never push her away in rejection. Even his endless questions about her past didn't bother her anymore, because she knew they weren't prompted by idle curiosity, but by caring.

Layla grinned as she slipped the keys into her purse and walked around to the street. Paul had missed his calling, she thought. He should have been a psychiatrist or maybe a priest. Her smile widened as she remembered how the last few evenings had ended and she was suddenly, fervently glad he wasn't a priest.

A minute later, she was knocking at the side door of his office.

"It's unlocked," he shouted, "come on in."

Paul slipped off his bloodstained white coveralls and turned to the sink as he heard the door close. He glanced over his shoulder, gave Layla a brief smile and turned on the taps. "Ready for the grand tour?"

"I've been looking forward to it," she replied, stepping up behind him and slipping her arms around his waist. She nuzzled the center of his back. "This is my big chance to see what treasures you've been hiding back there."

He turned off the water and reached for a paper towel. "I hope you won't be disappointed," he said, easing around to face her. "It's not all antiques and collectibles out there. There's still a lot of junk left over from when I bought the place."

His voice sounded apathetic. She stepped back and gazed at him. A worried frown crossed her face as she noted the deep lines of fatigue etched around his eyes. His hair was mussed and falling across his forehead and his mouth was a grim line. She smiled sympathetically. "You look so tired."

"I am," he admitted, wearily lifting one hand and pushing his hair out of his eyes. "Last night one of Ted Allison's horses decided to kick his way out of a stall. It took hours to patch him up."

"My goodness, I've never heard of such a thing. Is that normal?" Layla wished she knew more about animals. "Was he trying to run off or something?"

"No," Paul replied cautiously, his eyes riveted on her face. "Something spooked him. Ted thinks someone must have been in there, because the back door was wide open when he arrived."

"That's unusual," she mused, not liking the idea of some stranger prowling around the countryside. She'd felt safe living here. "You'd think this area would be too isolated for casual drifters. Did Ted check with the neighbors? Did they see anyone hanging around?"

"The Harrison place is just across the road. But Bud and Susan didn't see anyone prowling around and MaryBeth wasn't home."

"Maybe someone was trying to steal the horse? Is it valuable?"

"All the Allison horses are valuable. It's one of the best thoroughbred stables in the country. But I don't think anyone was trying to steal the stallion." Paul shrugged. He had a pretty good idea who'd been in Allison's barn and it wasn't a drifter or a thief. Jamming his hands into the pockets of his pants, he fingered the keys he'd found lying on the floor of the barn. "What time is Tank due back from Escondido?"

Layla's brows drew together in surprise. "Anytime now," she answered cautiously. Something was wrong here. Paul wasn't himself. "Is there a problem? He told me you said it was all right if he took the afternoon off. He has been putting in a lot of extra work hours lately."

"There's no problem," he replied. "I just need to talk to him."

"What about?" She watched him suspiciously.

He traced the edge of the key ring for a moment and debated telling her the truth. Then he decided against it. Layla was never reasonable where Tank was concerned and after a night without sleep he doubted his own ability to hang on to his temper.

"Nothing important," he replied shortly. He yanked his hand out of his pocket, walked to the back door and jerked it open. "Come on," he called over his shoulder. "Let's get this over with. That damned dance is tomorrow night and I don't want to spend the rest of the day worrying about decorating the school gym."

"Are you sure you wouldn't rather go home and get some sleep?" she asked as she followed him out.

"I'm sure," he said impatiently.

His abruptness hurt, but she told herself not to be so sensitive. Paul was tired and weary. His irritability wasn't directed at her.

The one hundred square feet at the back of the office was enclosed by a six-foot wooden fence with a gate leading to the street. A gravel driveway bisected the yard. On one side of the bottom of the yard, there was a metal storage shed. Between the shed and the back of the house, Layla saw the Model T, six huge barrels neatly sitting side by side, a calliope and what looked like several old-fashioned hot dog carts. On the other side of the driveway, a lattice overhang extended from the edge of the house to the fence at the end of the property.

Layla followed Paul beneath the overhang to an old hay wagon. The wood was weathered gray and the contraption was obviously ancient but it looked sturdy.

She ran her fingers over the side of the wagon and looked at Paul. He was gazing off into the distance, a frown on his face. Despite her certainty that something was out of kilter with him, she refused to give up and slink away. She lifted her chin and straightened her spine.

This was Paul. Not her father. If he was in a bad mood she didn't have to run and hide or bury her nose in a library book. She wasn't afraid of him.

She tapped the side of the wagon again and he turned toward her. "This is great," she said enthusiastically, determined to be cheerful. "We could find some hay and put it right on the dance floor. It's the right period and it'd look fabulous."

"Are you kidding?" Paul protested. "And let those high-school kids climb all over it?"

"But we wouldn't have to take it over there until right before the dance," she insisted. "Besides, most of the teenagers in Riker's Pass probably won't even be there. Let's face it. The Centennial Dance isn't going to be a big event on their social calendars. It's for the old fogies in town." She grinned. "Like us."

"Well—" he ran his fingers lovingly over the wagon "—if you think it'll be safe, maybe we could? But I'm mighty attached to this old thing."

She rolled her eyes heavenward. She had a feeling Paul was probably attached to everything he owned. "Let's see what else you have around here." She straightened and started for a large tarpaulin-covered object on the other side of the hay wagon, but Paul tapped her elbow, stopping her.

"This side," he said absently, waving across the driveway toward the Model T. "The only things under those tarps are the odd-size lumber and other building supplies that I inherited when I bought the place."

He turned and crossed the gravel toward the car. Layla shook her head. She told herself he was trying to be interested, but he was tired. He'd been up all night and he needed to sleep. But as she caught up with him and darted a quick peek at his face, she found it harder and harder to believe his mood was caused by fatigue.

Once again, his mouth was set in a grim line and his gaze was hooded and suspicious. Something had upset him. Something serious. And he wasn't telling her what it was.

Paul stopped beside the car and turned to face her, his mouth curving in a faint smile. She smiled brightly in relief.

"Now this is my pride and joy," he declared. "So don't even hint about taking it out of this yard."

"I wouldn't dream of it," she assured him.

They both heard it at the same time, a faint clink like glasses hitting against each other. It was coming from the other side of the car.

Paul stalked around the hood and Layla followed. He stopped so abruptly, she ran into him.

She gasped in surprise. Tank Mullins crouched next to the half-opened door of the car, a plastic bag in his hand. He stared at them, a look of horror on his face as the bag slipped out of his fingers and landed on the ground.

"What's in the bag?" Paul's voice was low, harsh and edged with fury. "And what the hell are you doing in here anyway? You're supposed to be seeing your probation officer in Escondido."

Tank's mouth opened, but no words came out.

"Answer me."

"Paul," Layla interjected in alarm. "Give the boy a chance. Whatever's in that bag might be personal."

He ignored her.

"Uh, I was just cleaning up in here." Tank dropped to one knee and snatched up the bag. "My PO's other appointment didn't show. I got out of there a little early and decided to head back here and get some work done."

Layla could see the Adam's apple in Tank's throat bob up and down as he spoke. His eyes were wide with fear and his face had turned a bright red.

Paul's eyes narrowed. "You're lying."

The boy flinched but said nothing. He slowly rose to his feet, his eyes never leaving Paul.

"Just a minute," Layla interjected, glancing from Tank's scarlet face to Paul's rigid features. "What is going on here? Tank," she prompted. "What's wrong? Just tell us what you're doing back here. That's all."

Silence.

She turned to Paul. "What kind of a game are you two playing? Why don't you say something? Why are you so upset because he's back here cleaning up. And why are you accusing him of lying?"

"I think Tank knows." Paul stepped forward and took the bag out of the boy's limp fingers. He looked inside and grimaced in disgust. Finally he raised his head and looked directly at Tank. "You're fired."

"Fired!" Layla yelped. "What are you talking about? What's in that bag?"

He shoved it into her hand. "See for yourself."

Peering inside, she gasped. There were half a dozen empty vodka bottles, the same kind that she'd found in the garbage cans behind her store. She raised her head, her expression stunned. "Tank," she said quietly. "What's going on here?"

Tank stepped toward her, his hands spread in a pleading gesture. "I swear," he said fervently, "those aren't mine. I found them in the Model T and I was just trying to get them out of here before you and Dr. Tressler saw them. But as God is my witness, those bottles aren't mine. I don't drink."

Paul shoved past Tank and yanked the door open the rest of the way. Puzzled, Layla watched him as he searched the car and rummaged around under the seat.

"And I suppose this isn't yours, either," he snarled, drawing out another bottle. It was full.

Tank shook his head.

Paul tossed the bottle to the ground in disgust and reached into his pocket. "What about these? I suppose they're not yours, too?" He dangled a set of keys under the boy's nose.

Layla stared at the keys for a moment before she recognized them. They were hers. An extra set she'd given Tank so he could lock and unlock the store and her house.

The color drained out of his face. "Those are mine," he admitted dully, almost as though he didn't expect anyone to believe him. "I lost them a couple of days ago."

Paul laughed harshly. "Yeah. I'll bet."

"Dr. Tressler," Tank said earnestly, "I know this looks bad. But those bottles aren't mine. I swear it. And I don't know where you found those keys, but honest, I really did lose them."

"Then whose bottles are they?" Layla asked. "You obviously know or you wouldn't have gone to so much trouble to try to get rid of them before we saw them."

His eyes filled with panic, then he dropped his gaze to the ground. "I can't tell you right now," he said quietly, his voice so low she could barely hear him.

Paul snorted. "That's a good one. What do you want us to do, give you time to think up some good lies?"

"No. Just give me a few days and I'll explain every-thing. The bottles, the keys, everything."

"No way." Paul planted himself between Tank and Layla. He glared down at the boy. "Time's run out for you now. You've had your last chance. Maybe I could have overlooked this. You haven't actually been drink-ing on the job and I'm not sure I give a damn if you want to get drunk on your own time. But I can't overlook everything else."

"Paul, what are you talking about? What do you mean, he hasn't done anything else," Layla snapped.

"Like hell! Ask him where he was last night? Ask him if he hasn't been sneaking around the Allison place try-ing to see MaryBeth."

Layla looked from Paul to Tank. The boy looked just as puzzled as she was. "Tank? Is that true?"

"I don't know what he's talking about."

"Don't give me that," Paul snapped. He stepped to-ward Tank, his hands on his hips. "Where do you think I found those damned keys? I found them on the stable floor. What've you been doing, hiding out in there and waiting for MaryBeth to come back from the library every night. Well, last night, your stupidity almost caused a horse to kill itself." He paused for breath. "Get off my property and don't come back. If I find you anywhere near my goddaughter again, I'll call your probation of-ficer myself. Is that clear?"

"But, Dr. Tressler," Tank pleaded. "All I need is a few more days. It's not what you think...."

"Get out. Now." Paul pointed to the gate.

"Just a minute," Layla interrupted. She tugged at Paul's arm. "All he wants is a few days. For heaven's sake, that isn't too much to ask. I believe him. If you fire him that probation officer of his will pull him in in a minute. You can't do it."

"Stay out of this, Layla."

She tugged harder on his arm until he glared down at her. "Paul," she whispered passionately, "if you care anything about me, we'll all go inside and discuss this rationally. You don't know what you're doing. You're too angry to think straight. You're tired. Please. Let's go inside."

"Are you threatening not to see me if I fire him?" he asked incredulously.

"Of course not," she replied, beginning to lose her own temper. "I'm just asking for a chance to discuss this situation calmly. Please. Is that too much to ask?"

Paul stared at her for a moment. "Yes." He turned to Tank. "I said you're fired."

Tank's shoulders sagged in defeat, but he turned and stoically walked toward the gate.

Something snapped in Layla. "Go to my house," she called. "Wait for me there. We'll work something out."

She refused to look at Paul until Tank had disappeared. Then, she turned furious eyes on him.

"I hope that makes you happy," she hissed. "You've crushed that kid without even giving him a chance to defend himself. All he wanted was a few more days. He'd have told us the truth, he'd have explained everything if you'd only given him some time."

"He's had enough chances," Paul countered. "And I don't appreciate your taking his side against me."

"Taking his side!" Layla repeated, so angry she couldn't think straight. "Of course I took his side. I'm the only one around here who believes in him. You've never really given him a chance, you've just been waiting for him to goof up so you'd have a good excuse to fire him." She stopped, took a deep breath and brought her temper under control.

"I didn't have to look for an excuse to fire him. He managed to mess up all on his own."

But Layla was determined to give it one last try.

"Please, Paul," she pleaded, "give him another hearing. I know there's more going on here than we realize."

"The only thing going on here is that kid's got the wool pulled over your eyes."

"No. It's not like that. Listen, a long time ago, I did something really stupid, but I was desperate. I could see that in Tank's eyes, the same kind of desperation, the same kind of fear. You've got to listen to him. Everyone deserves a fair hearing and all he wants is a little more time. If you fire him, he'll never get another job around here and he'll end up in jail."

"That's where he belongs," Paul shot back.

His words sent a shaft of fear racing down her spine. Hope drained out of her and she moved back, her eyes locked on Paul's unforgiving face. "You don't know what you're saying," she murmured, fighting off the painful memory of another time and another place. Only then it had been her that had done something stupid. Then it had been her father yelling "that's where she belongs."

"You can't mean that," she whispered. "You can't be that hard. Just let him explain. What can a few days hurt?"

But Layla could see by the way his face hardened that she wasn't getting through.

"Layla," he warned, "forget it."

But she couldn't. "This happened to me one time. I took some money from my father." She spoke faster, desperate to make Paul understand. "I was confused and frightened and all I wanted to do was to get away. It was right after my mother died and I was so lost. I took three hundred dollars from his desk. He caught me. He was going to send me to reform school, Paul. He didn't understand, either. But Miss Pine intervened. I called her and told her what happened and she came over. She talked to my father and kept him from sending me away. She gave me the chance I needed. Tank needs that chance now."

"I'm sorry, Layla," Paul said, his tone flat and final. "I can't do it."

"Why are you doing this? I never thought you could be this cold."

"Cold?" He laughed harshly. "You think I'm cold because I won't give that lying little punk another opportunity to hurt someone. I listened to you before, I gave him his chance because it meant so much to you, but he blew it."

"But you don't *know* that. You don't know that he's hurt anybody. You're convicting him on circumstantial evidence."

"Bull." Paul watched her through narrowed, angry eyes. "If you believe that, then you don't know me half as well as I thought you did." He turned on his heel and stalked into his office, slamming the back door behind him.

Blinded by tears, Layla ran to the gate, jerked it open and fled. She couldn't believe what had just happened. She couldn't believe the man she'd thought she was in love with could turn out to be so much like her father. So cruel, so uncaring, so willing to condemn someone to a living hell.

The threatening storm broke as she drove home. Over the sound of the driving rain, she let the tears fall. They streamed down her cheeks as she sobbed her anguish and betrayal. Because that's how she felt.

Betrayed.

Pulling into the driveway, she sat in the car for a moment until she had herself under control.

Tank sat unmoving on the porch. His slumped shoulders and defeated expression reinforced Layla's belief in him. His freedom and his job were important to him. She knew he wouldn't sacrifice either of them for booze.

Lifting her chin determinedly, she climbed out of the car. "Let's go inside."

Stanley met them at the door, his tail wagging. When he saw Tank coming in behind Layla, he whined in welcome.

"Hello, boy." Tank dropped to his knees and hugged Stanley to his chest. Layla tossed her purse on the couch and turned to stare at the two of them.

Tank had buried his face in the dog's neck. His arms were clutching the dog tightly and his frail shoulders were shaking. Layla's heart contracted and she hastily looked away, not wanting to embarrass the boy by letting him see she'd noticed he was crying.

A memory of a terrible night so many years before overwhelmed her. She closed her eyes, remembering. She was standing in her father's den. He was watching her with cold, hard eyes, as if she were an escaped convict who had crawled into his life and masqueraded as a blood relative.

She'd been alone, terrified and certain she was doomed. Then she'd called Miss Pine. Miss Pine who'd valiantly come to her rescue and offered to take her off her father's hands.

As far as Layla was concerned, Tank was innocent until proven guilty. A set of keys and some empty vodka bottles didn't prove anything. Least of all that he'd betrayed her faith in him. Didn't believing in someone mean keeping the faith against all odds, against all reason?

"I suppose you want me to explain." Tank's shaky voice brought her back to the present.

"Is there a reason you can't?" Layla leaned against the couch. She pushed her own pain to the back of her mind, she'd deal with that later. And she was amazed that it wasn't the memory of that night in her father's study that caused her heart to ache. It was the image of Paul's face when he'd refused to listen to either her or Tank.

Tank nodded and stood up to face her. "Yes," he replied somberly. "I can't tell you what it is, not yet. But I give you my word—I'll swear it on a stack of bibles if you want me to—that I haven't been drinking behind Dr. Tressler's office and I haven't been anywhere near Mr. Allison's place."

"When will you be able to tell me the truth?"

Tank dropped his gaze and stared at the floor. "Maybe next week," he said hesitantly. "I can't say for sure. This isn't just about me. Someone else is involved."

"Yes, I'd figured that much out." Layla wondered who he was shielding.

"But I promise, Layla—" Tank's eyes begged her to trust him "—I'll tell you as soon as I can."

Silently she debated his words. The evidence was against Tank. Paul could be right.

But she knew what her decision was. She was going to stand by Tank. If she was wrong, she'd live with it. But she wasn't going to walk away from him, she wasn't going to spend the rest of her life isolated. Trusting Tank meant taking a risk. The boy needed her. Needed her in a way that no one else ever had.

"All right, I'll take your word for it. But I do expect you to tell me what's going on. And soon."

"I will," he promised. "Like I said, all I need is a few days, then I can tell you and Dr. Tressler everything."

Layla shrugged, wondering why he'd included Paul. You'd think the kid would be so mad at the man he'd never want to speak to him again. But she kept the thought to herself.

Tank cocked his head to one side and stared at her curiously. "Can I ask you something?"

"Yes."

"Why are you sticking by me? No one else ever has."

She stared at him thoughtfully for a few seconds. "Because someone once stuck by me," she answered.

"Oh," he said, clearly intrigued. "Who?"

"A lady by the name of Violet Pine. She was the local librarian. I used to spend hours at the library. It was a good way of avoiding my father."

Tank snorted, "Yeah, I did that a few times myself when my old man was alive."

"Miss Pine and I became friends. She was really more of a teacher than a librarian." Layla smiled wistfully. "She spent half her time answering questions or helping us with our homework. She was always so positive, so encouraging. By the time I was ten, she was my best friend." She paused and fixed Tank with a level stare. "By the time I was fourteen, she was keeping me out of reform school."

His jaw dropped.

"Now," she said briskly, "we've got to figure out how to get you another job."

Tank sagged against the wall. "It's a sure bet that after people find out the doc fired me, no one else will take me on."

"Don't worry about that," she said. "I don't think he's going to broadcast it all over town." But that still didn't solve their problem. Even if Paul kept quiet, no one in Riker's Pass would hire Tank.

Layla's brow wrinkled as she thought about their options.

"Does that old car of your aunt's run well enough for you to get back and forth to Escondido every day? It's a sixty-mile round trip."

"Yeah. It's old, but I can keep it running." He grinned. "I'm a pretty fair mechanic."

"Good. Because you're going to have to drive there every day when you finish up at the store. There's dozens of restaurants and fast-food places down there. Every time I'm there, I see Help Wanted signs all over the place. You'll have to get a night job flipping burgers or busing tables. It's not much, but it'll have to do."

"But when they find out I'm on probation, they probably won't want to hire me," Tank said hopelessly. "Maybe I'd better just call Beals and tell him the truth, maybe he'll let it go as long as you keep me on."

She shook her head. "No, we can't risk that. It's not the probation officer's decision. It's the courts'. And they've already set the terms. But don't worry about it. You go in and apply—and when you're there, make sure you speak to the manager. I'll give you a letter of recommendation with my phone number. That'll help."

"And if it doesn't." He swallowed. "What then?"

"We'll cross that bridge when we come to it."

Chapter Thirteen

Layla was still so upset with Paul the next day, she almost didn't go to the dance. Saturday was the busiest day of the week for the store, so she was able to push him and their argument to the back of her mind for a few hours.

But as she closed the door behind the last customer and slid the bolt into the lock, she realized she had to go. Staying home smacked too much of her past. Argument or not, she refused to hide from Paul the way she'd always hidden from her father. He was being pigheaded and stubborn and just plain wrong, but that didn't mean she had to cower behind locked doors until it was safe to show her face again. And furthermore, she told herself as she stalked out to her car, she refused to have that kind of relationship with him.

If Paul was still angry at her, well, tough. She wasn't exactly happy with him right now, either.

* * *

The Centennial Dance was in full swing when Layla arrived. She stopped in front of the double doors leading to the gym, took a deep breath, patted her hair and then pushed inside.

She paused a moment in order to give her eyes time to adjust to the dim lighting. The room had been transformed. At one end, a makeshift stage had been set up and a band, dressed in turn-of-the-century costumes, played a tune she didn't recognize.

She smiled as she saw Paul's hay wagon, now filled with baled hay and sitting catty-corner between the stage and the red-and-white checked refreshment tables. Though the gym didn't have the air of an old-fashioned schoolhouse, the decorations were lovely, nonetheless.

Barrels were scattered around the perimeter of the room and covered by white linen tablecloths and topped with either a hurricane lamp or a basket of flowers.

In the middle of the floor, dancers attired in both period dress and modern clothes swirled around the floor.

Craning her neck, Layla scanned the whirling mass looking for Paul. But she didn't see him. She waved to Arnold Dunphy, who was doing a two-step with Lili Metcalf, then turned and surveyed the crowd around the refreshment table. Still no Paul.

Biting her lip, she smoothed her hand over her red silk skirt as her glance darted quickly from one huddled cluster of people to another. Then she spotted him coming in through the side door, a case of soft drinks in his arms.

Like her, he wasn't in costume but wore a pair of faded jeans and a blue-and-gray checked shirt. She watched him smile at Susan Harrison, who was serving the drinks, then drop to his knees and shove the carton under the table.

As he rose to his feet, their eyes met and his smile abruptly vanished.

Layla's mouth went dry. He didn't look overjoyed to see her. Butterflies erupted in her stomach but she gamely started toward him.

His gaze didn't waver as she crossed the gym. Layla was sure it was the longest walk of her life. But finally, she was standing in front of him, a tentative smile on her face. "Hello, Paul. The gym looks lovely."

"Thanks." He crossed his arms over his chest to keep from reaching for her. "I was afraid you wouldn't come."

"I almost didn't."

Paul raised his eyebrows but said nothing.

She hesitated and gathered her courage. "Can we go outside? I want to talk to you."

He stared at her a long time before replying. "All right. I've got a few things I want to say to you, too."

Taking her hand, he turned toward the side exit. "There are benches out by the parking lot. We can talk there."

Neither of them spoke as they left the gym and walked across the grass to a row of wooden benches. But Layla was aware of Paul's tension. She was nervous, too. But their relationship was important to her and she wasn't going to let it end because they'd had a fight. If Paul felt differently, if he wanted to walk away, she wanted to know now.

"Do you want to sit down?" Paul asked politely. He was determined to keep calm. He was also determined that a punk like Tank Mullins wasn't going to ruin his relationship with Layla. Couples had arguments all the time. He wasn't going to let her use it as an excuse to push him away. Not now. They'd come too far.

She shook her head. "No, I just wanted some privacy."

Carefully keeping his expression blank, he tried to control his impatience. "This must be serious."

"Paul, I...I—" She broke off, unsure of exactly what she wanted to say.

"You what?" he prompted. He tried to keep his tone neutral, but failed. Her eyes widened and she drew back and he knew she'd heard the impatience in his voice. "Look," he continued, "if you've come out here to tell me that we're through, forget it. We've had an argument, and I know you're mad as hell, but we're not going to call it quits because—"

"That's not what I was going to say," she interrupted quickly.

"It wasn't?" he replied, clearly surprised.

She shook her head, but before she could speak, a shrill voice sliced through the quiet night.

"Let go. I don't need you. Give me those keys back."

"No. I won't let you drive. You're drunk."

Layla jumped. She recognized the second voice. It was Tank Mullins. But Paul had recognized the first voice.

"That's MaryBeth!" Paul swiveled his head and scanned the parking lot. His eyes narrowed as he saw MaryBeth's car parked several rows back, beneath a lamppost. He took off at a run.

Layla raced after him. They'd almost reached the car when they heard MaryBeth again. "Give me those damned keys," the girl screeched.

They skidded to a halt by the car. "What the hell's going on here," Paul demanded.

Layla stared in amazement. Standing next to the driver's side was Tank. MaryBeth was sagged against the hood.

"Thank goodness you're here," Tank said, his voice relieved as he saw Paul. "She needs help."

"What's going on?" Paul moved closer to the teenagers, his expression confused. "What's wrong with MaryBeth? Is she sick?"

"Yeah, she's sick all right," Tank replied. He was breathing hard, as though he'd run a marathon. MaryBeth's hair was falling into her eyes, her mouth was hanging half-open and she was clutching the hood ornament like she'd never let it go.

As she realized Paul and Layla were there, she tried to straighten, swayed precariously and then slumped back against the hood.

"She's drunk," Tank continued quickly. "And I'm trying to keep her from getting behind the wheel of this car and killing herself or someone else."

"Oh, Tank's just doing his good deed for the day," MaryBeth said in a singsong voice. She lunged toward Tank's right hand, but he stepped out of reach. "He thinks poor, little MaryBeth is too tanked to drive." She laughed hysterically. "Get it? Tank thinks I'm tanked."

Paul was clearly stunned. He stared at the girl for a moment, taking in her disheveled hair and her rumpled clothes. "MaryBeth, have you been drinking?"

MaryBeth gave another high-pitched giggle. "Every chance I get, Uncle Paul. I love to drink. It's wonderful. It makes you forget how damned hard it is to always have to be so perfect. But don't tell my momma. Oh, no, I wouldn't want her to think her little girl isn't perfect."

She made another try for the keys in Tank's hand. This time, she actually managed to snag them. The boy tried to grab them back, but she deftly dodged to her right.

Paul caught her. He held her gently by the shoulders and stared into her glazed eyes. "It's okay, honey," he soothed. "Everything's going to be all right."

She gazed back at him for one long, confused moment and then her face twisted in grief. "No, it's not," she whispered, tears spilling down her cheeks. "It'll never be all right again. I can't stop, you see. I just can't stop. I've tried, I've tried so hard. But I can't."

Gently he pried the keys out of her hand and gave them to Tank. "Go get Bud and Susan."

"Did Tank give you the alcohol?" Paul asked as soon as the teenager was out of earshot.

"Him? Give me booze?" She laughed through her tears. "No. Oh, no. He never gives me anything but a lot of nagging. Booze. God, I wish. But all he ever does is bug me to get help, to dry out, to go into some stupid program, to tell my parents. Nag, nag, nag, that's all Tank ever does."

Over the girl's head, Paul's eyes met Layla's.

MaryBeth started to cry. "Get help, get help, get help. God I'm so sick of hearing that. He's supposed to be my friend. But all he ever does is take away my vodka and sober me up."

A few minutes later, Tank returned with a stunned Bud and Susan in tow. Paul gently sat MaryBeth inside her car before turning to her parents.

Layla and Tank tactfully retreated to the far side of the vehicle as Paul spoke quietly with the Harrisons.

She heard Susan cry out in shock, then, a few minutes later, the Harrisons left, leaving Layla, Paul and Tank standing in the parking lot.

Layla turned to Tank. "Would you like to tell us what's been going on?"

He sighed. "She's been drinking heavily now for months. I've been trying to help her, to get her to tell her folks so they could get her into some kind of program. But she can't quit."

Layla shivered and Paul slipped his arms around her shoulders. "Let's go to my place," she said. "I think we could all use a cup of coffee. You can tell us everything there."

Twenty minutes later, they were seated in Layla's living room, sipping instant coffee. Stanley was sitting on Tank's feet but the boy didn't seem to mind.

"Okay," Paul said softly. "I think it's time for that explanation. What's been going on?"

Tank closed his eyes and sagged, as though he'd just had a heavy burden lifted off his bony shoulders. "I've hated having to keep this to myself. But I promised her, I'd give her a chance to dry out on her own." He dropped his gaze and stared at the dog. "I should have known better."

"How did you get so involved with her problem?" Layla asked, peering at him over the rim of her cup. "I thought you didn't even see her these days."

"I couldn't avoid it. She was my friend, one of the few I've got. MaryBeth and I go way back. Up until high school, we were always in the same class and with both of us getting such good grades, we were thrown together on school projects and stuff like that. We've been close for years. But no one knew it. Her parents didn't like me."

He took a sip of his coffee. "The friendship kind of tapered off when I jumped ahead of her in high school.

Until I started tutoring her in math. Then we found out we had even more in common than straight *A*'s."

"No offense meant," Paul said, "but what could you possibly have in common with her? And what does that have to do with her being drunk tonight?"

Tank gazed at him uncertainly. "Everything. Mary-Beth and I discovered we both thought we had a lousy parent." He raised his hand quickly as he saw Paul's eyes narrow. "Don't get mad, Doc, but you asked. I'm not saying that Mrs. Harrison is anything like my old man used to be, I'm only saying that's what MaryBeth thought."

"Go on." Layla prodded softly.

"Anyway, we became friends again while I was tutoring her and then one day, I caught her drinking." Tank shook his head. "I was really peeved at her. I threatened to quit helping her but she promised she'd never do it again. She was lying, of course. A few weeks later we went to the movies, and she was clearly drunk again. It wasn't me that crashed the car, it was her. I wasn't even there. When I saw how drunk she was, I tried to get her to pull over and give me the keys. But she's clever. When I got out to go around to the driver's side, she took off like a bat out of hell. I hitchhiked back and went looking for her." He turned his gaze to Paul. "You found me back of your office because she'd told me it was one of her drinking holes. She'd sit in that Model T of yours at night and toss the stuff back like it was water."

"I knew you couldn't have wrecked that car and then just abandoned that girl," Layla cried.

Tank smiled briefly. "After that, I tried to stay away from her. But she kept coming back. Crying and carrying on and saying I was her only friend. I couldn't just turn my back on her. I begged her to tell her parents, because by then I knew she was like my old man. An alcoholic."

"Why didn't you tell someone?" Paul gave him a long, hard stare.

Tank's gaze was equally frank. "Would you or the Harrisons have believed me? Would anyone in town have believed me? Let's face it, everyone knew about my father and everyone knew about the time I got drunk and made an ass of myself. No one would have believed me, except maybe Layla, would they?"

"Probably not," Paul admitted softly. "But go on."

"A few weeks ago, she suddenly got a lot worse. She was drinking all the time."

"But how?" Layla interrupted, her brow wrinkling in confusion. "She lives with her parents. And where did she get the money to buy the alcohol? No one around here would buy it for her. And where did she go to drink? That's not the sort of thing you can do in the public library without someone noticing."

"MaryBeth's got plenty of money and she had a derelict down in Escondido buy the stuff for her." Tank shrugged. "As to where, well, she's an alcoholic. She's got lots of hideouts. Like I said, her favorite spot was the Model T. Two weeks ago, I caught her using that deserted area behind the store."

"So that's where those bottles in my trash can came from," Layla murmured thoughtfully.

Tank turned a bright red as he looked at Layla. "I've got to tell you something and I hope you won't get mad at me, but for those two Saturdays you two were together—" he reached down and patted Stanley "—I took MaryBeth to your house to try to sober her up. The first time was that day you went to Balboa. I found her boozing behind the store when I went to lock up. I took her to

Summer Reading
At Its Best

In July, Harlequin and Silhouette bring readers the Big Summer Read Program. Heat up your summer with these four exciting new novels by top Harlequin and Silhouette authors.

SOMEWHERE IN TIME by Barbara Bretton
YESTERDAY COMES TOMORROW by Rebecca Flanders
A DAY IN APRIL by Mary Lynn Baxter
LOVE CHILD by Patricia Coughlin

From time travel to fame and fortune, this program offers something for everyone.

Available at your favorite retail outlet.

GIFT OFFER

With Free Gift Promotion proofs-of-purchase from Harlequin or Silhouette, you can receive this beautiful jewelry collection. Each item is perfect by itself, or collect all three for a complete jewelry ensemble.

For a classic look that is always in style, this beautiful gold tone jewelry will complement any outfit. Items include:

Gold tone clip earrings (approx. retail value $9.95), a 7½″ gold tone bracelet (approx. retail value $15.95) and a 18″ gold tone necklace (approx. retail value $29.95).

FREE GIFT OFFER TERMS

To receive your free gift, complete the certificate according to directions. Be certain to enclose the required number of Free Gift proofs-of-purchase, which are found on the last page of every specially marked Free Gift Harlequin or Silhouette romance novel. Requests must be received no later than July 31, 1992. Items depicted are for illustrative purposes only and may not be exactly as shown. Please allow 6 to 8 weeks for receipt of order. Offer good while quantities of gifts last. In the event an ordered gift is no longer available, you will receive a free, previously unpublished Harlequin or Silhouette book for every proof-of-purchase you have submitted with your request, plus a refund of the postage-and-handling charge you have included. Offer good in the U.S. and Canada only.

MILLIONAIRE! Sweepstakes

As an added value every time you send in a completed certificate with the correct number of proofs-of-purchase, your name will automatically be entered in our Million Dollar Sweepstakes. The more completed offer certificates you send in, the more often your name will be entered in our sweepstakes and the better your chances of winning.

PRO1

your place and made her a pot of coffee.'' He raised his eyes to meet Layla's. "I'm sorry. I wasn't trying to pull one over on you, but I couldn't just leave her like that.''

"It's all right, Tank,'' she assured him, seeing his embarrassment. "I understand. You were trying to help her.'' She smiled wryly, remembering the morning she found the empty coffee can. "At least now I know what happened to those missing scoops of coffee. And it explains why she and Stanley are such good buddies.''

"Missing coffee?'' Paul asked.

"Never mind,'' Layla said quickly. "I'll explain it later.''

Tank turned to Paul. "And there's something else you'd better know. That night, when MaryBeth brought in her dog, she was the one who hit him. She was also the one who spooked Mr. Allison's horse. She was drunk.''

"How did she get your keys?'' Layla asked.

"Picked them up when I wasn't looking. After the doc told me he'd found them, I asked her. She wanted to be able to sneak into the store at night, when her parents thought she was at the library studying.'' Tank shook his head. "I'm amazed no one else spotted her drinking. The signs were all there.''

"What signs?'' Layla stared at him curiously.

"MaryBeth was always popping breath mints and she didn't wear that heavy perfume because she liked it, but because she thought it would keep people from smelling alcohol on her. Half the time her hands shook like a leaf and she's moodier than a crazy cat. God, it was so obvious to me. I kept hoping someone else would see it.''

Paul smiled cryptically. "It's too bad we didn't. Maybe things wouldn't have gone this far if we had.''

"Yeah,'' Tank said morosely. "It's too bad I didn't take a chance on telling you, Doc. But I honestly didn't think you'd believe me and I was trying so hard to give her a chance to dry out on her own. I thought I had her convinced to go to AA." He broke off and laughed harshly. "But she didn't. After you fired me, I gave her an ultimatum."

Layla gazed at him sympathetically. "To do what?"

"To go to her folks and tell them she needed help. It finally hit me that I was making the problem worse by covering for her. I was just keeping her from having to deal with the consequences of her own drinking." Tank looked disgusted with himself. "Threatening to snitch on her didn't feel good, but this time, she knew I was serious."

"Is that what brought on tonight's binge?" Paul asked.

"Yeah. I wasn't really surprised. Alcoholics do that. When they can't face something they get drunk. She knew I was serious about telling you the truth tonight and she knew that even if you didn't believe me, you'd start keeping an eye on her and eventually you'd figure it out. The Harrisons would listen if you told them the truth. She couldn't stand the thought of her mother finding out, MaryBeth's really scared of her."

"Susan wouldn't hurt a fly," Paul protested.

"Probably not," Tank agreed, "but she's put a lot of pressure on MaryBeth to be perfect. Wanting her to go to Stanford, pushing her to make good grades. MaryBeth's not going to get into Stanford, she's not going anywhere except to summer school. She's flunking math."

No one said anything. Then Tank put down his cup and stood up. "But at least now she'll get some help. I'm sorry I couldn't tell you the truth before this, but I hoped she'd do it on her own."

"It's all right," Layla said gently. "We know you were just doing the best you could for her. But it's up to her parents now. I'm sure they'll see she gets the treatment she needs."

"They will." Paul stood up, too. "Whatever pressures Susan put on MaryBeth, I know they love her."

"Let me give you a ride home." Layla picked up her purse as Tank headed for the front door.

"No." He stopped, one hand resting on the doorknob. "Thanks anyway, but I'd like to walk. I need the fresh air. I'll see you on Monday, Layla. Oh, and Doc, should I be at the office at my regular time?"

"Yes. That'll be fine."

After the door shut, Layla turned to Paul. "You hired him back?"

"Yes. I called him late this afternoon, after I'd had a chance to cool down." Paul sat back down on the couch, his face glum.

"But why?" Layla asked hesitantly. "I thought you didn't believe him."

"I didn't. But you had such faith in the kid that after I'd thought about it, it seemed like there was just an outside chance I might be wrong."

"I see."

Paul said nothing. Instead, he continued to stare morosely at nothing. Finally he raised his eyes to meet hers. "Do you?"

"W-well," she stammered, puzzled by his reaction. "I think so. I can imagine how you must feel. Tonight must have been a real shock. You didn't expect to find that Tank was shielding MaryBeth."

"No," he replied slowly. "I didn't. But then a lot of things have happened lately that I didn't expect."

Layla didn't know how to react to that statement; it could mean any of a dozen things. Paul was still staring off into space, his expression both thoughtful and troubled. "Are you all right?"

He nodded. "Yeah, I'm fine. You're right about one thing. This has been a real shocker. It makes me wonder."

"About what?" She sat back down in the chair.

He smiled sadly. "About how well I actually see people for what they are. About how well I know them. I was blind about MaryBeth and Tank both."

"You weren't blind, you were just convinced that your past perceptions about both of them were still true. No one can blame you for that. It's hard to know when people change. It's not like they carry a big sign or something advertising the fact."

"Yeah, but you noticed."

"But I had an advantage you didn't," she insisted, hating to see him taking so much of the blame. "I didn't have any preconceived ideas about them. And anyway, even I didn't catch on to the fact that it was MaryBeth that had the drinking problem. Tank was right, you know. The signs were there."

She stood up and walked over to the couch. Now that they were alone she was suddenly uncertain. She'd made it through the day on sheer determination and righteous anger. For the first time in her life, she hadn't run scared, she hadn't hidden away rather than risk an emotional confrontation. But now she wasn't so sure about what to say or how to act. Paul was still as tense as a coiled spring and she couldn't understand why. They knew the truth now, Tank and his problems wouldn't be between them anymore.

She stopped in front of him and smiled hesitantly. He stared at her somberly, reached for her hand and pulled her down next to him.

"Let's talk about this later," he said quietly. "Right now I've got to ask you something and I want you to be totally honest when you answer."

Her whole body went stiff in reaction, but she managed to nod. His eyes never left her face, and his gaze was so intense she couldn't have looked away if a hurricane blasted through the house. "All right," she agreed hesitantly.

"What were you going to say to me tonight? Before we were interrupted, I mean."

Layla almost sagged in relief. For a few moments, she'd been terrified. There were so many questions he could ask, questions she wasn't sure she was ready to answer. Not yet. Maybe not ever. "I was going to tell you that I thought you were pigheaded and stubborn and absolutely wrong about Tank, but that I still wanted to be with you."

Once the words were spoken, she realized they were the absolute truth. Despite her fear that he was going to ask her straight out for some kind of commitment, she was surprised by how free she suddenly felt. People *could* change. She'd seen the proof of that tonight. And hadn't she had a hand in shaping Tank's life?

Paul continued to stare at her and Layla knew a moment's panic. Her heart sank as it dawned on her that maybe her answer wasn't what he'd hoped to hear.

"Good," he finally said, "because that's the exact speech I was going to give you." He pulled her to him and crushed her against his chest, burying his face in her neck. "The last twenty-four hours have been the most miserable of my life. I was so scared you'd never speak to me again. That's why I didn't call you, I figured you'd come to the dance and I'd already made up my mind that come hell or high water, I was going to straighten things out between us.''

"I felt the same way," she murmured, giddy with relief. She managed to slide her arms around him. "Even though I was so mad, I couldn't think straight, the one thing I was sure of was that I didn't want to let you go.''

"We'll never let each other go," he vowed. He pulled back and held her at arm's length, his eyes searching her face. "I'm glad you still care. But the point is, how much?''

"How much?" she repeated with a puzzled frown. "What do you mean?''

"Let me explain. For the past few weeks, I've convinced myself you cared about me. No, that's not true, I'd convinced myself you were falling in love with me. But now, I'm not so sure. If I couldn't see what was right under my nose with Tank and MaryBeth, how can I make any judgments about your feelings? You haven't said anything.''

"Paul.''

"No. Let me finish.'' He sighed. "I pigeonholed Tank as an unstable delinquent and I refused to see that MaryBeth, my own goddaughter, had a serious problem. After I started seeing you, one part of me was convinced that if I just showed you how much I cared, how much I loved you, then all your problems would just disappear. But that's not the way it works.''

"Paul," she tried again.

"No, no," he interjected. "Don't say anything. You don't have—''

"*Paul!*" This time she shouted. "Will you listen to me?''

Surprised, he lifted his head and stared at her.

"Anyone could make a mistake about Tank," she said firmly. "You weren't the only one who was convinced he was Riker's Pass's answer to John Dillinger. The whole town thought he was no good."

"You didn't."

She ignored that. "The evidence against Tank was pretty convincing. There was a time or two when I wasn't so sure about him myself. And as for MaryBeth, why should you see something her own parents couldn't?" She paused and then added, "And you weren't wrong about me."

His mouth opened and then closed again. "I wasn't?"

"No." She smiled softly at the dazed expression on his face. "You were exactly right. You did show me how much you care and..." She hesitated, groping for words that wouldn't come. Words that were trapped behind that one last fragile barrier of fear. Words that she desperately wanted to say, but couldn't.

The phone rang, startling them both. Layla jumped to her feet and snatched it up. "Hello."

Her face paled as she listened to the voice on the other end. Alarmed, Paul came to stand beside her. Finally she said, "All right, I'll catch the first flight out in the morning, maybe I can even get one tonight. I'll call you."

She put the phone down but didn't say anything.

"Layla," Paul asked softly, "what's wrong."

She expelled the breath she'd been holding and turned to him. Her eyes were glimmering with unshed tears and he quickly pulled her into his arms. "What is it? What's wrong?"

"Oh, Paul," she said, the words muffled against his chest as she burrowed closer to his warmth. "That was my stepmother on the phone. My father's had a heart attack.''

His arms tightened around her and for a moment, he just held her. "Baby, I'm sorry," he whispered. "How bad is it?''

She sniffed and swiped at an escaping tear. "He's in intensive care. It doesn't...doesn't look good. I've got to go home.'' She stepped back and reached for the telephone. But his hand closed over hers.

"I'll call the airlines," he said. "You go make us a cup of tea. You need something to settle your nerves.''

"But there isn't time. I've got to hurry....''

"The airport closes in less than two hours. There's no way you'll get out tonight. Go on, do as I said.'' He gave her a gentle shove toward the kitchen. "Don't worry about a thing, I'll make reservations for the first flight out in the morning.''

When she came back with the tea, he was standing with his back to her. She saw him put down the phone and then he turned and crossed the room, taking the mugs out of her shaking hands.

"Sit down," he ordered softly, leading her to the couch. "I've got you on a seven forty-five flight tomorrow to Chicago, there's a half an hour layover and then a connecting flight to Cleveland.''

She nodded dumbly and reached for her tea.

"I've reserved two seats," he continued softly. "I'm going with you.''

Layla put her cup back down on the coffee table and smiled at him. She wasn't surprised by his announcement. One part of her wanted to hurl herself into his arms and shout yes, yes, yes. She would have liked nothing more than to have him with her, for she desperately wanted his strength and support, but she knew that was impossible.

"Paul," she began. "Nothing would please me more than to have you with me, but you can't. This is something I've got to do on my own."

He took a deep breath but before he could marshal the argument she knew was coming, she held up her hand. "Believe me, I've never been more tempted to say yes to anything in my life, but it's important that I face my father alone."

"That's ridiculous," he scoffed. "Why should you have to handle this alone? Why can't I go with you? Don't you want me by your side at a time like this?"

"Of course I do, but that's not the point. Please try to understand..." She faltered, not sure how to put her feelings into words. "It's important for us, for our relationship that I see my father by myself. It's hard to put this into words, but I feel like I've come so far. Yet there's still a barrier between me and the feelings that have been trapped inside me for as long as I can remember. I have the strangest feeling that the only way to get through that wall is to go back alone... Oh, heck, this doesn't make a lot of sense, but I know I'm right."

For a small eternity he didn't say anything. Then, he sighed and pulled her close. "All right. This goes against my better judgment, but if you feel that strongly about it, you're probably right."

He lifted her chin and their gazes met. Slowly he lowered his head and took her lips. The kiss was long, sweet and infinitely gentle. When it ended he said, "But if you need me, I want you to promise to call. I'll come."

Her eyes filled with tears again. "I promise."

Chapter Fourteen

Her stepmother was waiting at the gate when she arrived in Cleveland.

Ginnie Odell was a tall, heavyset woman with short curly blond hair, thick glasses and a brisk no-nonsense manner. "Hello, dear," she murmured enveloping Layla in a welcoming hug. "I'm so sorry you finally came to visit us under these appalling circumstances." She stepped back and plucked the overnight bag off Layla's shoulder. "The baggage claim is this way."

"How's Father doing? Is he going to be all right?" Layla asked.

"He's doing as well as can be expected," Ginnie replied. "The doctors are optimistic about his chances for recovery, but he still wanted you here." She hesitated and glanced at her stepdaughter. "He's been thinking about you a lot lately."

Layla didn't reply. She didn't know what to say. They arrived at the baggage claim and collected Layla's suitcase.

Both of them were silent as they crossed the parking lot and got into the car. After Ginnie had pulled out into the traffic, Layla's curiosity got the better of her. "How do you know Father's been thinking about me?" she asked. "Has he said anything?"

"Daniel's made a few comments. As you know, he's not the most talkative man on the face of the earth. But he's more communicative now." She checked her rearview mirror and changed lanes. "Did you know he's in a therapy group?"

Slowly, carefully, Layla turned to stare at her stepmother's profile. "Therapy?" she repeated in a stunned voice. "Father? You've got to be kidding."

"No, I'm not." Ginnie shook her head. "He goes to his group every Wednesday night. It's helped him enormously."

Layla couldn't have been more shocked if aliens landed in front of the car. "What made him do that?"

"Mainly, I think, it was going back to college."

"But I thought he was just taking a few horticulture classes. Something to help him with his gardening."

"No, he's been taking all kinds of subjects. Daniel's been bored since he retired, what with me still working and everything. Anyway, to make a long story short, during his first semester he took a political science class from this absolutely wonderful teacher, a Dr. Lanham."

Puzzled, Layla frowned. "I still don't get it. What does politics have to do with Father going into a therapy group?"

Ginnie shrugged. "From what Daniel said, the class wasn't really about politics, it was about political systems and how individual attitudes and behavior are shaped. I'm not sure of the details, but your father ended up doing a research paper on Appalachian child-rearing practices. He got fascinated and even after the class was over, he read everything he could on the subject. That class changed his life. If he hadn't come to a real understanding of why he was the way he was, he'd never have realized he could change."

Layla's head spun. Of all the things she'd expected, it wasn't to arrive and find that her father had switched personalities.

"Don't get me wrong," Ginnie said hastily. "He hasn't turned into Mr. Congeniality and he never will. But he's learned a lot about himself. And most importantly, he's learned that he isn't doomed to spend the rest of his life being miserable." She flicked Layla a quick look. "Did you know he'd been abused as a child?"

"No," Layla whispered. "I didn't. But somehow, I'm not really surprised. My grandparents were a couple of cold fish. We didn't see them very often and he never talked about them after they died. I certainly never asked." She paused and took a deep breath, steeling herself. "What kind of abuse are we talking about here?"

"Physical. Beatings mainly." Ginnie's voice hardened. "Your grandfather tended to use his fists, your grandmother preferred a razor strap. Between the two of them, they made his life a living hell."

"My God."

"However badly your father treated you," Ginnie continued earnestly, "he never once laid a hand on you."

They pulled up at a red light and Ginnie turned to Layla, her gaze direct and intense. "That's why I called and asked you to come. I know your life with him wasn't easy, but there's a chance he might die. He wants to make peace with you, just in case."

Layla's eyes filled with tears and she turned away. She didn't know why she was crying. Whether it was for herself or for her father. Whether it was for the cold, taciturn man who'd made her childhood a misery or whether it was for a human being who'd been trapped in a nightmare all of his own. She just plain didn't know.

"Layla?"

She sniffed and wiped at her eyes. "What?"

"Forgive him." Ginnie's eyes pleaded with hers.

Layla looked down at her lap. "Is he going to die?"

"Maybe. Maybe not. It's in the hands of God." Ginnie reached over and patted Layla's hand. "But he's getting the best possible care and he really *wants* to live. That counts for a lot."

They arrived at the hospital just as the doctor was coming out of her father's room. Ginnie introduced Layla and then asked, "How is he this morning?"

"Much improved." He smiled encouragingly at the two women. "Every hour that passes increases his odds." He peered at Layla over the rim of his glasses. "You can see him now, but only for ten minutes."

She nodded and walked to the double doors leading to the intensive care unit. She paused briefly and took a deep breath before going in.

He was lying in a glass partitioned cubicle. There was a tube in his nose, an IV running from his right arm to a suspended bottle and a variety of other paraphernalia that monitored his vital signs. Hesitantly Layla stepped to the bed and peered down at him.

Her throat closed and her chest tightened as she stared into his pale face. Gone was the imposing, domineering man she remembered from childhood. In his place was a tired, sick, and fragile human being she wasn't sure she knew anymore.

Her mind was still reeling from what Ginnie had told her. She remembered the letters he'd written her, how she'd thought them so different, so human. She thought of him nurturing a garden and going to college. She thought of the pain he'd endured at the hands of his parents and what it must have cost him in self-esteem and confidence. Then she thought of the pain she'd endured at his own hands and what it cost her.

He must have sensed her presence because his eyelids fluttered open. For a moment, he stared at her, his hazel eyes riveted to her face. "Layla," he whispered in a raspy voice. "You came."

"Of course I came, Father. How are you feeling?"

"Better," he replied, his gaze still locked on her face. "I'm going to get better. I have to. I've got so many things I want to tell you, so much I have to say." He tried to raise his hand, to reach for hers.

Layla could see what the effort cost him. Quickly she grasped the shaky fingers. "Lie still," she urged. "Don't exert yourself."

"Please stay. Stay long enough for me to talk to you."

"I will," she promised him hastily, "for as long as you need me."

Her words seemed to comfort him because he gave her one last smile and then fell asleep.

She and Ginnie didn't leave the hospital till after dark and by the time they got to the Odell home, Layla was physically and emotionally drained. But as tired as she was, she called Paul. She needed to hear his voice.

He answered the phone on the first ring. "Hello."

"Paul, it's me."

"Thank goodness you called. I was starting to get worried. I've been thinking about you all day."

"Of course I called. I promised I would, didn't I?"

"How's your father?" he asked quickly, ignoring her last statement.

"He's doing as well as can be expected," she replied cautiously. "We'll know more in a couple of days."

"Keep me posted, all right?" He paused, then added, "Are you all right?"

"I'm a little tired from the trip, but other than that, I'm holding up. It's my father and stepmother I'm worried about."

"I know," he murmured sympathetically, "but worrying isn't going to do any of you any good. Are you sure you don't want me to hop on a plane and fly out there?"

"No, I'm fine," she assured him, "but it's sweet of you to offer."

"I mean it, Layla," he said, "if you need me, all you have to do is ask. You sound exhausted. Go to bed and get a good night's sleep. Things will probably look better in the morning."

By Tuesday morning her father had improved so much he was moved from intensive care to a regular hospital room. As she went in to visit him, Layla wasn't sure how she would face him. For the past two days, he'd been too ill, too fragile to be anything except an object of compassion. But now that he was so much better, she knew things would change. Despite his being in therapy, despite all the alleged changes in his life, there was still a cold, hard core of anger in her gut. She didn't know if anything he said or did could make it disappear.

"Hello, Father," she said with forced cheer as she walked to his bedside. "How are you feeling this morning?"

He grinned. "Pretty good for someone who came that close—" he held up his thumb and index finger a quarter of an inch apart "—to meeting his maker."

Layla couldn't believe her ears. He was actually making a joke. In spite of her qualms, she chuckled. He looked so pleased with himself. "Well, thank goodness you didn't. But that was a close call. You had us worried."

"Sit down, dear. I want to talk to you." He looked pointedly at the chair that was next to the bed stand.

"Father, I don't think you're well enough—"

"Nonsense," he interrupted. "I've got a lot to say to you. And anyone who has come as close to dying as I have doesn't take one moment of his life for granted." He broke off and closed his eyes. "Please, it's important. To both of us."

Not wanting to upset him, Layla dutifully sat down.

Her father stared up at the ceiling. Somehow, that made it easier for her.

"I'm sorry." His words were soft and low and profoundly sad.

She cleared her throat. She wasn't sure what he was apologizing for. "About what?"

"Everything. About the way I treated you. About the way I treated your mother. About the miserable life I inflicted on all of us."

"Father—" she began, but he cut her off.

"Don't say anything," he pleaded. "It's taken me years to work up the courage to tell you this and this might be my last chance. So please, hear me out."

"You're not going to die," she protested. "Look I don't think this is the time for serious discussion. You've just had a major heart attack. You don't need any upsets."

He laughed softly. "Layla, I've been upset all my life. That's why I want to talk to you. I may or may not recover. I hope I do, but that's not the point. What's important is that I try to make things right with you before it's too late." He hesitated briefly and added. "Did Ginnie tell you I was in therapy?"

"Yes," she answered softly.

"Did she tell you why?"

Layla clasped her hands together. "She mentioned you had some problems and that it had something to do with my grandparents."

"You're hedging," he teased with a grin. Then his smile faded. "Don't be afraid to say it out loud."

"She said you'd been abused as a child." She gulped. "Physically abused."

"That's right," he nodded encouragingly. "Let's not hide the ugliness behind a euphemism. I didn't have 'some problems,' I was beaten. Frequently."

"Why?" she asked, her voice shaky. "Why did they do it?"

He sighed. "Because they were both obsessed with control. Because it was the way they'd been raised, because they were both miserably unhappy with their lives and they took it out on me. Maybe they were both a little crazy. I don't really know." He shrugged. "Back when I was growing up, no one did anything about it. The term 'child abuse' didn't exist."

"God, that's awful."

"Yes, it is," Daniel agreed. "That's why I swore it wouldn't ever happen to you. I won't lie to you and tell you I was happy about having to marry your mother. We were never in love with each other. But that's a separate issue. Right now, I just want you to understand what was driving me all those years. On the night you were born, I remember standing over your crib and vowing to Almighty God that I'd never lay a hand on you. I'd never, ever put you through what I had to endure.'' His voice broke.

Panicked, Layla leaped to her feet. ''Father, stop. This isn't good for you. You're not supposed to be upset.''

''Yes, it is good,'' he countered. ''Living with poison in your system is the real killer. Not letting it go.'' He waved her back into the chair. ''Don't worry, I'm not going to peg out on you right now.''

Watching him carefully, Layla surreptitiously picked up the call button for the nurse. If the worst happened, she could at least summon help.

''Even though I kept my promise and I never laid a finger on you,'' he continued, ''in my own way, I was just as bad as my parents had been. You see, they not only abused me physically, they abused me emotionally. So though I never hurt you, I didn't know how to love you. When you were growing up, I simply wasn't capable of it.''

''So what are you saying? That it was my grandparents fault?'' She heard the note of anger in her own voice and winced.

''God knows whose fault it really was,'' her father whispered fervently. ''It doesn't matter now. But it was a pattern. Though I broke the pattern of physical abuse, I didn't have enough awareness to realize the pattern of emotional abuse was just as damaging. And your mother was all too willing to play along.'' He looked at Layla. ''Don't get me wrong, I'm not blaming her. She was a kind, sweet woman who never had a chance to explore who she could really be. But all those times when I was cold and uncaring, all those times when I criticized or belittled you, she never once told me to shut up."

"She was scared of you."

"I know." A look of pain crossed his face. "You both were. But that's the way I thought families were supposed to be. It was only after I married Ginnie and she adamantly refused to put up with my criticism and silences that I began to realize how very wrong I'd been."

"Ginnie didn't take it?" Layla knew there was a reason she'd always liked her stepmother. For a moment, anger at her own mother flared deep inside her and then just as quickly disappeared. Because Layla finally understood that Elaine Odell had done the best that she could. Her mother had loved her, and that was really all that mattered.

"No. The first time I sat down for a meal at home with Ginnie she asked me if I'd lost my tongue," he confessed with a grin. "She literally forced me to have a conversation. It was hard, too. I wasn't used to sharing things." He turned his head and gazed directly at her.

"What do you want me to do, Father?" Layla asked in confusion. "Say that all is forgiven? That it's okay that you never once hugged me or kissed me or even had a kind word for me? That it's fine to be ignored and belittled and made to feel like I don't even belong on the face of the earth."

His face constricted in grief as she spoke. "No, I don't want you to say that. Life is never that simple. That easy. I just want you to stay for a while. Give us some time to talk, to be together, to try to get past some of the pain and the anger." He sighed deeply and glanced away. "I want you to give me another chance."

Layla saw him swipe at his cheeks. Then he looked at her again, his eyes pleading. "Just stay for a few days," he begged. "Give me a little of yourself. I know I don't have the right to expect it from you, but maybe we can get to know each other, maybe someday you can forgive me."

Anger and bitterness churned in her stomach. But as she stared into his hopeful eyes, she also felt the beginning of compassion and understanding. "I'll stay," she replied softly. "But I can't promise anything beyond that, okay?"

He smiled then. "That's more than enough."

A cold spring rain was falling as she walked out of the hospital. Ignoring the rain, Layla wandered across the street to the park, where she stood beneath the sheltering shade of a huge oak. She stood there for a long time, thinking about everything her father had told her.

Patterns. It all came back to patterns. She thought about her mother and her grandparents. And most of all, her father.

Then Paul's face would flash into her mind and she'd wonder if she was as guilty as her father. Her father had broken the pattern of physical abuse, but hadn't been able to take that one final step to break the whole pattern.

Until now.

Was she like that? Was she able to go so far but no farther? Wasn't she repeating the pattern just as her father had? She went so far with Paul, but no farther. She remembered how he'd said he'd loved her and try as she might, she hadn't been able to tell him what was in her own heart.

That she loved him, too. She had for a long time now.

Had she ever really allowed herself to trust Paul? Had she ever really faced what she felt for him? Was she ever really honest about her feelings or was she like her father, too terrified to take that one final step?

But her father had found the courage to break the pattern of his life. He'd changed. She could, too.

Even though she'd called him and told him when her flight was getting in, Paul wasn't at the airport when Layla got off the plane four days later. She tried hard not to let her disappointment show when Tank met her and explained that Paul had been called out on an emergency.

Tank talked nonstop all the way back to Riker's Pass. Layla tried her best to pay attention to what he was saying, but it was hard. She'd said goodbye to her father and Ginnie with affection, and they had discussed plans to come out and visit her in the summer, but now Layla's mind was on Paul and what she was going to say to him.

"Everything's fine at the store," Tank said brightly. "But it'll sure be good to have you back. Running the place on my own is kinda scary. Besides, I want to get back to the doc's office. I miss the animals."

"That's wonderful," Layla muttered absently. "I'm sure you've done a terrific job." What was she going to tell Paul? The truth? Could she do it? Did she have that kind of courage? Did she trust him enough to be that vulnerable?

"Stanley's going to go ape when he sees you," Tank said as he turned the car onto the gravel road leading to Paul's. "I took him over to your place earlier today. The doc only told me right before he sent me to pick you up that he wanted you to come back here."

"Fine, fine," Layla murmured, not really listening. Her pulse rate jumped as the front door opened and Paul stepped out. He came down the steps two at a time and trotted toward the car.

The instant she opened the door she was in his arms.

Paul held her tightly for a moment before lowering his head and taking her mouth. Oblivious to everything, including a grinning teenager, they kissed with unrestrained passion, in a frenzy of long-suppressed desire.

Tank cleared his throat. Loudly.

They broke apart to see him smiling sheepishly at them. Layla's suitcase was on the ground beside him. "Uh, I hate to interrupt," he said, "but I've got to get back to my aunt's."

"Good night," Paul said quickly as the boy slipped behind the wheel and started the engine. "And thanks for going to the airport."

"Thanks, Tank," Layla echoed. She watched the car until it turned onto the highway and then she turned to Paul.

He took her hand, picked up her suitcase and headed toward the steps. "How's your father? Still improving?"

"Yes, he's getting stronger every day."

Paul pulled open the door and led the way inside. Layla was surprised that none of the dogs were around. She moved farther into the room and then stopped. When she turned, she saw that Paul was leaning against the door staring at her.

Taking a deep breath, she decided it was now or never. She had to tell him before she lost her nerve. "Paul, I've got to tell you something."

He crossed his arms over his chest. "Okay, what is it?"

"I love you."

He didn't move, but his body stiffened. "What did you say?" he asked almost harshly.

Her heart was banging against her ribs like a jack-hammer and her stomach was turning flips. "I said, I love you," she repeated, surprised that her voice sounded normal.

He pushed himself away from the door and crossed the room until he stood right in front of her. His gray eyes were so intense they pierced her. "Are you sure about what you just said?"

"Yes," she whispered. "Oh, yes. I've never been surer of anything in my life."

With a low groan he pulled her into his arms and lowered his head until their lips met. Unlike the first kiss, this one was soft and sweet and exquisitely tender. He molded her against him, holding her body close and dragging his lips away from hers to cover her face with tiny kisses.

"Thank God," he muttered, feathering his lips across her nose, forehead and cheeks. "I've been so scared you'd never be able to say those words. I love you so much and when I finally worked up the courage to tell you, you had to leave. This has been the longest week of my life." He stopped and peered down at her. "Why the hell didn't you tell me this before? It would have saved a lot of wear and tear on my nervous system."

"I couldn't," she confessed. "I was too scared."

"Scared? Why?" He hugged her again and ran his hands lovingly over her back and shoulders.

"I've been scared to face the fact that I love you," she said earnestly, determined not to hold back. "I've loved you for weeks now. But in the back of my mind, I was terrified of getting close, of giving you that kind of power over me."

"Power?" He shook his head slowly. "My love for you isn't a power game. It's the way I feel, it's the way you make me feel. I only want to make you happy...that makes me happy. Don't you understand that?"

"I do now, but I didn't before. Don't you see? I saw love and need and commitment as a trap. As emotional incarceration. But as I got to know you, as you barged your way into my life, I got confused. Because instead of feeling imprisoned, I felt just the opposite. And then, when I saw how I'd made a difference in Tank's life, when I realized that patterns weren't set in granite, I felt even more liberated. But I still wasn't sure. I was still afraid and I didn't know why. But when my father got sick and I had to go back and face him, then I knew I could be free."

"How?"

"Because that was the final wall, the last barrier. If someone like him had the courage to change, to break the pattern that had been set years ago, then I could, too."

Paul pulled her closer again, enveloping her in a tight hug. "We'll do it together," he promised softly. "But don't change too much. I happen to love this particular Layla Jane Odell."

"And this particular Layla loves you, too."

They held each other tightly for a few moments. Then Paul abruptly let her go and headed for the hall. "Don't go anywhere," he called over his shoulder. "I'll be right back."

A few seconds later, he reappeared. She noticed he was holding something in the palm of his hand.

He hesitated a few feet away from her and she heard a sharp hiss as he took a deep breath.

"Paul?"

He took another step, stopping directly in front of her. "Layla, I know you've gone through a lot, what with your father and all, but, but..."

"Yes," she said. Her lips curved in a slow, knowing smile.

"I'm trying to ask you—" He broke off and ran his hand through his hair. "Damn. This is harder than I thought it'd be. Feels like I'm tongue-tied all of a sudden."

"Ha, that's a first. You haven't been at a loss for words since the day I met you. Go ahead, spit it out."

"All right, all right, give me a minute. I want to do this right."

"Do what right?" She'd never enjoyed a conversation more in her life.

"Ask you to marry me."

Now it was her turn to be tongue-tied. She wanted to throw herself at him and shout yes at the top of her lungs, but all she could manage was a feeble and shaky, "Oh, yes."

"This is for you." He handed her a small velvet box.

Layla's fingers shook as she picked it up and opened the lid. Her eyes filled with tears when she saw what was inside. "Oh Paul, it's the cameo ring." She threw her arms around his neck. "It's beautiful and I love you, I love you, I love you..." She couldn't stop saying the words, it felt so good, so liberating, so free.

He locked his arms around her fiercely. "I love you, too," he whispered. "I can get you a diamond, too, if you'd rather have that?"

"No, no. This is exactly what I want." She laughed in delight. "But it's been weeks since we were at that antique shop. I'm so touched that you remembered how much I loved this ring."

"I didn't have to remember," he said softly, nibbling at her ear. "I bought it for you the day we were there. Even then I was sure I wanted to spend the rest of my life with you. You were the one that needed convincing."

"Nonsense," she countered. "I'm a smart girl. I'd have eventually figured out we were meant for each other."

"Let's celebrate." He flicked his tongue on the sensitive spot at the base of her neck. "I've got a bottle of champagne in the fridge."

"Hmm..." She closed her eyes. From outside, Paul's dogs suddenly set up a howl. Layla straightened and jerked away. "Oh, my gosh," she gasped. "Stanley. He's all by himself and the poor darling's been alone all week."

"No, he hasn't. He's made out like a bandit since you've been gone. Tank brought him into town every day. That big mutt has spent his time lolling around my office. He's got everyone from my receptionist to the delivery man making over him and slipping him treats. The big ham's probably gained five pounds."

"But Paul," she protested.

"Humph." Paul hauled her against him and kissed her again. "Don't worry about Stanley. He'll be fine. He's probably already asleep."

He picked her up and started down the hall to his bedroom.

"But..." She laughed and twined her arms around his neck.

"No buts," he said firmly, pushing open the door and dropping her smack in the center of the bed. "This is one night we don't need a chaperon."

* * * * *

NORA ROBERTS

Love has a language all its own, and for centuries, flowers have symbolized love's finest expression. Discover the language of flowers—and love—in this romantic collection of 48 favorite books by bestselling author Nora Roberts.

Two titles are available each month at your favorite retail outlet.

In April, look for:

First Impressions, **Volume #5**
Reflections, **Volume #6**

In May, look for:

Night Moves, **Volume #7**
Dance of Dreams, **Volume #8**

Collect all 48 titles and become fluent in

THE LANGUAGE of LOVE

Silhouette®

LOL492

Silhouette Special Edition

salutes

MOMENTS OF GLORY

from Lindsay McKenna

In a country torn with conflict, in a time of bitter passions, these brave men and women wage a war against all odds... and a timeless battle for honor, for fleeting moments of glory, for the promise of enduring love.

February: RIDE THE TIGER (#721, $3.29) Survivor Dany Villard is wise to the love-'em-and-leave-'em ways of war, but wounded hero Gib Ramsey swears she's captured his heart... forever.

March: ONE MAN'S WAR (#727, $3.39) The war raging inside brash and bold Captain Pete Mallory threatens to destroy him, until Tess Ramsey's tender love guides him toward peace.

April: OFF LIMITS (#733, $3.39) Soft-spoken Marine Jim McKenzie saved Alexandra Vance's life in Vietnam; now he needs her love to save his honor....

Take 4 bestselling love stories FREE

Plus get a FREE surprise gift!

SILHOUETTE® *Desire*™

Silhouette Desire
10th Anniversary

Celebrate with a
FREE
classic collection
of romance!

In honor of its 10th Anniversary, Silhouette Desire has a gift for you! A limited-edition, hardcover anthology of three early Silhouette Desire titles, written by three of your favorite authors.

Diana Palmer   SEPTEMBER MORNING
Jennifer Greene   BODY AND SOUL
Lass Small   TO MEET AGAIN

This unique collection will not be sold in retail stores and is only available through this exclusive offer. Look for details in Silhouette Desire titles available in retail stores in June, July and August.

SDANN

FREE GIFT OFFER

To receive your free gift, send us the specified number of proofs-of-purchase from any specially marked Free Gift Offer Harlequin or Silhouette book with the Free Gift Certificate properly completed, plus a check or money order (do not send cash) to cover postage and handling payable to Harlequin/Silhouette Free Gift Promotion Offer. We will send you the specified gift.

FREE GIFT CERTIFICATE

ITEM	A. GOLD TONE EARRINGS	B. GOLD TONE BRACELET	C. GOLD TONE NECKLACE
# of proofs-of-purchase required	3	6	9
Postage and Handling	$1.75	$2.25	$2.75
Check one	☐	☐	☐

Name: _____

Address: _____

City: _____ State: _____ Zip Code: _____

Mail this certificate, specified number of proofs-of-purchase and a check or money order for postage and handling to: HARLEQUIN/SILHOUETTE FREE GIFT OFFER 1992, P.O. Box 9057, Buffalo, NY 14269-9057. Requests must be received by July 31, 1992.

PLUS—Every time you submit a completed certificate with the correct number of proofs-of-purchase, you are automatically entered in our MILLION DOLLAR SWEEPSTAKES! No purchase or obligation necessary to enter. See below for alternate means of entry and how to obtain complete sweepstakes rules.

SS1U

ONE PROOF-OF-PURCHASE
To collect your fabulous FREE GIFT you must include the necessary FREE GIFT proofs-of-purchase with a properly completed offer certificate.

(See center insert for details)